I0635869

Chorion Osiris

Ultra Meridian Series: Book 5

Theo Mann

invisible Publishing Company

Ultra Meridian Series

Book 1: Echo Omicron

Book 2: Artemis Rex

Book 3: Armageddon Core

Book 4: Terminus Anathema

Book 5: Chorion Osiris

Book 6: Atlas Arcane

Contents

Chapter 1	1
Chapter 2	7
Chapter 3	19
Chapter 4	31
Chapter 5	39
Chapter 6	43
Chapter 7	53
Chapter 8	59
Chapter 9	65
Chapter 10	71
Chapter 11	79
Chapter 12	87
Chapter 13	93
Chapter 14	99
Chapter 15	107
Chapter 16	113
Chapter 17	119
Chapter 18	125
Chapter 19	131
Chapter 20	137
Chapter 21	143

Chapter 22   151

Chapter 23   159

Chapter 24   165

Chapter 25   171

Chapter 26   179

Chapter 27   185

Chapter 28   191

Chapter 29   199

Chapter 30   205

Keep Reading   208

Sign Up Once--Get all Theo Mann's free books including brand new   210
releases

About Theo Mann   212

Also by Theo Mann (so far)   213

Chapter 1

The Reserve Wing Stalwart *Remorseless* raced between asteroids in the Terigon Hyrax field off the Ichthys Pelma Vein. The ship was too big to maneuver well and its speed kept making the ship crash from one asteroid to another.

"Be careful, Bandit!" Rodeo barked from the bridge command station.

"Do you want to fly this hunk of junk?" Bandit bellowed from the pilot's station. "You can take over anytime you like."

Rodeo changed the subject by turning to Lyons at the station next to him. "How far out are we?"

"At least another half hour in the asteroid field before we get clear enough to make a break for Ultra Meridian."

"Four more Stalwarts are cutting around the field to head us off!" Emmett called from a different bridge station. "We won't be clear enough to make a break for Ultra Meridian."

"We need a different plan," Rodeo decided.

"The Reserve Wing will follow us no matter where we go," Lyons told him. "This Stalwart is too recognizable. The Reserve Wing can track it anywhere."

"This is the only ship we got," he countered. "It isn't like we can just up and swap it for another ship."

"Yes, we can." She attacked her controls. "I'm sending you the coordinates of a smuggler's market where we can trade it."

Bandit took his eyes off the controls long enough to read the coordinates. "Acrolith Diastema. That's all the way on the other side of the Hyrax field. I would have to turn around and......"

That moment of distraction made the *Remorseless* crash into another asteroid. "Bandit!" Rodeo roared.

Bandit seized the controls and hauled the Stalwart around another massive asteroid just in time to avoid a head-on collision. "I'm trying, man!"

"Turn us around and head for Acrolith Diastema," Rodeo ordered.

Bandit started to turn around to stare at him. "Seriously? Do you realize how long it took us to get here?"

He remembered his mistake in time to face front. He skirted another asteroid, but at that moment, a barrage from the pursuing Daggers pummeled the asteroids nearest him.

The shots deflected off four enormous boulders and sent them wheeling into the *Remorseless's* path. Bandit hit the throttle and slalomed between them, but he was still no closer to freedom.

"Turn around, Bandit," Rodeo ordered again. "We can't get to Ultra Meridian like this."

No one on the bridge said a word when Bandit took a turn around one of the giant rocks in his path and pulled the *Remorseless* back the other way. He gunned the engines and took off at high speed through the field.

The Daggers followed and the rest of the Chorion Team opened fire with the ship's Howitzers. Gunshots pelted through the asteroid field, struck the asteroids in the *Remorseless's* wake, and they tumbled into the Daggers' path.

The Daggers had to fly in wild courses to avoid colliding with the asteroids. One of the Daggers didn't adjust in time and detonated on a giant rock rolling straight into its path.

The explosion distracted the other Daggers and the *Remorseless* separated a little farther from the pursuit. Another Dagger exploded and the pursuit dropped back.

"The Stalwarts are holding their position," Lyons reported. "They aren't coming to cut us off."

"Set course for Acrolith Diastema, Bandit," Rodeo ordered.

"And then what?" Emmett asked. "How does this help us get Fiddler back—and Dice and Davenport?"

"Once we get a ship the Reserve Wing can't trace, we'll be much better placed to help all of them." Lyons rested her hand on his shoulder. "Don't worry. We'll get them back."

He swallowed hard and turned away. "We better."

She turned to her own station and used the controls to scan the planet ahead. Bandit had to weave his way through parsecs of asteroid field to get to a part of space well clear of the Reserve Wing pursuit.

The delay gave Lyons all the time she needed to check that everything was the way she remembered it on Acrolith Diastema.

"Where can we get a ship to trade for this one?" Rodeo asked on the way there.

"I know people there," Lyons told him. "We can talk to them about it and see what's available."

"Make it something fast," Bandit called over.

"And small." Rodeo made a face at the bridge around him. "This thing is way too big."

"If we trade it for something smaller, we'll probably have enough money left over to buy weapons and any other supplies we need," Lyons told him.

"Even better." Rodeo stood up. "I'm going downstairs to brief the boys. Lyons, you can tell Bandit where to set down."

He was just about to leave the bridge when the door opened and Marshall Lawrence Healey walked in. "Are we at Ultra Meridian yet?"

"We aren't going to Ultra Meridian," Rodeo told him.

"We're going to Acrolith Diastema," Bandit added from his station.

Healey raised his eyebrows. "Is that a good idea?"

"Do you know about it?" Lyons asked.

"Everyone knows about it," Healey replied. "It's the biggest steaming smugglers sewer in the whole Confederacy."

"Except for Pandora's Needle, right?" Emmett interrupted.

"We can't go to Ultra Meridian," Rodeo told him. "The Reserve Wing is already lying in wait for us and this Stalwart is too recognizable. Lyons says we can trade this ship for something else at Acrolith Diastema. What do you think of that plan?"

Healey glanced over at Lyons and they shared a moment of silent communication. Lyons had never spent this much time around lawmen in her life.

Now she saw instantly that Healey understood. Lyons was a smuggler. Healey was a Confederate Marshall.

They would have been blood enemies if they hadn't both gotten caught on the wrong side of Admiral Killian Joyce's cockamamie plan to blow up the Confederacy.

Healey looked away and shrugged. "I suppose it's as good a plan as any."

"You better stay hidden, Marshall," Rodeo told him. "If the place is crawling with smugglers and we plan to negotiate with smugglers, they won't be happy to see you."

Healey snorted. "They won't be happy to see you, either, son. Besides, I can pull some strings with the local sheriff and get us a stamp to buy weapons and anything else we need. Being a marshall on Acrolith Diastema won't be all bad."

Rodeo only shrugged. "If you say so."

He walked out and left Lyons and Healey looking at each other. She broke eye contact first and went back to studying her controls.

She searched the planet ahead, but she couldn't see what she wanted to know about it from up here. She would just have to wait until she got down on the ground. That should be interesting.

She was just hoping Healey would leave the bridge, but instead, he came over to her station, looked over her shoulder, and pointed at the screen. "Why are you researching Yuki Duetis? Why are you reading his criminal record?"

"I know him," Lyons muttered without looking up. "I was just checking to see how active he still is."

Healey raised his eyebrows again. "He's active, all right. He's very active."

"I know," she mumbled.

"How do you know him?"

"The smuggling word is close-knit." She changed to a different screen. "Everyone has to trade and negotiate with each other all the time. It's impossible not to know almost everybody if not literally everybody."

Healey shrugged. "If I ever crossed paths with Yuki Duetis, one of us wouldn't be going home that night."

Lyons looked up in surprise. "You know him?"

Healey snorted. "How could I not?" He bent over the list she'd been reading. "I know quite a few people on this list—and not in a nice way."

"Maybe it's better if you don't go out there, then."

"I'll have to if I want to visit the local sheriff."

"We don't need a stamp," she pointed out. "We can buy the stuff under the table. We'll blend in better that way. Having a stamp will only make us more noticeable.....and you're as wanted as we are. The local sheriff will try to take you into custody."

"I doubt that. I know him, too."

Lyons went through some more records on her controls. "Sheriff Lurin Kagne. I don't know him."

"Count your lucky stars. He's a true-blue lawman. He can't stand people like you."

Lyons cracked a grin. "People like me. That's a good one considering we're on the same ship running the same mission now."

He smiled at her, but he held eye contact way too long. He studied her in a way that made her uncomfortable—almost as if he could see all the things she wasn't telling him—or anyone else.

He inclined his head in the other direction as if he wanted to ask her something, but he stopped himself and then Bandit interrupted. "I'm coming out of the Hyrax field now. Tell me where to go."

She bent over her controls again. "I'm sending you coordinates to land outside of town. Keep clear of the houses so you don't squash anybody."

He grimaced, twisted up his mouth in the wrong shape, and angled his head back and forth while he sneered in a sing-song voice. "Be careful you don't squash anybody, Bandit!" He changed back to his normal voice and muttered, "Like I don't know how to land a ship."

She laughed and he spun around to stare at her. She nodded toward his controls. "You might want to watch what you're doing so you don't squash anybody."

He faced front, steered the ship out of the asteroid field, and then sprinted the last dozen parsecs to Acrolith Diastema.

He hovered in orbit for a while, but there was nothing down there. Lyons scanned the surroundings. The Reserve Wing didn't follow the *Remorseless* here.

"Something isn't right," Healey muttered. "They should have followed us."

"I know," Lyons murmured. "Maybe if we get a ship they can't track, we'll be able to sneak away before they find out where we are."

He shook his head. "They know where we are. This is the only refuge for lightyears around. It wouldn't be too hard for them to track us from here, either."

"So what are we supposed to do?" Bandit asked. "We can't just keep flying around in this bucket of bolts."

"Take us down," Lyons ordered. "We have to dump the *Remorseless* either way and we won't be able to do that up here."

Chapter 2

Lyons left the *Remorseless's* bridge and went downstairs. She planned to arm herself from the Stalwart's weapons locker, but when she passed one of the ship's many crew lounges, she heard voices yelling in there.

She stopped at the threshold to see Rodeo in full confrontation with the rest of the Chorion Team. They all surrounded him yelling at once.

Lyons couldn't make out what they were arguing about. The four young women from the Armageddon Core sat around on the couches watching and listening.

Lyons stood in the doorway. She didn't want to get involved in whatever these boys were so agitated about.

Rodeo finally held up his hands. "Shut your holes!" he thundered. "We don't have a choice about this!"

"What were you thinking—bringing us back to Acrolith Diastema?" Alla snapped. "Didn't we get into enough trouble here last time?"

"What part of, 'we don't have a choice,' did you not understand?" Rodeo snapped. "It was either come here or fly straight into the Reserve Wing's guns."

"I'll take the Reserve Wing," Axel returned.

"Then it's a good thing you aren't in charge," Rodeo countered. "We're already on the planet. The only question is whether you boys are going to go out there and get your heads shot off or if you might at some point display enough intelligence to stay on the ship and stay hidden."

"That won't make a difference if Yuki Duetis comes after us," Coon pointed out. "If you go outside and he sees you, he'll realize we're all here. Hiding on a Reserve Wing Stalwart won't stop him from coming after all of us."

"Don't you think I've thought of that?" Rodeo fired back. "I wasn't planning to go out there, either. Lyons knows people here."

"Actually," she interrupted from the doorway, "the people I know here *are* Yuki Duetis....and a few other people."

"You see?" Laub interjected. "This is a disaster waiting to happen."

"So.....you all plan to stay on the ship?" Lyons looked back and forth between them. "All of you? That means I'll be going out there alone."

"*We're* definitely staying on the ship," Flack chimed in from the couch. "You won't catch me going out there and showing my face anywhere the Reserve Wing might see me."

"The Reserve Wing won't see you," Lyons told her. "The Reserve Wing isn't here."

"Famous last words," Fizzle muttered.

Lyons threw up her hands. "Hey, if none of you wants to go out there, I'll go alone."

"No, you won't." Rodeo turned around. "I'm going with you."

Another outbreak of yelling erupted from the other Chorions. Rodeo stood in front of them and took it without saying anything this time.

He propped his hands on his hips and waited for them to shut up, but they didn't. They kept going off on him until Healey and Emmett came downstairs from the bridge with Bandit.

"What's going on?" Healey asked over the noise.

"These boys know Yuki Duetis," Lyons told him. "They don't want Rodeo to go with me to negotiate for the ship. The boys are worried Yuki will come after them as soon as he realizes they're on the planet."

Healey waited for a break in the argument and asked, "Why don't you all go after Yuki instead? If you all rolled up on him, he wouldn't be able to come after you. You could make it out that you don't care if he comes after you or not because you could put him down if he did."

"That would lend quite a dose of credibility to my negotiation," Lyons added.

Rodeo waved at them. "You see? I'm not the only one who wants to face Yuki."

"I never said I wanted to face Yuki," Healey corrected. "You won't catch me setting foot in the same room with the man."

"Me, either," Alla replied.

"What's your problem?" Rodeo countered. "Yuki is half your size. You could swallow him in one gulp."

"But not his whole army," Alla pointed out. "If we take out Yuki, the rest of his people will come after us in revenge."

"Actually, they won't," Lyons interrupted. "Not if you're with me."

All eyes turned to stare at her. "They won't?"

She raised her hands in surrender. "It's a long story. Who's coming?"

Dead silence fell over the lounge for a second before Rodeo said, "I'm definitely going."

The other boys exchanged glances.

"Oh, come on," Rodeo chided. "You can't all be that chickenshit. Axel, you come with me. Wolf, Laub, and Alla can come, too. Breeze, you stay here."

"Definitely," Lyons added and a few of the boys snickered.

"Go arm up," Rodeo told them and turned to the others.

"We're staying here," Friend told him.

He only shrugged. "Fine. What about you, Emmett?"

"I guess I'll come. I have nothing else to do."

Rodeo turned to Healey. "And you're splitting off for the Sheriff's Office, right, Marshall?"

"Right."

Rodeo nodded and the crew dispersed—at least, they split into two groups. Those staying behind stayed behind.

Lyons, Healey, Emmett, Rodeo, Wolf, Alla, Axel, and Laub went downstairs to the ship's hold where they loaded themselves with weapons.

Lyons got herself a nice shiny new XQ-62. She was just loading it when the group heard a clunk through the bulkhead nearby.

Laub spun around. "What was that?"

"I think Beauty is working on the ship," Lyons told him.

"Wonderful," Alla muttered. "We won't have a ship to trade when he finishes with it."

"But the buyer will never know that," Lyons told him and snapped her ammo cylinder into the magazine. "Beauty knows how to work on ships."

"That might be the only thing he knows." Healey stuck his loaded weapons into his holsters and headed for the hatch. "I'll see you people on the other side. Make sure you come back alive."

He walked off across the open ground to the town in the distance. Lyons and the others approached the hatch more slowly.

Laub puffed out his cheeks in a deep breath. "I never thought I'd come back here."

"Neither did I," Lyons murmured.

Emmett glanced at her. "What do you know about this place?"

"What *don't* I know about this place?" She stepped outside. "If we're doing this, let's get it done so we can get out of here."

She set off toward the town in the distance. Memories flooded her as she got nearer to it. The sounds, the smells of roasting food, the hubbub of voices coming from the market—they all brought back memories good and bad.

Walking back into this place felt like walking into the past.....except this wasn't the past. She was coming back here with the Chorion Team....and Emmett.

They kept her anchored in the present. She wasn't the person she had been when she left Acrolith Diastema.

She hadn't been back to this place in years. She never thought she'd ever come back.

Now she was coming back as a fugitive from the Reserve Wing, but she couldn't bring herself to feel any shame about that.

She was prouder of becoming a fugitive from the Reserve Wing than of anything else she'd ever done in her life. She finally did the right thing by helping Davenport.

She was still helping him now by helping the rest of the crew retrieve the Ziprothil. She might not be as good as Davenport, but she could at least help him when he couldn't carry on his mission himself.

She had to remember that at all costs. She couldn't let all the sights, smells, sounds, and memories of Acrolith Diastema break her focus from her current mission—and the person she'd become to carry it out.

She wasn't the same person she'd been when she started this. She wasn't the same person who'd taken the Ithium on board the *Echo Omicron*.

She knew then that whoever stole the Ithium from Helios Sanctus planned to use it for something bad. She told herself that their plans didn't concern herself. Her only job was to transport the Ithium—nothing more.

Those days felt like a hundred years ago. She couldn't even think of herself making a decision like that now.

She never would have thought to put herself in danger to help a lawman before. The person she'd been then never would have stuck her neck out to stop Admiral Joyce from carrying out his plot. She would only have cared about protecting herself.

She had to struggle to stay oriented when she walked into the market. She saw plenty of people she knew. She smiled and waved at them. It would be so easy to slip right back into this life and go on the way she did before.

Then she noticed people glaring at Wolf and Rodeo. The stallholders and customers definitely recognized them.

"Maybe you boys shouldn't have come," Emmett muttered.

"No, we definitely should have," Rodeo growled. "If any of these people tries anything, they'll regret it."

"They must know that or they would have tried it already," Lyons pointed out. "Let's go see Yuki. The sooner we get a ship, the sooner we can get out of here."

She set off through the streets heading deeper into town, but the tension kept rising the farther she walked.

Wolf growled in her ear. "Someone is following us," Emmett muttered.

Rodeo angled his ear slightly farther to the right. "More than one someone."

"How many?" Lyons asked without turning around.

"A lot. Wait for it....."

The words barely got out of his mouth before someone charged the party from the right.

Lyons didn't see who it was until a giant man dressed all in black plunged out of the crowd, raised a giant curved sword, and brought it down with a crushing blow right on Rodeo's head.

At the last possible moment before it cleaved his skull in half, Axel thrust out his arm above Rodeo's head. The blade crashed down on Axel's wrist, but it didn't cut him.

It clanged off and sparks flew from the spot. The blade bent from the force of the swordsman's strike and the guy staggered back gaping at his crumpled blade.

Just as fast, more attackers converged from all sides. The five Chorions sprang into a square surrounding Lyons and Emmett.

Lyons braced herself for a fight, but before any of the attackers could get near the party, Alla lunged forward, opened his mouth to a massive size, and inhaled ten men, weapons and all.

He swallowed them and the rest of the mob drew back for a second. "Come on, you bastards!" Rodeo bellowed over the crowd. "You want some of this? Come on!"

At that signal, the crowd surged in again and all hell broke loose. Wolf let out a chilling yowl, sprang out of position, and dove into the heart of the mob. Screams, shrieks, and ripping sounds came from the spot where he vanished under a hill of bodies.

Alla cleared a space around him by swallowing everyone who came near him. Axel stood alone surrounded by twenty swordsmen all attacking him at once. Their blades clanged and pinged off his head, shoulders, and back.

His arms whirled so fast that they became a blur. He grabbed any blades he could get his hands on, twisted them out of shape, and turned them on their owners.

Lyons didn't see what Laud and Rodeo were doing. She dropped her XQ into position and unloaded on the mob closing from all sides. She blasted away anyone in front of her, and when she saw the locals getting too close to the Chorions, she hammered them, too.

Emmett moved into position next to her and leveled his XQ at the crowd. He pivoted sideways so their combined firepower cut huge swathes through the mob.

Lyons didn't take the time to check who she was shooting. She didn't care until another wave of people rushed past her heading back into the market. Alla charged after them, cracked his mouth to an enormous size, and gulped down another twenty of them before they could get away.

The others ran for their lives. Lyons held her fire and turned back to the others, but the fight was over. Bodies surrounded Axel in a ring of gore. More people ran away bleeding from where Wolf had shredded at least thirty assailants to death.

More townspeople stood around the periphery watching with huge eyes. None of them dared to take a step forward.

"Is everyone all right?" Lyons panted. "Is anyone hurt?"

Wolf spun around, bared his teeth at the onlookers, and gave them a hideous snarl. They reared away from him and a few people ran for it, but most just stood there gaping.

Rodeo clamped his hand on Wolf's shoulder and steered him back into their group. "It's all right. They won't come back now."

"They're braver than I gave them credit for," Lyons remarked.

"They're always trying something," Axel muttered. "They never learn."

"Are you sure you want to do this?" she asked. "Are you sure you want to face Yuki?"

"More than ever," Rodeo replied and he cocked his head to listen to the market.

"Was he the one who sent these men out to attack us?" Alla asked.

"How could he?" Laub asked. "We just rolled into town. He won't have heard yet that we're here."

"He will now." Rodeo waved Lyons ahead. "Go on. Let's get this over with before he does find out and sends out the big guns."

"What do you know about him?" she asked on their way through town.

"We did business with him in the past. That's all I can say about it."

"Why is he so against you?" she asked.

"Let's just say he doesn't like it when he can't hurt someone when he wants to," Rodeo replied. "He likes to be able to inflict his punishment on anyone whenever he wants. He found out the hard way that he can't do that with us."

"Why did he want to punish you?"

Laub laughed and Axel bit back a smirk. "He also doesn't like it when he finds out someone is smarter than he is," Laub replied. "Yuki met his match with Ekol Thaine and Yuki came out the loser. He didn't like that."

Lyons didn't pursue the matter any further. She had left Acrolith Diastema for a reason. Now she remembered why she never wanted to be part of this life—just in case she'd forgotten.

She couldn't get out of seeing Yuki now that she was actually here. No one else dared to mess with the party when she led the way to a nearby building, entered through a plain, unmarked door in the side, and climbed the stairs.

The stairs exited on one of the building's top floors. All the interior walls had been removed to make a giant apartment covering the whole story.

Fifty or sixty aliens crowded the room. They all talked and drank while they stood around mingling with each other. Alien waiters filed between the guests serving everyone.

Lyons stopped on the threshold to watch and let the memories flood over her. She'd been in this room a thousand times if she'd been in it once. She knew almost everyone present.

A few people noticed her, Emmett, and the Chorions. The guests stopped talking and a widening circle of hushed silence spread outward from the stairs as everyone present realized who it was that just walked in.

She stepped forward and the staring crowd parted to let her and the Chorions through. The guests backed away on both sides and left a wide-open aisle down the center of the room.

Lyons advanced and stopped in front of a short man with satin-black hair down to his shoulders, sloping almond black eyes, and smooth light brown skin. A thin mustache curved down both sides of his upper lip.

He couldn't have been more than twenty-five and he barely came up to Lyons's chin. He was busy talking to some of his alien guests and he didn't stop talking when everyone else did.

He was still talking when Lyons halted in front of him. Yuki only stopped talking when his guest glanced over at her and then gave Yuki a pointed look.

He glanced over his shoulder and his eyes flew open. "Lyons! What a pleasant surprise!"

He stepped toward her, squeezed her arm, and kissed her on the cheek. "Hi, Yuki," she murmured. "It's good to see you."

"I missed you!" He burst into a beaming smile. "Nothing has been the same here since you left."

"I don't know about that. Things look the same out there."

His eyes darted to her right and left and his expression darkened. "You got a lot of nerve coming back here, Rodeo."

"It wasn't by choice," Rodeo snapped and he tilted his head to one side to listen to the room behind him. His milky blind eyes stared in a different direction away from Yuki.

"What are you doing with *them?*" Yuki asked Lyons.

"They're my friends. We're flying together now. I know you have history with them, but I'm asking you to let it pass for now. We're flying a stolen Reserve Wing Stalwart. We want to change it for something and then we'll all be out of your life. You'll never see these boys again."

"I don't know if I can do that," Yuki replied. "I have a vendetta against the Chorion Team."

"I'm asking you, as a personal favor to me, in honor of our past together, that you let it go," she repeated. "For me."

Those words made him jolt and his eyes snapped back to her face. He glared at her for a second and then he softened. "I shouldn't, but I guess I can do it for you."

"Thank you," she exclaimed. "I won't forget it."

He smiled again and the color rushed to her cheeks. "I should make you stay here with me in exchange for letting them live."

"I can't do that," she replied. "I have a few other things I need to take care of."

He cast another exaggerated glance over the people around her. "You aren't still flying with Dice and Beauty, are you? You can do so much better."

She stiffened at those words. "Who I fly with is my business. If you're going to fit us out with a ship, I'd appreciate it if you could do that now. We're in a hurry."

"You're always in a hurry. Share one meal with me before you leave. That's all I ask. I'll do everything you say including putting aside my beef with the Chorion Team. Just sit down and eat one meal with me. Then you can leave."

Lyons glanced around the room. Everyone stood in silence and listened to their conversation.

She sighed. "All right. One meal."

Yuki snapped his fingers at one of the alien guests nearest him and the person handed him a handheld computer device. Yuki tapped on it. "I'll give you a Valiant-class heliopod. That will be faster than a Stalwart or even a Nitrol."

Lyons had to bite back a gasp. "Thank you, Yuki."

He grinned at her over his device. "We'll call it a token of my affection. Now come over here and sit down."

He walked away to a line of cushions propped against one wall. No one else was sitting down.

He sat down and the rest of the guests went back to talking and hobnobbing the way they were before, but Lyons definitely noticed people giving her and the Chorion Team the side eye.

She sat down next to Yuki. The rest of the Chorion team sat on her other side so she would be between them and Yuki.

They filled the available space. Emmett had nowhere else to sit, so he sat on Yuki's other side, but Emmett made sure to leave a healthy gap between himself and the smuggler baron.

The alien waiters came over immediately and served everyone, including Yuki. Then some more waiters came and set up a row of small tables in front of the party.

The waiters started piling the table with dozens of plates, each one loaded with a different delicacy from different cultures all over the Confederacy.

Lyons held her tongue when she saw unique dishes that would have cost a fortune. Yuki took some skewered Chetis tentacles, so Lyons helped herself to a few Vilvillon eyes.

As soon as she started eating them, the Chorions helped themselves, too. The tension started to dissolve.

"Have you heard from Leron?" Yuki asked with his mouth full.

Lyons shook her head. "Not since he left Acrolith Diastema. Have you?"

"He contacted me about a year ago. He said he'd finally tracked down the crew that killed your father and threw our syndicate into turmoil. Leron said only three of the original hit team were still alive. He planned to bring them back so we could interrogate them about who hired them to hit your father. Then I never heard from Leron again."

Lyons looked down at her plate. "I guess that's another reason to just let it go and leave it alone."

"We can't do that," he countered. "You know we can't. Rizarth Hudan was the king of this syndicate. Whoever put out a contract on him must have been trying to take down the whole syndicate. They even tried to kill you to stop you from taking over in his place."

"I remember," she mumbled. "You don't have to remind me."

He stretched out his hand to pick up a bowl of Lubbichi squares. Lyons had just been about to snatch them herself, but Yuki got to them first.

"You could have become the most powerful smuggling kingpin in the sector if you'd taken over in his place," he went on. "Instead, you ran off to become a lowlife gunrunner with Dice and Beauty and I had to step into your father's place."

She tried to smirk at him, but her resolve failed. She became painfully aware of Emmett and the Chorions listening to her whole sordid history.

"You did a great job taking over," she told Yuki. "You deserved this.....but we both already knew that when I left. I couldn't have done as good a job as you've done."

He didn't smile back. "Rizarth took me in when I was orphaned as a boy. He was as much my father as he was yours. We could have ruled together if you'd only stayed."

"I couldn't," she murmured. "I couldn't stay here."

"You broke my heart when you left. You know that, right?"

She couldn't look at him. She already knew that. He wasn't telling her anything she didn't already know.

She should have known this meal would turn into a trip down memory lane. She *did* know it would turn into a trip down memory lane, but she owed him at least a few minutes of her time before she abandoned him and Acrolith Diastema again.

"Is there any way I can change your mind?" he finally asked.

"No, I'm afraid not," she replied. "I have a few things out there that hold a higher obligation over me than anything on this planet, including you. I'm sorry if that hurts you, but my life is elsewhere now."

"So what are these obligations?" He pretended to look around. "Where are Dice and Beauty? Don't tell me they were too afraid to come and face me. I thought we got along pretty well the last time they were here."

"They aren't afraid to face you. Beauty is on board our ship doing some repair work and Dice....." She trailed off. "Let's just say he's one of the obligations I need to fulfill before I settle down anywhere."

Yuki rolled his eyes. "I'll never understand what you see in that guy."

She looked away again. "No, you wouldn't."

"So where is he? Tell me he isn't hiding from me."

"No, he isn't hiding from you. He doesn't know I'm here."

"I can see you don't want to tell me where he is." He put the Lubbichi squares back. Lyons was just about to pick them up when Rodeo snagged them right out from under her hand.

She spun around, but he was already taking one of the few remaining squares and passing the rest to the Chorions down the row. Alla took the last one. So much for that.

Just then, one of the alien guests came over, bent across the table, and whispered in Yuki's ear.

He stiffened to high alert. "Excuse me, Lyons. I have to go. It seems there's a new Confederate Marshall in town who is asking questions and making life interesting at the local station. I'll have my people bring the Valiant over to your Stalwart so you can load up. I'm supplying the Valiant with everything you'll need so you don't have to worry about buying the rest. I hope I'll see you again before you leave."

Before she could reply, he picked up her hand and kissed the back of her knuckles before he hurried away and vanished into the crowd.

Chapter 3

"**H**oly f-in' shit!" Rodeo breathed. "Rizarth Hudan was your father?! I don't believe it!"

"Believe it," Lyons murmured back. "I was born here and grew up in this syndicate. My father raised me and Yuki as brother and sister, but Yuki always wanted it to be more than that."

"That is wild!" Axel whispered. "All this time, we've been flying with one of the greatest smuggling kingpins of all time!"

"Not me," Lyons replied. "I'm nothing. I never wanted to take over after my father died. Everyone else wanted me to, but I just wanted to have a normal life. That's why I signed on with the *Echo Omicron*. They had another crewman who just got killed a few weeks before, so Dice was looking for a third person to join their crew."

"You could have been ruling the criminal underworld and you walked away?!" Laub countered. "You could have been rolling in money."

"Did you ever stop to think that might be why someone put out a hit on my father? I would have had a price on my head for the rest of my life, which is exactly what Yuki has. I didn't want to live like that."

"Well, now you have a price on your head anyway," Rodeo pointed out.

"Are we done talking about this?" Lyons asked. "Can we go now? We have a ship waiting for us, and if Yuki has anything to say about it, there will be a whole posse of armed aliens gunning for Marshall Healey when he comes back to meet us."

"Yeah, let's go," Laub replied and picked one of the Vilvillon eyes.

Alla attacked the table and scooped up a whole handful of the Chetis skewers. Laub grabbed a box of Tarte Tatin on their way out of the room.

None of Yuki's guests paid the slightest attention when the party left the building and stepped out onto the dusty streets.

"I can't believe we're getting out of here so easily," Axel murmured when the friends squinted toward the market.

"Don't speak too soon," Lyons told him. "We're still here. We haven't gotten away yet."

"Let's get out of here," Alla added. "I don't like this place."

"That makes two of us." Lyons turned away from the market and headed back to the outskirts of town where they'd left the *Remorseless*.

The Valiant was just coming down to land next to the Stalwart. Someone must have sent word to the ship because, as soon as the Valiant touched down, Bandit, Coon, and Beauty came out of the *Remorseless* and headed for the Valiant instead.

They crossed the space between the two ships and waved when they saw Lyons and the others coming closer. She waved back, but just then, gunfire broke out behind her.

Everyone spun around to see Healey sprinting across the ground followed by a mob of armed aliens. They waved swords and other household implements at him and a few guns went off in the crowd.

He dodged the shots, hurdled random obstacles, and then took off at high speed heading for the Valiant.

Rodeo pushed Lyons away. "Get to the *Remorseless* and get everyone over to the Valiant! We'll cover you! Hurry!"

She veered away. Rodeo and the others barreled for the Valiant.

She pounded up the ramp and through the hold just praying to God the Armageddon Core was still in the lounge. She didn't look forward to searching the whole damn ship to find them.

They were in the lounge. Breeze stood in front of them twisting his limbs in complicated knots, contorting himself into grotesque shapes, making faces, and making the four women laugh.

"We gotta go!" Lyons blurted out. "Follow me! Hurry! We're changing ships!"

They bolted after her and she charged outside just as Healey made it halfway across the ground from town. He would never make it before the townspeople caught up with him.

More gunfire erupted from the townsfolk. Some of it hit the Valiant. Lyons straightened her arms to push the Armageddon Core back inside the Stalwart, but at that moment, the Valiant's engines blasted to life.

The ship leapt off the ground, spun around, and opened fire. Those shots would have flattened Healey, but he ducked, rolled, and the Valiant's fire hit the townspeople instead.

They started to drop back, but they didn't leave. Healey raced the rest of the way to the ship and Lyons herded everyone forward. "Go!" she yelled and pushed everyone into the open. "Go!"

The four clones took off running for the ship even though the Valiant was still fifty feet off the ground.

The ship laid down a brutal carpet of gunfire to hold the townsfolk at bay, but it didn't work. More and more people poured out of town to come after the crew.

Lyons didn't let herself think about why all these people were coming after the crew. Yuki better not be trying to stop her from leaving—or maybe he decided to get his revenge on the Chorion Team after all.

Lyons herded Breeze and the clones closer to the ship, but it had to stay aloft long enough for Healey to join them. Then the Valiant buzzed a little way in front of them and continued to pound the townsfolk while the ship drifted down to land

Lyons pushed everyone on board. The ship was bigger than a Drifter like the *Artemis Rex* had been, but not as big as a Dagger.

Bandit, Rodeo, and Coon occupied three seats in the spacious cockpit up front. The ship's onboard cannons operated from seats set up in rows behind the cockpit.

"Mount up!" Rodeo yelled back. "We can expect groundfire as soon as we get airborne!"

"What do you mean by groundfire?" Emmett yelled back.

The townspeople answered him because, right at that moment, Bandit punched the throttle and launched into the atmosphere. At the same instant, ground artillery opened fire from somewhere inside Acrolith Diastema.

One shot clipped the Valiant in the ass and sent the ship somersaulting head over heel.

"I don't think Yuki likes you as much as he says he does!" Rodeo hollered over his shoulder.

"What the hell are you talking about?!" Bandit yelled back.

"Just fly the damn ship, boy!" Lyons hollered. "Open fire on the town!"

Coon actually turned all the way around in his seat. "You want to open fire....on a civilian outpost?"

"It isn't a civilian outpost, fool!" she countered. "It's a criminal syndicate and, in case you hadn't noticed, *they're* firing on *us*! Aim for the buildings north of the market!"

The rest of the crew strapped into their seats. Axel, Laub, and Wolf got their cannons aimed first and bombarded the buildings Lyons indicated.

By the time she buckled her harness and turned her own weapon in that direction, the Valiant was already burning up the parsecs and putting too much distance between the crew and Acrolith Diastema anyway.

"Head back to Terigon Hyrax," Rodeo ordered. "We're going to Ultra Meridian come Hell or high water.

Silence fell over the compartment for a few minutes, but when nothing happened, the others unbuckled themselves and went into the back to pass the time doing something else.

Lyons stayed where she was and watched Acrolith Diastema getting farther away in the Valiant's vapor trail.

She wasn't sorry to leave it behind—again. She always felt in her gut that she didn't belong there.

Now she knew it was true. Yuki sent his people after the crew and then he opened fire with his ground artillery to shoot down the Valiant he'd so faux-generously given her. He could have killed her.

Maybe that's what he wanted. Maybe he wanted to kill her to stop her from leaving. She wouldn't have been surprised.

The three boys in front of her brought her back to reality. "Did you see that?" Bandit pointed at something on the controls in front of Rodeo.

"I saw it." Rodeo cocked his head to one side. He didn't look at the controls. "Did you identify it?"

"I can't identify it," Bandit replied. "What about you, Coon. Do you recognize it?"

Coon rested his fingertips on the console, but he didn't look at the controls, either. Silver filaments merged his fingers with the controls.

"It isn't Confederate—either Reserve Wing, Confederate Core, or Sheriff's Service. It doesn't belong to Yuki Duetis or any other criminal syndicate, either."

"See if you can identify it." Rodeo's sensitive fingers danced over the controls. "He's definitely following us."

"What do you mean by 'he'?" Coon asked. "The ship is reading thirty crewmen."

"I can't identify what species they are," Rodeo added.

"What the hell difference does it make what species they are?" Bandit interjected. "We have to shake them off!"

"Forget it," Rodeo snapped. "We're going to Ultra Meridian to get that Ziprothil. We've delayed too long already."

Bandit pursed his lips and hunched over the controls. "Then we'll have to shake him off. Pull out, Coon. I don't want you tempted to intervene."

Coon withdrew his filaments from the controls and Bandit gunned the engines again. The Valiant took off at a brutal pace and Bandit went into one of his lunatic runs through the asteroid field.

He zoomed around rocks and boulders. The Valiant's speed made the asteroids roll and tumble out of position so they pivoted into the pursuer's path.

"Stand by to fire, Lyons!" Rodeo ordered. "We'll need you to either blast our way through or shoot some asteroids to slow him down."

"Who is he?" Lyons asked. "I mean who are they?"

"No idea," he replied. "Stand by."

Lyons's eyes riveted to her targeting grid. She really wished now that some of the others would come back so she wouldn't be the only gunner facing this......whatever it was.

She saw right away that Coon was right. The ship following the Valiant didn't belong to any Confederate law enforcement agency. In fact, the Valiant's database couldn't identify the pursuing vessel at all. It was completely unknown.

The scanners detected the crew, but nothing else beyond that. That on its own was unusual. The ship wasn't much bigger than this Valiant. The thirty crewmen on board must have been sitting on top of each other.

Bandit kept whizzing between asteroids and making them tumble and crash into each other right in front of the pursuing ship. He picked up speed, soared faster, and cut corners tighter, but the pursuit kept pace with him all the way.

"He's one hell of a pilot. I can tell you that much," Bandit growled.

"Ultra Meridian coming up!" Coon called. "You'll need to break out into the open if you want to get there."

"Do it!" Rodeo ordered. "Open fire, Lyons!"

"On what?!" she hollered back.

"Follow my signal. I'm sending you targeting coordinates."

"But that's....."

"Just do it!" he barked. "Shoot where I tell you to shoot—now!"

A river of data poured across her controls and she threw caution to the wind. She went into a trance shooting at any coordinates he fed her.

She tried not to think about the fact that she was taking her targeting cues from a blind man. He couldn't even see what he was telling her to shoot at, but man! Could he ever target!

She jerked her cradle back and forth shooting in a mindless flurry. Her shots struck asteroids all around the Valiant and sent them ricocheting into each other. They exploded each other and came perilously close to crushing the pursuit ship.

The pilot dodged every collision and Bandit ripped the Valiant out of the asteroid field into open space.

The instant he broke clear, he put on speed for Ultra Meridian, but the pursuing pilot only copied him. The strange vessel burst out of the asteroid field right on the Valiant's tail and opened fire.

Pounding gunfire struck the ship in the side and jolted it off course. Lyons hauled her cradle around to return fire, but Bandit was already punching the ship into a dead race for the planet.

Axel, Laub, Alla, and Wolf sprinted up front and dove into their cradles. "Who are we shooting at?" Laub asked over the noise.

"Does it matter?!" Bandit yelled over his shoulder. "Just shoot the bastard! He's....."

More gunfire erupted from the pursuer and peppered the Valiant's underbelly. The impact hurled Lyons hard against her harness. The controls flickered. She couldn't target for a second.

The distortion cleared and Bandit drove the ship into another bone-crushing race for Ultra Meridian. The pursuit ship dropped back and then gunned its engines to burn up alongside.

All the gunners spun around to return fire, but the pursuit ship was bigger and better-armed.

"We can't land near the cave!" Rodeo hollered in Bandit's ears. "We can't let them follow us to the Ziprothil."

"I hate to be the one to tell you this," Bandit bellowed back, "but we'll be lucky to land anywhere with this asshole on our tails!"

Rodeo tried to argue, but another barrage from the enemy cut him off. Lyons and the other gunners did their best to keep up, but the enemy slammed every shot back at them.

A punishing crash struck the hull right next to Lyons. She pulled her cradle around to shoot in that direction, but the enemy was already whizzing off somewhere else.

The enemy pilot put Bandit to shame by circling the ship in crazy rings, hitting the ship from all sides, and then skimming off somewhere else before the gunners could target him.

He coiled around the Valiant's fuselage and skidded to a halt right under the ship's belly where the Valiant's guns couldn't hit him at all.

He delivered a cruel shot straight into the ship's underside. "Hull breach!" Coon hollered. "You better get us on the ground in a hurry!"

"What the hell do you think I'm trying to do?!" Bandit countered.

"Take us closer to the Blood Calliope!" Fizzle yelled from the back. "The rocks will hide us!"

No one answered her except another vicious barrage from the enemy. He nailed the ship from underneath again and blew the starboard engine.

"Brace for a bumpy landing!" Bandit roared. "You all might want to get in the back, arm and supply up, and get ready to make a run for it before our friend comes back for us."

Some of the others unbuckled and hustled into the back, but Lyons stayed where she was. She tried a few more times to shoot at the enemy ship, but the strange crew never let up the incessant hammer blows of explosions pulling the Valiant apart.

"Get in the back, Coon!" Rodeo ordered. "You, too, Lyons! Go!"

She finally dragged herself out of her seat, but she had to hold onto the walls and the other seats to make it into the back. The ship kept pitching back and forth from one side to the other. She couldn't walk more than a few steps at a time, and even then, she staggered.

Coon followed her. They found the rest of the crew standing by the Valiant's rear hatch. They were all taking out the weapons that Yuki so generously left for them. Maybe he must have known the crew would never get a chance to use these weapons against him.

He wouldn't have sent out this strange ship to hunt the crew down. If Yuki wanted to kill Lyons and all her friends, he would have wanted her to know exactly who did it. He wouldn't hide what he was doing by hiring someone she couldn't identify and flying them after her in a ship the scanners couldn't penetrate.

She attacked the weapons locker and grabbed as much as she could carry, but the crew didn't have time to gather any other survival equipment that would help them cope with Ultra Meridian's harsh climate.

Another deafening boom struck the ship from the side and pitched the Valiant over on its port wing. Everyone fell over each other, and then the ship slammed down onto the ground.

Lyons dragged herself out of the dog pile just as Bandit and Rodeo stumbled back from the cockpit. "Everybody outside!" Rodeo ordered. "Come on! Move it!"

He stood up straight, cupped his hands around his mouth, and bellowed back up toward the cockpit. "Beauty! Get off the ship now! We're making a run for it."

Rodeo spun around, slammed his hand on the hatch release, and the ramp crashed down on the ground.

"Everybody out!" he roared. "Run for it! Lead us into the rocks, Flack!"

Lyons tripped over Breeze on her way outside. She might even have stepped on him, but no one cared about that. They bolted outside. She waited just long enough to make sure Beauty got off the ship before the whole crew raced away into the desert.

Lyons couldn't see where she was going with all the dust blowing in her eyes. She could just barely squint enough to see Beauty, Emmett, and the Chorion Team charging after the Armageddon Core up ahead.

The four clones slowed to make sure the group stayed together. Beauty outpaced everyone and ran ahead to the front of the line.

Blistering, sandy wind struck Lyons in the face and body. The wind bit straight through her clothes and got into her nose, mouth, and eyes. She didn't have any mask or goggles to protect her. None of the crew did.

The friends made it ten feet from the destroyed Valiant before gunfire erupted from the nearby rocks. Lyons recognized where they were. The crew was in the canyons near the Blood Calliope wreck. She couldn't see well enough to tell if the crew was running toward the wreck or away from it.

Lyons raised her XQ to shoot back at whoever was attacking the crew, but Axel grabbed her and pulled her forward. "Come on! Keep moving! We can't fight them all!"

She almost asked what he meant, but more gunfire answered that question for her. It came from the canyon rims above the fleeing party. Gunfire burst out from multiple locations. It sounded like a whole army up there.

The clones led the way into a steeper canyon and turned a corner where the gunmen couldn't hit them, but in a second, more gunfire burst out up ahead. The enemy was following the crew.

The canyon became so narrow that gunshots pinged off the rocks, but they didn't penetrate this far down. More guns went off from every side.

Flack pulled everyone into a tight crack a mile from where the Valiant went down. "They have a lot more than thirty people," she panted.

"We can't go near the cave with all these people after us," Rodeo gasped. "We need to hide."

"I'm taking you to one of Friend's tunnels," Flack told him. "It will take us back to the cave without anyone seeing us."

"I don't want to trust that," he replied. "The Reserve Wing knows we're here which means they know the Ziprothil is here."

"This isn't the Reserve Wing," Coon pointed out. "This is someone else."

"Who the hell cares who it is?" Alla interrupted. "Whoever it is wants to kill us."

"I don't think so," Rodeo countered. "They want to scare us. They know we're here to snag the Ziprothil...."

"You're assuming they're involved in the Ziprothil plot," Lyons pointed out. "What if they aren't? What if they're just some random person who wants to kill one or all of us? That could be a lot of people."

Rodeo started to shake his head, but just then, the gunfire changed to a different direction. It pinged down the canyon from another angle and one of the shots deflected dangerously close to the crew's position.

Flack pulled everyone away, but they didn't go back out into the main canyon. "I know a way we can get to the tunnels," she told everyone. "Come on. Follow me!"

The canyon walls blocked most of the wind, but the crew still had to hike a long way under constant gunfire. The crew stopped a few times to return fire, but no one could see who they were shooting at.

Flack finally led the crew to a crevice twisting upward into the rock. "The tunnel is at the top of this rise. Then we can get to the cave."

Lyons glanced down the canyon and gulped when she saw what looked like hundreds of people swarming up it from below. They were coming from the route the crew just used to get here.

"No way!" Bandit murmured. "How the hell did they get here? There weren't that many people on the pursuit ship and there was only one of them."

"Give me your weapons!" Rodeo held out his hand to Lyons, Emmett, and the Armageddon Core. "I'll make a stand here and hold them while the rest of you get into the tunnels. I'll create a diversion to throw them off the trail. Get the Ziprothil and split."

"I'm staying, too," Bandit added.

"We all are," Axel insisted and Wolf growled in agreement.

"I'm staying with you boys," Healey announced. "You'll need every gun you can get fighting all those people."

Frost handed over her weapon. "We'll come back for you."

"No, don't," Rodeo told her. "Get the Ziprothil and get off the planet any way you can."

"How?" Fizzle asked. "The Valiant is totally wrecked."

"I bet you that guy's pursuit ship is still perfectly good," Coon pointed out. "You could steal that."

"Steal whatever you want." Rodeo gathered weapons from Lyons, Healey, Beauty, and the Armageddon Core. "Just get that Ziprothil away from these people. Nothing else matters."

"Thank you, Rodeo," Lyons exclaimed.

"Get the hell out of here." He hefted an XQ, faced down the canyon, and cocked his ear to listen. "This canyon is narrow enough for us to defend it."

"If you get away, you'll find the tunnel at the top of this crevice," Flack told him. "You can take it back to the cave."

"Just make sure you don't lead the enemy back there," Friend chimed in. "Make sure none of them follow you and find out about the tunnels."

He nodded. "I got it. Now go. We'll be all right. Just execute the mission and go."

Lyons would have liked to say more, but he only turned his back on her. Healey and the other Chorions moved into line with him and they all leveled their weapons at the mob of strangers coming from farther down the canyon.

Frost pulled Lyons away. She followed Emmett, Beauty, and the four clones, but she hated to break up the crew like this. Everyone kept going in different directions.

Now she didn't even know if she would ever see Davenport or Healey again. What would she and her friends do with a cartridge full of Ziprothil when they finally found it?

They would need to find some trustworthy law enforcement officer and now they didn't even have that.

The group scrambled up the crevice. It got steeper and Lyons didn't see the top of it where the tunnel might be.

Right then, gunfire erupted behind them. The walls amplified the noise and made her jump. She spun around, but Emmett pulled her away even more firmly. "Come on!" he told her. "Keep moving! We can't stay here!"

She whirled around to face front, but the boom of guns echoing up the walls racked her nerves. She couldn't walk away from those people while they faced an overwhelming force of advancing enemies.

She didn't have a choice. Healey and the Chorions sacrificed themselves so she and the rest of the crew could retrieve the Ziprothil. She had to follow through on that and make good on their sacrifice. That was her mission now.

Chapter 4

Healey pounded the enemy with gunfire, but no matter how many people he and the Chorion Team shot down, more of them kept coming.

"We gotta move!" Rodeo yelled. "We can't hold them off from here!"

"We can't lead them into the tunnels!" Healey countered. "We gotta take a different route!"

"I can't hear over all this noise! You show us where to go!"

Healey didn't remind him that none of them knew where the hell they were. None of the crew knew how to navigate Ultra Meridian.

Now the Armageddon Core was gone and Healey and the Chorions were on their own.

He took a chance, tugged Rodeo's sleeve, and signaled the other boys to fall back. The party kept dumping gunshots down the canyon onto the advancing enemy, but they just kept coming.

The canyons created a choke point the enemy had to file through to get near the crew. The enemy would have overrun the crew in minutes if not for that.

Healey backed away. The walls closed even tighter, but that worked in the Chorion Team's favor. Healey and Laub stood shoulder to shoulder. Between the two of them, they could protect the others' retreat.

The boys clambered up the steep crevice with the others surrounded Rodeo. He couldn't do anything with all this noise blocking his hearing. He was truly blind now.

The boys passed a few caves on the right. Healey assumed those caves led to Friend's tunnels, but the boys paid no attention to the caves. With luck, the enemy wouldn't pay any attention to them, either.

"Get up on the rims!" Healey yelled over his shoulder. "Double back and flank these assholes!"

"You got it, Marshall!" Axel yelled.

Breeze bumped into Healey from behind. "Let me go down there, Marshall! I can slow the enemy down for you!"

"It's too dangerous!" Healey told him. "The boys will start shooting and you'd be in the line of fire. Just hold off a little longer....."

Healey had to stop talking and concentrate on shooting. He and Laub held the line against the advancing enemy and then, without warning, more gunfire exploded from the canyon rims above Healey's head.

Axel, Alla, Wolf, and Bandit sprinted along the walls shooting downward at the enemy. The boys kept going until they got all the way behind the advancing strangers—or where Healey supposed would be behind the strangers. He couldn't be sure since he couldn't see that far.

Coon ran down the other side of the canyon. The boys planted themselves in protected spots up there and bombarded the enemy from above.

More of the strangers swarmed up the canyons getting closer to Healey's position. He could see the strangers now, but they all wore masks. They looked human, but he couldn't identify them.

Without warning, Breeze stuck his head up above one of the curved walls farther down the canyon. Healey had a split second to see Breeze aim a massive XQ-85 straight for Healey and Laub.

Healey opened his mouth to yell out, but Breeze was already pulling the trigger.

The shot smashed into the walls right at the choke point where the enemy was trying to storm Healey's position. The rock detonated and caved on both sides. Tons of rubble and debris rained down on top of the enemy and blocked anyone else from getting through.

Healey and Laub hesitated for a second and then opened fire even more ferociously on the remaining invaders on this side of the barrier. Ten of them got caught on Healey's side and he and Laub gunned them down in seconds.

The other boys raced back and forth on the canyon walls finishing off the rest. They took ten minutes to do the job before they came running back down the crevice to rendezvous with Healey.

"They're retreating, Marshall," Axel told him. "We killed a bunch of them. The rest are making for their ship."

Healey turned around to see Rodeo huddled against the wall with his hands over his ears. Healey touched his shoulder. "It's all right, son. It's over."

Rodeo straightened up and turned his head from side to side to listen. "They're....they're running away." He frowned. "Something's weird."

"Forget that," Healey told him. "We gotta get into the tunnels before they get their ship and circle us from the other side." He called up the walls. "Come down here, boys!"

They all came back and the crew went into the caves. "Where's the tunnel?" Alla whispered.

"I think I hear it over here." Rodeo turned to his right.

He led the way through three more caves. The last one looked like all the others, but when the crew stepped into it, an invisible force jerked Healey forward.

He wavered trying to catch his balance, but just as quickly, whatever it was spat him out in a different cave. He and the Chorion Team were back in the Armageddon Core's secret hideout.

Rodeo went over to Friend's table full of computer equipment. "I'm not reading the others on the planet. You're the only human on the planet, Marshall, which means Lyons, Emmett, and the clones got away."

"Can you pick up the Ziprothil anywhere?" Healey asked.

"Friend said it was in this cave, but it isn't here."

"Does that mean she took it with her when she left?" Coon asked.

"I don't know. Maybe you can tell us. Is the Ziprothil anywhere on this planet?"

Healey didn't know what Rodeo meant, but Coon did. He went to one of the walls, rested his fingers on the wall, and his silvery filaments burrowed into the bedrock.

He pulled out in seconds. "No, it isn't here. It isn't anywhere on the planet. The clones must have taken it."

"Then it's just a question of us getting off this planet, too," Healey crossed the room to the computer workstation. "Can you find us another ship?"

"Make it so we steal those attackers' ship," Laub chimed in from the other side of the room. "We have a reputation to protect as Ekol's team. No one gets away with shooting at us."

Healey snorted. "Since when?"

"The pursuit is gone, too," Rodeo replied. "They probably realized that we were just a diversion."

"Is it possible they captured our people and the Ziprothil?" Healey asked.

"There's no way to tell." Rodeo frowned at something, sat down on Friend's stool, and scrolled back through some of the records.

"What are you looking at?" Healey asked.

"There's something weird about those attackers," Rodeo muttered.

"You mean besides the fact that they were shooting at us?" Alla countered.

Rodeo ignored him and ran through some of the records from the battle. "These scanner readings don't look right. They don't identify what species all those guys were."

"Why are you so set on finding out what species they are?" Axel asked.

"The Valiant couldn't identify them, either," Coon replied. "Any scanner equipment should have been able to pick it up."

"They looked human to me," Healey remarked.

"There are plenty of other species that look human," Rodeo inclined his head the other way and then sighed. "I guess we'll never find out now."

"We need a ship to get out of here," Laub pointed out. "Where are we going to get one?"

"Typhon Elexor and Mount Refractory both have ships," Rodeo replied. "I'm sure I can find one of Friend's tunnels that will take us straight there."

Healey's eyes popped. "You want to steal a ship.....from Typhon Elexor or Mount Refractory? Do you know how dangerous they are?"

"We can be dangerous, too." Rodeo stood up and turned around.

Alla, Coon, Breeze, Wolf, Axel, Laub, and Bandit had broken into one of the Armageddon Core's crates of supplies. The boys stood in a circle around the crate helping themselves to the food.

Healey and Rodeo stopped in their tracks to watch. "Let me guess," Healey teased. "You won't mount your assault on a dangerous criminal organization until after you eat."

"We need our energy," Laub replied with his mouth full.

"It wouldn't pay to mount an assault on an empty stomach," Coon agreed.

"The clones won't use this stuff anyway," Alla pointed out. "They aren't even on the planet."

Healey and Rodeo exchanged glances. "I guess it couldn't hurt," Rodeo finally admitted.

Breeze held out a handful of Griffin Cakes. "Do you want some?"

Rodeo took them, sat down on another crate, tore them open, and started eating.

"What do you want, Marshall?" Laub asked.

"I'm not hungry," Healey told them. "I'm gonna take a look around this place."

He left them to their food and searched the caves. He found a few Skimmers stashed in another chamber behind this main area.

He also found a crap ton of weapons and storehouses loaded with supplies. The Armageddon Core really had been arming for doomsday, which is what they got.

He returned to the main room to find all the boys sitting down. Healey sat down on the crate next to Rodeo. Rodeo handed him three Griffin cakes and Healey finally ate them. What else did he have to do?

"So how are you going to assault Typhon Elexor to steal a ship?" he asked.

"That's easy," Bandit replied. "All we have to do is trespass on their wind farm. Typhon Elexor will send out ships to shoot us and we'll nab one then."

"Nab how?" Healey asked. "How will you nab one when it's in the air and you're on the ground?"

"And don't say you're going to shoot it down," Coon added. "We need a ship that's intact enough to fly away from this rock."

"That's the other question," Breeze chimed in. "Where are we going to go after we leave here? We need to lie low for a while."

"It would be better if we met back up with the rest of the crew," Healey pointed out. "They might need our help to deal with anyone coming after the Ziprothil."

"We still need a ship for that," Laub argued.

"And yet Bandit says that will be easy," Healey countered.

"It will be easy," Coon replied. "I'll bring the ship down without damaging it."

"Yes!" Axel and Laub both thumped him on the back. "Coon's our man!"

He blushed. "It's nothing."

"So what are we waiting for?" Healey surveyed the group. "Have you all had enough to eat?"

Breeze peered into the crate and frowned. "We could open another one of these....."

Bandit pulled him away. "No! You might explode all over the battlefield and ruin the ship."

"Or he might explode inside the ship," Rodeo suggested. "That would be disastrous." He went back over to Friend's computers. "Friend has a tunnel that goes into Mount Refractory territory."

Healey jerked his thumb over his shoulder. "There are some Skimmers in there."

"Perfect. We'll take those." Rodeo waved to the others. "Arm up, boys. We're going shopping."

The Chorions couldn't fall over each other fast enough to get their weapons ready and they all clapped Coon on the back and told him he was gonna kick Typhon Elexor's ass.

They grinned and giggled in excitement on their way into the other room. Rodeo, Healey, Bandit, and Axel mounted their Skimmers. Wolf and Coon climbed on behind. They were both small enough not to weigh the Skimmer down too much.

The others spread themselves out between the other Skimmers and everyone fired up their engines.

Healey didn't see where Rodeo said Friend's tunnel was. Rodeo throttled his Skimmer out into the main room and then streaked away into the winding gullies and ravines making his way across Ultra Meridian toward the west—away from Typhon Elexor territory.

Healey followed him. Axel and Bandit fell in line. The crew wove and dodged through multiple canyons until Rodeo hit the gas and plunged straight into a sheer wall.

Healey was driving so fast that he didn't stop in time. The Skimmer plowed into the wall and burst through into another dizzy tube of some mysterious force pulling him out of control.

It spat him out in another canyon somewhere. All these canyons looked exactly alike.

Rodeo pulled up somewhere under an overhang and shut off his engines. "Typhon Elexor's wind farm is directly above us. As soon as we go up there, we'll be trespassing and they'll send out their ships to stop us."

Healey turned to Coon. "Are you sure you can do this without exhausting yourself?"

"I won't do anything until the ship comes up on us."

"You'll probably have to take care of any other ships Typhon Elexor sends after us," Bandit pointed out. "We wouldn't get lucky enough for them only to send one."

"I'll take care of them....." Coon glanced over at Rodeo. "Unless you want me to capture more than one ship."

"It might not be a bad idea," Laub agreed. "More can't hurt...."

"One is enough," Rodeo decided. "We might get separated if we had more than one ship."

"On the other hand, it would be harder for anyone to kill us all in one shot if we had more than one," Bandit pointed out.

"Just get us one," Rodeo insisted. "We aren't running a fleet of gunships here. Let's go....and if you start to get too tired, Coon, you pull out and we'll take care of the ships another way."

"Is it possible for us to go on one of these missions without you treating me like I'm made of glass?" Coon fired back. "I can handle myself."

Rodeo raised both hands. "Fine. You can handle yourself. Let's go."

Chapter 5

Rodeo led the way to the end of a defile that split off the main canyon. The crew had to climb another steep incline.

Rodeo crouched behind another corner at the top. "Here we go. Coon, you get to the nearest windmill as soon as we break cover. The rest of us will defend you as much as we can, but as soon as the ships come out, you're on your own."

Coon nodded. "No problem. I can take them."

"Good boy." Rodeo gripped his shoulder. "Go!"

Coon hopped over the side and sprinted away before the others made it out onto the surface. Healey scrambled up with the others. Coon was already halfway to the nearest windmill.

They towered over the barren landscape and their blades thumped the air. Scouring wind howled across the tops.

Healey really wished now that he'd brought a mask and goggles from the Armageddon Core's supplies, but if this worked, he and the Chorions wouldn't be on this planet for long.

Healey and the boys pivoted outward to aim their guns at the skies. The group backed toward the windmills while Coon darted into place near the pedestal of the nearest giant machine.

Healey's nerves tensed to the breaking point waiting for Typhon Elexor to attack. They wouldn't let anyone trespass on their territory.

The others rotated their guns at the skies. They didn't have to wait long.

The crew barely got into position before four gunships shrieked out of the distance. Healey couldn't see through all the sand to tell where those ships came from.

"Hold your fire!" Rodeo bellowed. "Don't shoot until Coon brings them down!"

The sound of engine noise triggered Healey's defensive instincts. He raised his weapon to his shoulder anyway and aimed for the gunships.

The rest of the Chorion team did the same, including Rodeo, but no one fired.

Healey held his breath waiting for something to happen. The gunships wheeled in front of the crew and angled their weapons downward to fire.

The Chorions stood in a semi-circle around the windmill's pedestal. Did the gunships even see Coon crouching near its base? Did the Typhon Elexor pilots understand the damage one thin, frail boy could do to them?

The gunships closed ranks and then it happened. The windmill came to life. Its blades stretched into flailing, whipping arms that cracked and hissed through the air.

One of them lashed around the nearest gunship, snatched it out of thin air, and ripped it away into the sky. The ship's engines screeched to their highest pitch.

The other three gunships turned their weapons on the windmill that now became a living, moving thing. It snaked its blade arms in all directions.

One of the gunships opened fire and a blade-arm cracked through the air and batted the gunship far away over the landscape. A faint puff of dust showed the spot where the ship crashed into the ground.

The other two gunships floundered trying to figure out what to do. The windmill reared off its pedestal and turned into an enormous metal monster. It grabbed another gunship and smashed it flat into the rock directly in front of Healey.

The whole scene shocked him so much that he couldn't move. He couldn't have fired if his life depended on it. None of the other Chorions moved, either. They all stared at the windmill in stupid horror.

The fourth and last gunship dodged a few vicious strokes of the blade arms and fired its guns into the windmill, but that only seemed to enrage the monster. It heaved off its pedestal and its pilons took one menacing step toward the gunship.

The pilot changed his mind, yanked his ship away, and raced for cover toward the north.

The windmill gave an agonized groan, stepped back onto its pedestal, and resumed its former position. It used its blade-arm to lower the first captured gunship to the ground.

Healey and the boys swarmed the ship aiming their guns at the cockpit window. The two pilots inside raised their hands in surrender. Laub forced the rear hatch open and he, Axel, and Bandit stormed inside to take control of the ship.

Healey, Wolf, and Rodeo ran over to the windmill's pedestal where they found Coon slumped on the ground. "Hey, boy!" Rodeo called. "You okay?"

Coon looked up and gave a weak smile. "I'm okay! That was fun!"

"Come on. We're getting out of here." Rodeo hung his gun over his shoulder, and got under one of Coon's arms, and supported him to get on board the ship.

The other Chorions drove the Typhon Elexor pilots out at gunpoint and left them standing on the cliff edge while Healey and the others clambered on board.

Bandit sprang into the pilot's seat. "Here we go! Shut that hatch and let's beat it before they come back."

Laub shut the hatch. Rodeo lowered Coon into a safety seat against the rear hull. This ship didn't have any compartments or cabins or any other amenities. Six guns stuck out of its sides from the only compartment.

Bandit occupied one of two seats up front. Rodeo took the other.

Healey and the other boys got behind their guns and Healey braced himself to go out shooting, but no one came after the thieves. Bandit hit the throttle and the ship rocketed into space.

"Now we gotta hook up with the Ziprothil," Rodeo decided and started working on the controls.

"It's gonna be tough to track a ship with six humans on board," Bandit pointed out.

"See if you can identify Beauty's species and scan for him," Healey suggested.

"Good idea." Rodeo got busy on the scanners and then snarled. "I don't believe it!"

"What's wrong?" Bandit asked.

"That cocksucker is following us again," Rodeo muttered. "It's the same asshole that followed us to Ultra Meridian."

Bandit spun around. "That's impossible."

"He's flying the same ship and he has thirty crewmen on board again. He's a persistent son of a bitch. I'll give him that."

"Why is he following us when we don't have the Ziprothil?" Healey asked.

"You said he realized the diversion and went after the other crew," Axel pointed out. "If he was after the Ziprothil, he shouldn't be interested in us at all."

"Use your brains," Rodeo countered. "He probably wants to question us about where the others took the Ziprothil. If Lyons, Emmett, Beauty, and the four clones got away with the Ziprothil and gave this idiot the slip, then he probably thinks we know where they went. Maybe he thinks we're planning on rendezvousing with them."

Bandit leaned over and checked whatever Rodeo was working on. "He isn't attacking. He's keeping his distance."

"He probably wants us to lead him to the Ziprothil."

"What do you want me to do?" Bandit asked. "We can't fight him in this gunship. If the Valiant couldn't take him, we don't stand a chance in this."

"We need to take refuge somewhere.....somewhere he'll never follow us." Rodeo bent over his charts.

"Where would that be?" Healey asked.

Rodeo didn't answer right away. He worked on his instruments all while staring off in another direction. His fingers danced over the controls without him ever looking at them.

He was still working on them when he cocked his head the other way. "Keep your speed steady, boy. Don't speed up. Just hold steady and let him follow us."

"Sorry," Bandit muttered. "I didn't realize I was speeding up."

"He isn't doing anything but following us." Rodeo inclined his head the other way. Everyone in the back watched and listened to their conversation.

"Come on!" Bandit growled. "Give me something! This bastard is getting on my nerves."

Rodeo didn't answer right away. Then he said. "I got it. We'll take him back to Chorion Osiris."

Healey's head shot up. "No!! We can't go there!"

"We'll be fine," Rodeo replied over his shoulder and turned to Bandit. "Set course for the...."

"NO!!" Healey interrupted. "We are NOT going to Chorion Osiris! Hell no!"

Rodeo turned his head ever so slightly, but he didn't turn all the way around. He didn't answer Healey at all.

Rodeo only jutted his chin at Bandit and said, "Do it," in a way that Healey understood only too well. He'd been overruled. What in God's name was he thinking flying with a bunch of Chorions?

None of them thought twice about going to Chorion Osiris. Why should they? It was their home planet.

Healey gulped. He couldn't go there. It was too dangerous. Some people thought Chorion Osiris was too dangerous even for the people who lived there.

It was definitely too dangerous for humans to go there. No humans ever went there—not any humans who wanted to survive to tell the tale.

Bandit adjusted course, but he didn't change his speed. Healey buried his face in his hands. Just when he thought this trip couldn't get any worse, this had to happen.

Chapter 6

Healey told himself not to look up when Rodeo said, "There it is. We're coming into orbit now."

"Where do you want me to set down?" Bandit asked.

Healey looked up without him thinking about it first. He stared through the gunship's cockpit window at a lush, green planet covered all over in thick, impassable jungle.

Everyone in the whole Confederacy knew about Chorion Osiris. The place was the stuff of legend and nightmares.

A single exploration mission had landed on the planet when the Confederacy first incorporated this part of space. The mission lost twenty of its thirty members before the survivors found a way to escape with their lives.

After that, no humans ever set foot on Chorion Osiris. No one of any other species set foot there, either. Chorions left the planet to join the rest of the Confederate population, but no one went down there.

Healey gulped more than once when Bandit brought the gunship into orbit.

"He's still following us," Rodeo muttered. "He isn't breaking off to keep away from the planet."

"Get us on the ground," Coon called from the back. "I'll get rid of him for you."

Rodeo only nodded and pointed to something on Bandit's controls. "Land over there."

Bandit descended without a word. No one in the back said anything, either. What did all these Chorions think about returning to their home planet?

Healey kicked himself for not finding out more about these boys before now. He didn't even know why they left their home planet in the first place.

He would have thought any sane person would want to get away from a place as dangerous as this, but none of them protested coming back here.

The Chorions on the crew didn't protest nearly as much about coming here as they did about going back to Acrolith Diastema. They definitely didn't want to go back there.

Bandit lowered the ship deeper into the atmosphere. Healey thought he saw things moving around in the jungle canopy, but he couldn't be sure. Great, heaving waves undulated across the surface, but that might just have been the wind.

Just then, another crack of gunfire smacked the ship from above. That shot punched the ship deeper into the atmosphere and another two shots drove the ship almost to the treetops.

"Get us on the ground—NOW!!" Coon bellowed again.

Bandit said something else and then another vicious boom forced the ship all the way down through the branches.

The engines still held the ship up and Bandit stabilized enough to hover there under the canopy's protection. "Set us down!" Coon snapped. "Hurry up!"

Bandit only nodded and set down between the trees. The jungle was so dense that he could barely find a spot big enough for the ship to fit.

Coon sprang out of his seat, dove for the rear hatch, and plunged outside in an instant. He didn't seem too concerned about the danger.

Bandit stayed where he was to power down the ship. All the other boys unbuckled their harnesses and went outside to follow Coon.

Healey followed more slowly, but he didn't dare to set foot on the planet. He should not be here. He was the last person who should have been here.

Coon ran a dozen yards into the jungle and dropped on one knee between the trees. He crouched there facing east and a break in the canopy gave everyone a view of the sky. A line of mountains cut off the horizon in that direction.

The pursuer's ship hovered there in the atmosphere. He seemed to understand the danger well enough not to land. He didn't descend, but he didn't fly away, either. He just hung there waiting for something.

Out of nowhere, a massive, jointed metal tentacle snaked out of the mountains, whipped through the air, and caught the enemy ship in an unbreakable grip. The engines flared, but it was too late. The tentacle retracted and pulled the ship down to the ground.

Coon stood up and faced friends. "Let's go. I can hold him there until we get there and find out who he is."

Rodeo glanced around, and for the first time, he actually looked at everything with his eyes. "We have a few hours before sunset. We should be able to get there in time." He turned to Bandit who was just stepping out of the ship. "Is the ship still fully operational?"

"It's fine," Bandit replied. "It will be fine if we leave it here."

"Let's go, then."

Rodeo turned to Wolf. "Is anyone around—anyone that could come after us?"

Wolf sniffed the air and then said in a perfectly intelligent voice, "There are four families in the area, but they already know we're here and they're hiding from us. We won't have to worry about them." He shot a glare at the jungle around him. "It's everyone else we have to worry about."

"Right. Let's get moving." Rodeo started walking and then spun around to stare at Healey.

Rodeo's milk-white eyes locked directly on Healey. That gaze made Healey squirm. This was the first time Rodeo had ever looked at Healey directly and Healey understood in that moment that Rodeo could see. He was back on his home planet and all these boys' powers worked perfectly here.

Coon's ability to manipulate metal didn't exhaust him here. Rodeo could see. Wolf could talk and think as clearly as any normal person. On this planet, he *was* normal. They all were.

Rodeo strode back to the hatch and looked up at Healey with that impenetrable gaze of his. "You need to stick close to us, Marshall. Do you understand?"

Healey had trouble getting his voice working. He didn't even care if the boys saw how petrified he was. "Yeah," he husked. "I understand."

"Come on, then—and don't use weapons. The species that live here can turn your weapons against you. We'll protect you." Rodeo waved Healey out of the ship. "Come on. We can't wait any longer."

Healey stepped down to the ground, and almost instantaneously, a living vine shot out of nowhere heading straight for Healey's neck.

Before he even realized what was happening, Alla cracked open his enormous mouth and chomped it down on something Healey didn't see.

Alla bit something out of the air from a nearby branch, and before anyone could react, Alla had it in his mouth and started chewing it up. "Nice try," he muttered.

Axel moved closer to Healey. "Stay between us, Marshall."

The boys closed around him and the party moved off into the jungle. They'd only gone another twenty feet before some monster Healey didn't recognize dropped out of the canopy directly over Healey's head.

A demon straight out of Hell opened a mouth full of razor fangs. It would have bitten Healey's head clean off, but Axel lunged for him and thrust his arm into the air over Healey's head. The creature clamped its jaws around Axel's arm, but the teeth didn't harm him.

Axel yanked the creature away, shook it off his arm, and then kicked it into the undergrowth.

More horrific creatures attacked the party every few seconds, but the boys always managed to deflect them before they got to Healey. A few local monstrosities attacked the boys, but they always defended themselves.

Healey did his best to hold it together. He was utterly defenseless on this planet. He couldn't even care that the boys had to keep him alive. He was too grateful for their protection. He would have been dead within minutes without them.

They hiked for two hours before they found the enemy ship. The tentacle holding it down still lay wrapped around the fuselage. The tentacle held the ship so tightly that the hull had crumpled under the pressure. Other than that, the ship was intact.

The boys circled it to the rear hatch. "It's empty," Bandit observed. "The crew must have hidden in the jungle."

"There's only one of them." Wolf crisscrossed the area sniffing the ground, the trees, the wind, and every rock and plant around the downed ship. "And he's a Chorion." He straightened up and peered into the undergrowth to the east. "He went that way."

"How can he be only one person when there were thirty people on that ship?" Bandit asked.

"There were hundreds at Ultra Meridian," Healey observed.

"If he's a Chorion, maybe he can multiply himself," Rodeo suggested. He narrowed his eyes at the surroundings. "It's too dangerous out here. We need to withdraw."

"Not yet." Coon approached the hatch and went on board the ship.

Healey, Rodeo, and Bandit went inside and found Coon sitting in the pilot's seat in the cockpit. His filaments had encased his arms halfway up to the elbow.

A solid mat of the same fibers had invaded all the ship's controls. The fibers covered the console in a solid mat of glowing threads.

"What are you looking for, Coon?" Bandit asked.

"The pilot....." Coon's glazed eyes darted back and forth. He stared into space and colored lights flickered across the controls under his hands. "He.....he met with Admiral Joyce......a week ago...."

"A week!" Healey exclaimed. "That was before Joyce captured Dice, Davenport, and Fiddler."

"Joyce....hired this Chorion to come after us.....and find the Ziprothil. The pilot has been following us. His contract is to eliminate us when he retrieves the Ziprothil. He's even supposed to eliminate Marshall Healey."

"Son of a bitch!" Healey muttered.

"We gotta bring this cocksucker down," Bandit muttered. "I don't care what it takes. A guy this evil has no business running around alive."

"Can you take the evidence with you, Coon?" Rodeo asked. "Can you copy it and remove it from the log records?"

"I'm doing that now." He fell silent for a while.

Healey glanced toward the hatch. What else was out there waiting to kill him?

Rodeo read his mind. "We need to find some shelter where we can spend the night."

"What about the gunship?" Bandit asked. "It's better than nothing."

Rodeo made a face. "It isn't what I had in mind."

"I found it," Coon interrupted and started withdrawing his filaments from the ship's controls. They retraced into his hands and the light went out of the ship's instruments.

He took his hands away and sat back, but he didn't collapse the way he did before. He remained bright-eyed and alert. He pulled a memory card out of the console and put it in his pocket before he stood up. "I'm ready to go."

The four of them went back outside to find Wolf still sniffing everything. "Can you find us somewhere to spend the night?" Rodeo asked. "Somewhere other than sleeping on the floor in the gunship?"

"I can find somewhere," Wolf replied. "It might not be any more comfortable."

"Just make it somewhere safe," Rodeo told him. "I don't care about anything else."

"Follow me," Wolf replied and set off through the jungle.

The boys closed around Healey again. They took turns deflecting, killing, or in Alla's case, eating whatever came out to kill them.

The local creatures must have picked up instinctively that Healey couldn't protect himself. They concentrated their efforts on him especially.

He went numb with all the forces threatening him. On that long, long hike back through the jungle, he made peace with the fact that he probably wouldn't survive to get off this planet. He was going to die here. The boys wouldn't be able to protect him forever.

The party returned to the part of the jungle where they started, but Wolf didn't lead everyone back to the ship. He took off to a different area.

Healey couldn't keep track of where they were going, but after another two hours of hiking, Wolf led the group into a set of curved rocks. They weren't as high as the cliffs at Ultra Meridian, but they formed channels that ran in crooked directions over miles of terrain.

Wolf followed them and finally entered an open, sandy area surrounded by these walls. He approached a cave on the far side and held up his hand for the others to stop.

The crew came to a halt and Wolf advanced more slowly. He inched one careful step at a time toward the cave, tilted his head back, and gave a spine-chilling yowl like an animal.

He did it again and again getting louder and more threatening and ferocious sounding. In the end, he swelled out his chest, threw back both arms, and bellowed into the treetops.

Dead silence answered him and then, very slowly, two little faces appeared out of the nearest cave. They were covered all over in black fur with bright, sparkling eyes and flat, round faces.

They studied Wolf over the rim of the cave. One looked like a girl with finer features and more pointed ears. The other had a boyish look despite his dark fur.

Wolf took a few more steps toward them and yowled again and again, but this time, it sounded like he was speaking another language—a feral language of pure wildness.

He got within twenty feet of the cave when, without warning, a woman shot out from the deepest shadows. She exploded from the darkness at full speed, collided with Wolf, and tackled him to the ground snarling, spitting, and baring her teeth.

She looked like a normal woman to Healey, but the way she acted was not normal. She wore tattered clothes that had been ripped in multiple places and dirt smudged her face, arms, and neck.

She slashed her teeth at Wolf, bowled him across the ground, and then sprang clear, rolled up onto her feet, and stood upright like a regular person. Wolf rolled into a crouch and stayed there coiled to spring.

He glared at her, bared his teeth, and snarled in hideous threat, but they didn't attack each other. The woman took a step forward and gave an answering growl in the same strange language.

Wolf didn't move, but just then, the two young ones bounded from inside the cave. They sprang across the ground on all fours, but as soon as they got near Wolf, they stood upright, too, and bounded around him like normal human children.

"Did you just come, Wolf?!" the boy exclaimed. "Did you bring us any presents?"

He stood up immediately and hugged them both. "I am your present, pipsqueak," he replied and made them laugh. He rubbed their heads and cuffed them a few times.

The woman stood off to one side watching them. She didn't approach them until the children settled down.

Wolf looked up and saw her staring at him. His expression softened and he made another yowling noise in his throat.

She burst out laughing and her whole demeanor changed. "You haven't forgotten, Wolf."

"How could I forget?" He beamed at her, broke away from the children, and crossed the sandy ground to hug her. "I smelled you earlier. Is everything all right with these two?"

"Everything's fine." The woman waved toward the rocks. "Viper is out there somewhere."

"That's good." Wolf turned to the rest of the crew. "This is my sister, Mave, and these two rascals are Dodger and Shade." He rubbed the children's heads again, first the boy's and then the girl's. "These are my friends. This is Marshall Lawrence Healey of the Confederate Sheriff's Service and these are Rodeo, Breeze, Alla, Laub, Axel, Bandit, and Coon."

Coon raised his hand. "It's nice to meet you."

"Thank you for seeing us," Rodeo told Mave. "We were just seeking shelter for the night. We didn't mean to put you in danger."

"You can't put them in danger," Wolf interrupted. "Mave has the ability to establish fields of protection around herself at certain distances. She's charged these rocks with the field so nothing can enter if it means any harm to her or the children."

"You might as well come inside," Mave told everyone. "We don't have much, but what we have, you're welcome to."

"Thank you," Rodeo replied.

She headed back to the cave. Healey still found it nearly impossible to believe that such a normal-looking woman could be Wolf's sister.

Then again, apart from his dark fur, he was acting so normal now that Healey shouldn't have been surprised. He shouldn't have been surprised by anything on this planet.

The children kept bouncing around Wolf bombarding him with questions and demands. "Where did you find a Confederate Marshall, Wolf?" Dodger asked. "Are you in trouble with the law?"

Wolf laughed. "If I was, you would be the last people in the galaxy that I would ever tell."

"Are you going home to Griva, Wolf?" Shade asked.

"I hadn't really thought about it," he replied.

"Have you seen any of the rest of the family?" Mave asked.

"I haven't had time to. I just landed a few hours ago."

The crew followed Mave back to the cave entrance where Healey had first seen these children. They acted so feral outside, but they behaved like normal children now.

They approached a fire pit in the center of the cave and a fire burst to life inside it without anyone doing anything.

Wolf laughed. "Which one of you did that? Was it you, Dodger? That will be a useful skill to have out in the jungle."

"It was me," Shade replied, and just to prove it, five more fireballs exploded all over the cave in random spots. They flared and died out just as quickly as if they'd never been there.

Wolf rumpled the fur on her head and smiled down at her affectionately. "That's fantastic. I can see you're going to be just fine."

Mave crossed the cave to the carcass of some animal hanging from the ceiling. Healey didn't see how it had been secured. Enough of the carcass had been hacked off that he couldn't recognize what it had been when it had been alive.

She took out a knife and started carving off a huge section of the meat. "Did Viper bring you that?" Wolf asked.

She shot him a grin. "Don't start acting all big-brother protective about him, Wolf. He's taken very good care of us since we came out here."

"I never said anything about it," Wolf countered.

Mave jerked her chin at Healey. "Where *did* you find a Confederate Marshall? I never thought I'd see one in the flesh."

"I never thought I'd ever set foot on Chorion Osiris, either," Healey replied and everyone burst out laughing.

He didn't see what was so funny about it, but Wolf only grinned at him. "Sit down, Marshall. You look exhausted."

Healey glanced around the cave. He almost asked if it was safe, but he could see that it was. He still couldn't get himself to relax.

In the end, it was Breeze who pulled Healey over to the fire and dragged him down to sit on the bare stone floor. "You're safe here. Mave's protection will stop anyone from coming."

"What about Viper?" Wolf asked.

"He comes and goes as he pleases," Mave replied over her shoulder. "He's no threat to us. I'm sure he already knows you're here."

"Chorions usually live in isolation," Breeze told Healey. "Mothers usually live in the jungle with their children to protect them from both the environment and their fathers. Fathers usually keep away in case the children get jealous of his contact with their mother and try to kill him."

Healey gasped. "Does that actually happen?"

"All the time," Axel interjected. "If the baby doesn't develop an ability to protect itself early on, it won't survive. Twins are even better because that's three people against the environment instead of two."

"You didn't say where you got the marshall," Mave repeated.

"He was on the ship with us when we landed here," Wolf replied. "He didn't want us to come here."

"Why did you come?" Dodger asked. "We thought you'd never come back."

"I came back to find someone. Maybe you know him. He can copy himself as many times as he wants."

Dodger frowned. "Interesting ability. I would definitely know if I'd seen anyone like that."

"Maybe he isn't from this part of the country," Rodeo suggested. "Maybe he's only here because Coon pulled him down here. Maybe our boy ran off back to his own people."

"He'll be looking for some other way off the planet," Coon added.

"Or maybe he just wants to wait until *we* leave the planet," Bandit chimed in.

Mave came over to the fire, skewered the meat, and put it over the flames. "I don't know anyone like that."

"Could you help us find him?" Wolf asked.

"I can't leave the children, but you could ask Viper to help you. He's really good at tracking."

Wolf scowled into the flames. "Maybe."

Chapter 7

Healey leaned back against a rock and fought to keep his eyes open. The two Chorion children lay curled up asleep on the bare rock floor. Their mother draped some furred animal skins over them, but the family didn't use any cushion underneath to pad the surface.

Breeze, Alla, Coon, Laub, Axel, and Bandit lay curled up on the other side of the fire in exactly the same way. None of them acted like this was anything unusual. None of them even seemed to notice the fact that Mave and her children were living in a cave and cooking over an open fire like primitives.

The Chorions all treated this as so normal that Healey had to admit the truth. The whole population must live like this. Maybe their planet was so dangerous that they'd never developed the technology to live any other way.

Healey knew that wasn't true. The Chorions had space flight. Chorions came and went from the planet via spacecraft all the time. They were some of the smartest, most resourceful people in the whole Confederacy.

And yet it all started here—in these caves. These boys must have all grown up like this—isolated from each other in tiny family pockets where they could protect themselves from all the dangers threatening them.

Wolf and Mave sat off to one side growling at each other in an undertone. It sounded like hushed whispers of conversation because it was. They spoke a language all their own.

Rodeo sat by the cave mouth training his ears into the darkness. He'd been sitting there for hours without moving.

Healey would have liked to ask a thousand questions about all these people's lives—like whether it was really true that Chorion children were in as much danger from their parents as from everything else in this hostile environment.

Healey couldn't figure out why he should doubt that. Everything else on this planet posed a threat to children—and anyone else who couldn't protect themselves—like him. He was more defenseless than the tiniest Chorion baby.

He was just about to get really depressed about that when Rodeo suddenly stood up, strode back into the cave, and halted by the fire. He frowned at Healey, the other Chorions, and finally at Wolf and Mave.

"There's another family out there," Rodeo announced. "I know them. I'm going out there to question them about the pilot. I'll be back before morning."

Healey struggled to his feet. "I'm going with you."

"No, Marshall," Rodeo snapped. "You can't go."

"Aw, come on," Healey chided. "I can't keep sitting here on my ass. Let me come with you. I won't slow you down, get you into any additional danger, or get myself killed. I swear it."

Wolf stood up. "I'm coming, too. If your friends know about the pilot, I want to hear what they have to say."

Rodeo scowled at him and then at Healey. "All right, Marshall. If you really want to come, I won't stop you. Just be ready to defend yourself. Understand?"

Healey nodded. "Yes. I understand."

"Come on."

He left the cave. Rodeo, Wolf, and Healey closed in a tight bunch. Wolf and Rodeo moved fast through the jungle and made no effort at all to keep their location a secret. They thrashed straight through the undergrowth.

Healey pushed himself to keep up with them, but he realized after an hour of bushwacking that their speed made it much more difficult for anything to attack them.

A few night creatures darted out of nowhere and went for Healey's face, neck, or tried to lash around his body.

Wolf and Rodeo were too intent on covering as much territory as possible. They walked in front of him and didn't see these attacks. Healey had to fight the creatures off with his bare hands, but pretty soon, he got into the habit of seeing the attackers before they struck.

The three men had been working their way deeper into the jungle for almost two hours before Wolf pulled Rodeo to a stop. "Ssh!" Wolf whispered. "Keep quiet!"

Healey held his breath, but he couldn't hear anything over his heart pounding. Wolf turned his head from side to side sniffing the air. Rodeo frowned at him. "I don't hear anything. What is it?"

Wolf bared his teeth and whispered. "It's Viper. He's here."

Before either Healey or Rodeo could react, Wolf shot off the ground in a mind-blowing leap. He sailed upward into the dark canopy and landed squatting on a branch directly overhead.

Healey didn't realize until Wolf landed there that another man was already squatting on the same branch. He must have been up there watching and listening to the three friends storming through the jungle.

Wolf landed easily next to this stranger. They squatted next to each other in the shadows for a few seconds and then they both jumped down.

The stranger wore the same tattered, torn clothing that Mave and the children wore. This man had shaved his hair on the sides and in the back, but that had been long enough ago that it had grown out to almost an inch long.

The top thatch hung over his eyes and gave him a feral, primitive look.

"This is Viper, Mave's mate," Wolf whispered. "He's been patrolling this area to protect Mave and the children."

"We're looking for another Chorion," Rodeo told Viper. "He can copy himself an infinite number of times—hundreds of times. Do you know him?"

"I've heard of him, but I don't know who he is," Viper replied in an undertone. "I've never seen anyone doing that. I wish I could help you. Is he dangerous?"

"Only to us," Wolf replied. "I would have smelled him if he was in the area. He went somewhere else."

Viper nodded. "If he comes here, I'll kill him."

"Do you know Silver?" Rodeo asked. "She's camped over there with her two babies. I heard them earlier."

"I know them," Viper replied. "You better be careful going near her. She doesn't like visitors."

"What about Fox, her mate?" Rodeo asked. "Is he in the area, too?"

"He's dead. Their younger twin boy killed Fox a few minutes after the twins were born."

Healey had to fight back the urge to gasp. Rodeo's features hardened. "How did it happen? Fox was a friend of mine."

Viper only shrugged. "You know how it is. The boy has a forked tongue. He can shoot out his tongue and kill things with it. He was crying and his tongue shot out and killed Fox. It was a freak accident and the boy was only a few minutes old. He had no idea what he was doing. It just happened."

Rodeo looked away. "I see."

Wolf squeezed his shoulder once. "Do you still want to see Silver?"

"I have to." Rodeo nodded at Viper. "Thank you for seeing us. You have a beautiful family."

Viper shot off the ground just as fast as Wolf. Viper rocketed into the air and landed in a squat on the same branch. He stared down at Wolf, Rodeo, and Healey for a second and then Viper blasted off into the shadows and vanished.

Rodeo turned away. "We better move fast. It will be dawn soon."

He took off through the undergrowth again. Healey and Wolf had to work even harder to keep up with Rodeo. He didn't turn around or look at or speak to them again until they made it to a high rock outcropping buried deep in the jungle.

A tiny glimmer of a fire burned in the darkness below them. Healey could just make out a woman squatting by the flames. She didn't live in a cave. She camped out in the open where anyone could see her.

Two little baby boys played and crawled and fumbled in the dirt right next to the fire. She watched them in between putting sticks on the fire and turning something in a long metal skewer that looked like a short sword.

One of the boys rolled onto his back and a long, snake-like tongue slithered out of his mouth. It coiled through the air before he pulled it back in.

The other boy crawled a few yards away from his mouth, and when he put his chubby little hand on the ground, a deep thump shook the soil under his hand.

He crawled to some nearby rocks, put out his hand, and it thumped again. It created such a deep concussion that it shattered the rock and blasted the fragments into the undergrowth.

The little boy laughed at his own ability, crawled to another rock, and did the same thing. The mother watched both boys, but she didn't smile at them. She had a hard, fierce expression.

She took her eyes off her sons to scan the darkness until, without warning, her flinty dark eyes shot upward toward the rocks where the three men stood watching her.

"Wait here," Rodeo growled and took off at a fast walk toward the fire.

"Should we do anything?" Healey asked as soon as he left.

"Yeah, we should wait here." Wolf squatted down. "Pull up a seat, Marshall. This could take a while."

Healey remained standing, but in a minute, he sat down and watched Rodeo approach the camp. Silver stood up as he got closer, but Healey saw right away that Viper was right. She wasn't happy to see Rodeo at all.

"Do you know her?" Healey asked Wolf.

"No, I never saw her before in my life."

"So.....you boys didn't know each other before you left Chorion Osiris?"

"We met on the transport ship leaving the planet. We didn't know each other before that. Rodeo belongs to a different tribe. We all belong to different tribes."

"Why is Silver in this area, then?" Healey asked. "Why is she so close to your family?"

"She probably wanted to get away from anyone who knew her. It happens like that with some mothers. They want to keep their children away from anyone or anything that might threaten the young ones."

Healey didn't ask any more questions. He didn't understand all this, but that was the point, wasn't it? He would never understand what it was like to grow up on a planet where everything was trying to kill you, including your own people.

Rodeo advanced to the ring of firelight, but he didn't try to approach Silver. She stood across the fire glaring at him.

"Can you hear them?" Healey asked.

"No, they're too far away. He would be able to, but I can't."

Rodeo and Silver talked across the fire at each other for what seemed like a long time. Then the younger twin crawled over to Rodeo and used Rodeo's leg to stand up. The little boy tottered there for a second and then his tongue darted out of his mouth.

He would have wrapped it around Rodeo's leg, but Rodeo shot out his hand and grabbed the tongue in a death grip. The boy tried to yank it back and then started howling when he couldn't.

Wolf chuckled under his breath. "Lesson number one, kid. Don't mess with Rodeo."

Rodeo let him go and the boy crawled away to sulk. Rodeo and Silver kept talking through the whole incident.

Healey expected their confrontation to end in a standoff, but after a few more minutes, Silver dropped back down into a squat and stared into the flames.

Rodeo reacted instantly, circled the fire, squatted down next to her, put his arm around her shoulders, and talked earnestly into her ear.

Rodeo stroked Silver's hair back from her face and then kissed the side of her head. She said something else and he pulled her in to hug her against his body.

Healey watched in silence. He regretted coming out here. He shouldn't be here watching this, but it was too late now.

Wolf must have been thinking the same thing. He stood up. "Come on, Marshall. Let's head back."

Healey followed without a word. They hiked for a long time and eventually made it back to Mave's cave. Mave was asleep.

Wolf curled up on the floor next to her, shut his eyes, and went straight off to sleep.

Healey sat down by the fire, but it took him a long time to settle down. He stared into the flames thinking over everything he'd seen and learned.

He might be the only human alive in the whole Confederacy who had seen this much of Chorion domestic life. How many people in the Confederacy knew what it was like on this planet?

After a while, his eyes felt heavy enough for him to lie down and go to sleep. Rodeo still wasn't back by the time Healey drifted off.

Chapter 8

Healey sat up and saw sunlight streaming through the cave opening. He also saw Rodeo sitting there in the same place as though he'd never left. He faced outward into the jungle listening to all the noises out there.

Healey stared at the back of Rodeo's head. Rodeo obviously didn't sleep last night.

The others took a long time to stir, and in all that time, Rodeo didn't move.

Healey didn't disturb him or ask if Rodeo had found out anything about their mystery pilot. Healey realized now that Rodeo hadn't gone out into the jungle in the middle of the night to find out about the pilot at all. He went to see Silver.

Healey would never know what happened between them and Healey didn't want to know. He almost wished he wasn't finding out so much about these boys' personal lives.

Mave and the children woke up first. They made so much noise that they woke up everyone else.

Wolf played with the children while Mave roasted another piece of meat for breakfast. Healey was having trouble deciding what to think of all this when Viper came in.

He carried another dead animal over one shoulder and dropped it on the floor next to Wolf. Viper squatted down by the fire and skinned, gutted, and cleaned the carcass.

He talked to Wolf nonstop while he worked and told Wolf all about people they knew, who had paired off with whom, who was living where, and all the people they knew who had died since Wolf left Chorion Osiris.

The others listened without interrupting. Viper hung the second carcass next to the first and then joined everyone for breakfast.

Rodeo didn't leave his place or even turn around when Viper entered the cave. Rodeo continued sitting there and didn't enter when Mave cut the meat up and served it to everyone else.

After they ate, Wolf stood up and said goodbye to his sister, Viper, and the children. He hugged them all and told them he hoped he would see them before he left the planet again, but he couldn't make any promises.

Healey and the other boys took their leave from the family, thanked Mave for everything, and walked out. Rodeo stood up and joined them when they left the shelter of the rocks.

The party walked for a long time without saying anything. Healey didn't know where they were going and he didn't ask.

He distracted himself by practicing defending himself against all the creatures and even plants that tried to kill him when he walked through the jungle.

He was getting better, but the job turned out to be infinitely more difficult in daylight. More creatures spent the daylight hours actively hunting.

Rodeo finally asked, "Where are we going?"

Breeze spoke up. "I know someone who can help us. Follow me. His camp is down the river."

He turned off and the other boys followed him with no argument or protest. No one offered any other suggestion.

That day's hike turned out to be considerably longer and more arduous. Breeze led the way downhill into some more mountainous areas of the jungle. The party had to climb multiple hills, down into ravines, and then back out.

They eventually came to a broad river lined on both sides with rock beds. Breeze followed it downriver, but that didn't make the going any easier.

By late afternoon, the hills on both sides closed on both sides of the river. The crew had to walk through the gravel beds.

They walked almost all day. Toward evening, Healey realized that Breeze hadn't tripped or done anything clumsy since the crew landed on this planet. Did he only act that way away from Chorion Osiris?

He followed the river to the point where the two towering mountains on either side came together in a sheer cliff. The river fell over the edge in a curtain of water.

Breeze walked straight up to the cliff to where an indentation in the rock led the way into a cave behind the waterfall. The deafening pound of water shook the rock on all sides.

Breeze crouched low and led the crew deeper into a series of caves until they widened out into a room buried under the mountain. A thin shaft in the ceiling let in a ray of sunshine.

A scruffy, greying man sat on a wooden stool in front of a worktable stacked with electronic equipment. Most of it looked derelict and obsolete.

The man didn't wear the same tattered, homemade clothing Healey had seen yesterday. This man wore a greasy, ancient Confederate mechanic's jumpsuit. The seat and thighs were so stained with grease that they had congealed into something more like solid armor.

The man was in the process of screwing something onto a fan motor. It wasn't hooked up to anything.

Breeze rushed forward and hugged the man. The man gasped in astonishment and then his eyes welled up with tears when he saw Breeze. "My boy!" He clasped both of Breeze's cheeks. "My boy! You came back! You're here!"

The old man hugged Breeze again and then glanced at everyone else. Breeze grinned from ear to ear. Healey had never seen him so genuinely delighted, not even when he clowned around to entertain his crewmates.

"This is my father, Jairo," Breeze told everyone and then he introduced his father to everyone by name.

Jairo stepped forward and held out his hand to Healey. "It's an honor to meet you, Marshall. You have my undying gratitude to you for looking after my son."

"Actually, he's the one who's been looking after me. He's a credit to you. You would be proud of him."

"I am proud of him." Jairo cupped Breeze's cheeks again and gazed into his eyes. Then Jairo sprang away. "But never mind all that. Come in, come in! Sit down. I have some food here."

He rummaged under his worktable and hauled out a giant steel chest locked with a massive industrial padlock. He collected an equally enormous ring of keys from his table and spent way too long hunting through them for the right key.

Breeze left to go into some other cave and came back with two regular wooden chairs. He propped them around the chest and went back and forth to bring in more seats for everyone.

Healey and the others lowered themselves into the chairs while Jairo fiddled with the lock. He finally popped it open, heaved back the crate lid, and revealed an absolutely bewildering array of every kind of wrapped, packaged Confederate food imaginable.

Healey stared at a mountain of ChunkyTenders, JuicyPies, Griffin cakes, Maltese Chipmunks, Duckwats, and countless other things. There must have been five hundred packages in that crate.

Healey scrambled to get his brain to accept what he was seeing. This whole episode contradicted every impression he'd gotten from his visit to Mave's cave and what he'd seen at Silver's camp.

Were the Chorions primitive people living in the Stone Age or were they Confederate citizens with access to electronic equipment and processed, packaged Confederate food?

"Help yourselves," Jairo insisted and he did help himself to a Griffin cake.

The boys each got themselves something to eat, too, and they all ate while Breeze and Jairo caught up on everything Breeze had been doing since he left home.

Interestingly, Breeze didn't varnish over the parts where he'd gone to work on Ekol Thaine's payroll. Breeze didn't doctor any of the details to make his employment in a murderous criminal syndicate sound more glamorous or upright than it really had been.

For some reason Healey couldn't for the life of him figure out, Jairo acted just as pleased by Breeze's tales as if Breeze had told his father that he'd spent that time saving humanity.

Jairo beamed at his son in overflowing pride and exclaimed over Breeze's exploits. Breeze did *not* tell his father about the whole Ithium scandal and everything the crew had been doing since Ekol assigned the Chorion Team to work for Davenport.

"Breeze's mother died when he was a baby," Jairo told Healey without any introduction. "I was watching them from a distance and I stepped in to raise Breeze alone after that."

"That's amazing. I'm impressed," Healey replied. "Your hard work certainly paid off. He's a fine young man."

"We're looking for a Chorion who just landed here yesterday," Breeze interrupted. "He can multiply himself and we know he's on the planet somewhere. Can you help us?"

Jairo rubbed the back of his neck. "I might be able to help you with that. Which way did he go?"

"His spacecraft crashed in the northern Kocha mountains and he headed southeast from there."

Jairo frowned even more deeply. "Kocha, huh? That's a dangerous area."

"We know," Rodeo replied. "We don't want to go there if we can find out that the pilot went in a different direction."

"If he can multiply himself, he could be anywhere," Axel pointed out. "He could have copies all over the planet."

"Then why hasn't anyone seen him?" Laub countered.

"Because no one has seen him multiply himself," Axel replied. "If he multiplies himself when no one is looking, then no one would realize that they're all the same person."

"Wouldn't they notice a couple hundred people who all look like the same guy?" Coon asked.

"Not if he can make the copies look different from each other," Rodeo suggested.

Jairo laughed. "That would definitely be a useful skill to have."

"That's why we need you, Father," Breeze told him. "No one beats you for tracking."

"Oh, all right. Since you asked, I'll do it."

"Thank you!" Breeze grabbed his hand. "I knew we could count on you."

Chapter 9

Healey woke up lying on a comfortable bed with sheets, blankets, and pillows surrounding him. He couldn't remember being this comfortable since he'd left Pandora's Needle.

He looked up at the ceiling and remembered where he was. He was on Chorion Osiris, but he didn't feel like he was in any danger here.

Jairo, Breeze's father, had put the crew up in a series of cave rooms winding back from the waterfall. Healey didn't see the end of this complex of caves.

Jairo had set up multiple rooms as bedrooms—or maybe someone else set them up that way and he just moved in and started living here.

Healey got up and made his way back to the room with Jairo's worktable in it. All the wooden chairs sat around the crate full of food.

Alla, Coon, Breeze, and Laub were already there eating. "You didn't eat it all yet, Alla," Healey teased. "I'm pleasantly surprised."

"Very funny, Marshall," Alla sneered. "I had to save some for you, didn't I?"

Healey laughed and helped himself to a ChunkyTender. "I appreciate you thinking of me."

"Don't worry about eating too much," Breeze told them. "Father can get as much of this as he wants."

"Where does he get it from?" Healey asked.

"He steals it from Confederate Corps vessels," Breeze replied. "Father belongs to a raiding crew. They leave the planet, raid Confederate Corps vessels, steal their supplies, bring everything back here, and sell it all to the locals."

Healey choked on his ChunkyTender. "You might not want to say stuff like that to Confederate law enforcement officers, son."

"Why not? It isn't like you or anyone else would ever be able to stop them. No one sees them. No one knows they exist. They use their abilities to stay hidden."

Healey's head shot up. "Seriously?"

"Of course. Everybody has to make a living. Why shouldn't they use their abilities to do it?"

Healey bent over his ChunkyTender and didn't say anything. He didn't ask what Jairo's ability was—or what any of his raiding crew's abilities were.

Healey had enough to worry about just dealing with Admiral Joyce and the Ithium. Some Chorion raiding crew ripping off Confederate Corps vessels was someone else's problem.

The other boys showed up in a few minutes. They all sat around eating and talking for another half an hour before Jairo dragged himself in.

His hair stuck out in odd directions and he shuffled his feet when he walked. He wore the same grease-impregnated jumpsuit as yesterday. He probably never took it off.

He didn't respond when anybody spoke to him. He flopped into a chair, pulled a JuicyPie from the crate, and stared into space while he munched it.

The boys kept talking while they waited for him to come back to his senses. Healey watched Jairo in fascination. Healey tried to guess what Jairo's special ability was. It must be something that allowed him to conceal himself. That would definitely be a useful skill to have.

Everyone on this planet had some skill that allowed them not only to thrive, but also gave them a unique edge when it came to earning a living. They developed these abilities in childhood and then exploited them later in life.

Jairo finally woke up from his trance, crammed another JuicyPie down his throat, and stood up. "We better make tracks if we want to make it to Kocha by dark."

The crew followed him back outside. Then they spent the rest of the day bushwacking back north to the crashed mystery pilot's vessel.

They got there late in the afternoon, but Jairo didn't show any sign of slowing down. He stuck his head into the vessel's open hatch and then took a tour around the area to survey the surroundings.

The tentacle that brought the ship down wasn't there anymore. Coon must have made it go back inside the mountain.

Jairo stopped in front of the vessel. "You're right. He went southwest. You boys start walking that way. I'll meet you over there."

The boys started walking, but Healey hung back. He wanted to see what Jairo did that made him such a great tracker and raider.

The minute he stopped talking, he sank into the ground and vanished. Healey looked down at the spot and saw what looked like the outline of Jairo's face moving under the dirt. It undulated away into the trees toward the southwest.

Then, out of nowhere, Jairo rose up out of the dirt thirty feet away from Healey. Jairo looked around, scanned the countryside, and then sank into the ground again.

The boys didn't seem to notice anything unusual about any of this. They just kept walking southwest the way Jairo told them to.

Healey hustled to catch up with them. They hiked for another ten minutes before Jairo reemerged from the dirt the way he did before.

"He's turning directly east toward Kocha," he told the boys. "It looks like he belongs to the Kocha tribe."

He made this announcement and immediately sank into the ground. He kept popping up at random spots along their route and redirecting the boys to follow the pilot's trail.

The party climbed a steep ridge, and after another hour and a half of hard hiking, Jairo reappeared right in their path. "This is the Kocha boundary. This is as far as I go. If you have any sense, you'll turn around and go back home. Don't go down there. It's too dangerous."

"We have to keep going," Rodeo insisted. "Someone put a contract out on our lives. If we don't stop the guy, he'll just keep coming after us—and he'll keep going after the clones. He won't stop until he gets the Ziprothil."

"Ziprothil!" Jairo fired back. "What does this have to do with Ziprothil?"

"Rodeo is right, Father," Breeze interjected. "We have to go on."

Jairo's face contorted in misery. "No, son! Not you! Don't go down there. You don't know what these people are like."

"*I'm* Kocha," Rodeo snapped. "Your son has been riding with me for years."

Jairo barely looked at Rodeo. Jairo wrung his hands and whimpered in despair. "Just come home, son. Please! Ekol Thaine is one thing, but this!" He shook his hands and moaned. "No, please, no!"

Breeze's features hardened. "If we don't stop these people, they'll use the Ziprothil against the Confederacy, Father. I have to go. We've covered too much ground already."

"Come with us," Healey urged Jairo. "You can help us. We could really use someone like you."

Jairo cast a terrified glance down the hill behind him and shook his head fast. "I couldn't! I couldn't go into Kocha. It's too dangerous there."

"It's no more dangerous there than it is everywhere else on this planet," Rodeo countered. "You've been listening to too many ghost stories."

Jairo didn't hear him. "You can't go down there, Marshall! Come back to the waterfall with me. Going down there would be suicide for you."

"He has to come." Rodeo turned to Healey. "You have to come, Marshall. You're here as a Confederate law enforcement officer. You can arrest the pilot and take him back to the Confederacy. He can give testimony that Joyce hired him to carry out a hit on us."

"Somehow, I don't think arresting the pilot will work," Healey remarked. "Not here."

"I'm certain that it won't work," Rodeo returned. "Chorions don't accept Confederate law on their own planet. The only law is blood and death which means one of us will have to challenge the pilot in open combat."

"What the hell?!" Bandit countered. "Which one of us did you have in mind for that? Don't even think about volunteering me for that."

"Cool your jets, boy," Rodeo growled. "This is my tribe and these are my people. It has to be me. Now come on. We're losing daylight here."

He set off down the hill. Healey would have liked to know what Rodeo meant by insisting that Healey attend as a Confederate law enforcement officer if Chorions didn't recognize Confederate law, but Rodeo didn't give anyone a chance to question anything.

The boys hesitated and then followed him one after the other. Jairo kept making little moaning noises of anguish. He kept doing it when Breeze hugged him. "I'll see you later, Father. Thank you for your help in bringing us this far. I really appreciate it."

Breeze broke away. The boys headed down the hill and Healey went with them. He was in this thing up to his eyeballs now. He wouldn't be able to back out, now when it really counted.

Jairo burst into a fresh convulsion of hand-wringing and wretched sobs watching Breeze walk away. Breeze gave one last backward glance and then passed down the hill where his father couldn't see him anymore.

"Why is the Kocha tribe so dangerous?" Healey asked after a while.

"They live as a tribe," Rodeo replied. "They're the only group on Chorion Osiris that lives together in one place. It amplifies the danger of accidents."

"And *not* accidents," Alla added. "The Kocha are also warlike and aggressive. Most Chorions are retiring and prefer to live alone. The Kocha are not like that at all."

"So....did you lie to Jairo when you said it was no more dangerous than everywhere else on the planet?" Healey asked.

"It isn't more dangerous because there are plenty of things that want to kill you no matter where you go," Rodeo replied. "You just need to stay on your toes."

Healey glanced at the other boys, but none of them took this as anything particularly noteworthy. They just accepted it as fact.

Chapter 10

The tension mounted as the party ventured further into Kocha territory. Healey didn't notice anything different about the terrain until they came to the flat ground at the base of the mountains.

The countryside became more domesticated, and toward dusk, the party approached a village in the distance. It looked placid and serene in the glow of the setting sun.

All of that went out the window when the group entered the village. The noise built to an ear-shattering din as the party got closer. Rodeo walked right into town on the main thoroughfare and the crew entered a hellscape of horrors unlike anything Healey ever dared to imagine.

Fights broke out in the street between the houses with people shoving, throwing punches, and then descending into vicious brawls while others stood around laughing and pointing.

People led monstrous creatures around on leashes. These creatures attacked each other, random bystanders, and the people leading them. No one seemed to consider this at all unusual.

The people leading these creatures stopped them in front of houses and carved off sections of the creature's flesh to hand out to anyone who wanted it.

Then housewives and a few men started cooking this food over open flames while the creatures went into rages from pain, fury, and in frustration at their own captivity.

Things took a turn for the surreal when the party ventured deeper into town and Healey saw people setting these creatures on children to fight in the middle of the street.

One man held a stout rope looped around the head of a giant creature covered in shaggy fur. The man jabbed the creature in the flank with a long sword and the creature thrashed in all directions baring its fangs and gnashing at anyone who came within range.

The man darted out of the way laughing and retreated to the end of his rope. Then he pushed a little boy toward the creature, pointed, and then the man sat down to watch.

The boy couldn't have been more than eight or nine. He wore nothing but a piece of some animal's hide tied in a loincloth around his waist and his matted hair stuck out from his head.

Dirt and grime covered the boy from head to foot and he advanced to face the creature with nothing but his bare hands.

The man who was obviously the boy's father sat at the end of the creature's rope and yelled for the boy to get at it right now. The boy flexed his legs into a crouch.

The creature thrashed in all directions, but everyone else backed away and left the boy alone to face the monster.

Healey turned away feeling sick. "Do we really have to watch this?"

Rodeo smiled at the scene. "It brings back memories."

"Did you used to do this?!" Healey gasped. "It's barbaric!"

"We did it all the time. We grew up playing this game."

"You call this a game?!" Healey snarled in a strained whisper. "That kid is gonna get slaughtered!"

"No, he won't," Rodeo replied. "Watch."

Healey didn't want to watch. Watching this was the absolute last thing he wanted to do, but he couldn't exactly walk away, either. He had to stay with the boys no matter what else he did.

Rodeo whistled through his teeth and clapped. "Come on, kid!" he yelled. "Break its neck!"

The other boys watched, too. Healey couldn't tell if they were as horrified as he was. Healey couldn't decide if he was more horrified by the scene or by Rodeo himself.

The fact that Rodeo's parents must have put him against some monster like this when Rodeo was blind and too small to defend himself—it boggled Healey's mind.

And yet here Rodeo stood—tall, strong, smart, and unquestionably rock-solid capable of defending himself against anything. Maybe his parents had the right idea after all.

Healey shook that thought out of his head, but he didn't have time to think about it before the monster gave a ground-shaking bellow and charged the boy.

He stood his ground until the last minute and then took a flying leap. He landed one foot on the monster's head. The monster roared again, tossed its head trying to chomp the boy, and the boy used the creature's momentum to vault clear.

He soared over the creature's back and dropped. He landed on the ground next to the creature's side, and as the boy fell, he stretched out his hand and dragged his fingers through the creature's fur.

The fur parted and the boy's hand sliced a deep gash in the creature's side. The wound gushed blood all over the place and the creature thundered in pain as it whipped around to face the boy.

The monster dove for the kid and tried to bite the boy in half, but the boy struck out a second time. He slashed another brutal wound down the creature's neck using only his bare fingers.

Healey stared in fascinated horror as the boy leapt clear again and landed in another tense crouch ten feet away.

The crowd went ballistic. Rodeo yelled himself hoarse and pumped his fist in the air whistling and clapping.

The creature shook itself all over, but anyone could see it didn't stand a chance against this kid. Blood poured from both wounds. The kid could have severed the creature's throat and ended the fight in seconds, but he didn't. He was toying with this creature.

The monster gathered its resolve, growled low under its breath, and narrowed its eyes at the boy. The boy coiled every muscle for the killing blow that would bring the creature down.

The creature lowered itself closer to the ground and then lunged for the boy, opened its mouth, and bared all its fangs to slash and tear.

The boy rocketed off the ground. He didn't use the creature as a vault this time.

The boy took another flying leap, landed one foot on the creature's neck, and from there, spun around to balance on the creature's back.

The boy wavered as the creature thrashed and tossed underneath him. The creature reared and contorted trying to grab the boy.

The boy waited until the creature threw back its head one more time and then the boy caught the creature by the fur on the back of its neck.

He held the animal there with its head pried all the way back. The creature burst into a fresh convulsion of struggling and yanking to free itself.

The boy didn't let go. The scene hung suspended in time and Healey saw that the boy was showing off for the crowd. He was riding this creature to entertain everyone and it worked.

The crowd cheered him. Those cheers filled the whole village.

Time stood still until, at some unseen signal, the boy pried the creature's head back just a little more, dove forward, and passed his bare hand across the creature's throat.

Black blood spurted from the wound and the creature buckled to the ground still trembling in its death throes.

The boy rode the body to the ground and then sprang off onto the ground. People charged him, surrounded him, clapped him on the shoulder, he beamed at them when they congratulated him.

Then all the village people surrounded the creature's body and started cutting it up into pieces. The father stood up, congratulated the boy, and went over to take the rope off the creature's head. The show was over.

Rodeo turned away with a sigh. "He did very well."

"Do you recognize anyone, Rodeo?" Coon asked.

"I recognize a lot of people. None of them can multiply themselves."

"Maybe we're misjudging this guy," Healey pointed out. "Maybe it's something else besides him being able to multiply himself."

"He might not be native to this tribe," Alla remarked. "He might have gone to a different village."

"No, he's here," Rodeo murmured. "I'm certain of it."

"Then who is he?" Bandit asked. "Do you sense anyone new, unfamiliar, or out of place?"

"No, it's just a gut feeling."

"How do we find him?" Healey asked.

Rodeo opened his mouth to answer when a deafening roar echoed through the village. "RODEO!!"

Everyone spun around and dead silence fell over the village when a hulking man with bulging, muscular shoulders stepped out of the crowd.

"RODEO!!" the man thundered. "I swore you would die if you ever set foot in this village again!"

All eyes followed the guy as he stormed up to Rodeo. Rodeo didn't move, not even when the stranger halted an inch from Rodeo's nose and snarled in his face. "You're a dead man, Rodeo."

"Prove it," Rodeo murmured.

The stranger bellowed even louder, but Rodeo didn't flinch. "CHALLENGE!!" the stranger roared. "CHALLENGE RIGHT NOW!!"

"Accepted," Rodeo murmured under his breath.

The guy spun away, spread his arms, and strutted around the village roaring in wordless aggression.

Rodeo stayed where he was. "What's happening?" Healey hissed.

"Back off, Marshall," Rodeo snarled through his teeth. "Keep out of the way."

Alla took hold of Healey's arm and pulled him away. Healey didn't want to find out what this challenge was, but he didn't want Rodeo fighting anybody, especially not a man twice his size.

Rodeo didn't even blink. He glared at the challenger as the guy kept barging around the village with his arms stretched out to both sides. The man widened his eyes at everyone and roared at the top of his lungs.

The sound threatened to snap Healey's last nerve, but when he tried to break out of line, the other boys grabbed him and held him back.

The challenger came storming back and clenched his hands into fists. He stomped toward Rodeo in such obvious menace that Healey flinched.

Rodeo didn't even raise his hands to defend himself. He stood still and waited for his challenger to come.

Without warning, an absolutely gigantic Chorion stepped out of the crowd. This man stood taller than the nearest house and he dwarfed the challenger by a mile.

The giant took two steps between Rodeo and his challenger. The challenger was already picking up momentum to attack Rodeo and the challenger nearly collided with the giant.

The giant raised one enormous hand, brought it down on the challenger with a crushing blow, flattened the guy to the ground, and held him there.

Some kind of sizzling reaction bubbled under his hand and his touch melted the challenger to a steaming puddle of goo on the ground.

Healey stared at the scene with his mouth open. The whole thing happened so fast that his brain took a second to catch up.

A dangerous silence fell over the village as everyone watched the challenger disappear under the giant's hand.

Rodeo stood still behind the giant's back. Rodeo didn't even move his head to one side to see what happened to the challenger.

The giant pressed the goo down into the dirt and then straightened up, wiped his hand on his ragged pants, and cast a brutal glare around at the onlookers.

Healey shrank from that look. Healey didn't want this guy touching him—whoever he was.

The boys cowered away from the guy, too, and the next minute, everyone in the village turned away and went back to whatever they had been doing before.

A few people looked over their shoulders at Rodeo and his friends, but no one came out to interfere anymore.

Healey couldn't go near Rodeo. Healey was starting to doubt if he'd ever known Rodeo at all. In fact, Healey was certain that he didn't. He'd been under a complete misapprehension about who and what Rodeo was. Maybe no one could understand Rodeo.

The giant stayed there planted in front of Rodeo. The giant glared at everyone to make sure everyone went back to their own business. Only then did he turn around and face Rodeo.

The two men leveled each other with a direct stare.....and then they both burst out laughing. The giant lunged for Rodeo and Rodeo lunged for the giant. They threw their arms around each other and embraced laughing their heads off.

They both broke apart and held each other at arm's length. "You still got it, you big dope!" Rodeo exclaimed.

"And you're just as stubborn as you ever were," the giant boomed. "You really would have fought him, wouldn't you?"

"Of course!" Rodeo exclaimed. "He challenged me. He should have known better."

"You would have broken him and left him maimed and alive. I know you!" The giant slammed his beefy hands on Rodeo's shoulders. "You're a fool for coming back here."

"I know!" Rodeo laughed again. "Anyway, you're here so it was worth it."

They hugged each other again and finally, finally Rodeo turned to face the rest of the crew.

His cheeks glowed with pleasure and his eyes sparkled in ways Healey had never seen. "This is my good friend, Talon," Rodeo announced. "Talon, this is everybody."

"You are lucky to have Rodeo as a friend," Talon told everyone. "He's saved my life many times."

"Stop it!" Rodeo muttered.

"Having good friends is important here," Talon went on.

"That reminds me," Rodeo told him. "We're looking for someone—a guy. He can multiply himself and make copies of himself. We know he came into Kocha in the last day or two. Have you seen any new people around—anyone you don't know or anything like that?"

Talon frowned. "No, nothing like that. No one new ever comes to Kocha. You know that—except for *these* people." He tossed his head at Healey and the other Chorions.

"Yeah, I know," Rodeo replied. "That's gonna make him difficult to find."

Talon got serious. "You know......about that other thing....."

"Yeah," Rodeo replied. "I guess there's no time like the present."

Chapter 11

"What is he doing?" Healey whispered to Coon.

"I have no idea," Coon replied.

Healey and the Chorion Team followed Rodeo and Talon to a nearby house. Healey didn't see anything special about the house except that, when the crew got near the door, he heard a whole lot of noise coming from inside.

Talon pushed the door open and Rodeo ducked under the low doorframe to get inside. Healey and the others followed, but it took Talon plowing his way in to force the crowd apart.

So many men packed the house that Healey and the others got caught crammed right up against the wall. Healey craned his neck to see where Rodeo was.

Lighted oil lamps lined the house walls to keep it bright in the gathering evening. Dozens of voices throbbed through the crowd when the crew got in, but that noise died as Rodeo forced his way deeper into the crowd and eventually stopped in the center.

Some people moved back to give him space and the outward surge knocked Healey into the wall. His calf bumped into something else, and when he looked down, he saw a log brace in the wall that held up the support post.

He stepped up on the log and could finally see what was going on over everyone's heads.

Rodeo stood at the center of the house with at least a hundred men surrounding him. Seven older, more distinguished men sat on one big, long cushion against the far wall.

These men didn't look like anything special, but as soon as the crowd parted to reveal Rodeo standing there, the man on the far righthand end of the cushion sprang to his feet and rushed into the open.

"Challenge!" he yelled. "Challenge!"

An older man on the cushion held up his hand. "Silence, Dane. You'll have your turn to speak."

Dane spun around to stare down at the man and then whipped the other way to glare at Rodeo. Dane faced outward into the crowd and Healey saw for the first time that one huge mask of scar tissue covered Dane's face.

Rodeo didn't look at Dane at all. Rodeo focused on the older man sitting on the cushion. "I accept the challenge. We can carry it out right now if Your Excellency wishes."

The old man held up his hand a second time. "One moment, please. You fled the village to escape justice, Rodeo."

"I never fled anything, Your Excellency," Rodeo countered. "I had no reason to flee from Dane. I won our last challenge and we both know it."

"You bastard!" Dane roared. "You did not win that challenge! You should have killed me—not leave me scared, alive, and in disgrace."

"And yet here you are," Rodeo replied in the same smooth tone and still without even looking at the man. "Here you are sitting at your father's right hand as one of the head men of this village. It looks to me like I did you a favor."

"You traitorous rotten scum!" Dane bellowed. "I challenge you! I'll tear you apart!"

"You'll try, you mean," Rodeo murmured. "You won't succeed. You accused me of sabotaging your father's rule last time. You challenged me, but you've never been able to beat me before and you won't be able to now."

Dane roared again, but the man on the cushion interrupted. "Dane! Be silent!"

Dane backed off instantly and the man on the cushion turned to Rodeo. "Why did you leave the village if you weren't fleeing from Dane? You left within a week of your last challenge."

"I got a job offer off the planet," Rodeo replied. "I'd been seeking work off the planet for over a year. It just happened to come through right after the challenge. It had nothing to do with that—as you can see by me coming back now. If I feared Dane, I would never come back."

"You fear me!" Dane roared.

Rodeo laughed, bowed his head, and then shook it, but he didn't turn to look at the man he'd so badly disfigured. "What is there to fear from you? You're a harmless mouse."

Dane bellowed again, and this time, he lunged for Rodeo. Four men jumped out of the crowd and grabbed Dane's arms to hold him back.

"Can you verify your claim that you left to take work elsewhere?" the man on the cushion asked. "Can you call anyone to corroborate your story?"

"There are three men standing in the back of this room right now who can verify it," Rodeo replied. "They were with me on the transport and they all shipped out to the same job with me. We all had to apply for the position six months before we shipped and we all got the call at the same time. They can corroborate that my departure was not sudden nor was it taken out of fear of anyone."

"Who are these men?" the older man asked.

"Their names are Breeze, Axel, and Coon."

The man on the cushion waved his hand again. "Bring them forward."

Everyone turned around to stare. Then every man present had to smash themselves even tighter against the walls to make room for Breeze, Axel, and Coon to make their way to the front.

Rodeo didn't turn around at all. He didn't look at his friends. He stared straight in front of him through it all.

"Do you know this man?" the old man asked the three crewmates.

"Yes, Sir," Axel replied. "We met him the day we all shipped out to Nox Anonyma."

"I do not know that name," the old man returned. "Did you apply for jobs there six months ahead of your date of departure?"

"Yes, Sir," Axel replied. "It happened exactly as Rodeo says. The job came out a year before that and we had to apply by the six-month deadline. Then we got called up three days before the ship was due to leave. We had to be there on the launch pad or miss our shot. We all went out on the same transport."

"And Rodeo went with you to the same job post?"

"Yes, Sir," Axel replied. "He's been with us the whole time. He's never worked anywhere else. None of us have."

The old man frowned. "I see. That puts a different spin on it."

"If you really want me to accept a challenge from Dane, I will, Your Excellency." Rodeo dragged his white eyes over to Dane for the first time. "You might not want that, though."

"You son of a bitch!" Dane roared. "I'll kill you!"

The man on the cushion waved them both away. "Do it....and finish the job this time, Rodeo. This fool has been insufferable since you hurt him last time."

The whole house erupted in noise. Rodeo turned his back on Dane and strode toward the crowd. Everyone shuffled their positions and spread out to clear a space in the center of the building.

People jostled and shoved both to get out of the area and to get into positions where they could see better. Healey hopped off his support post and had to elbow his way to the front where he could get near Rodeo.

Rodeo stood off to one side pulling off his shirt. Talon bent over him yelling in his ear. "Just do what you did last time! Nothing fancy. Don't play with him. Just finish it."

"You just said do what I did last time and finish him, but I didn't finish him last time," Rodeo pointed out.

"Will you stop screwing around?!" Talon thundered. "He'll kill you if you make a mistake."

"I won't make a mistake."

"You can't fight this guy!" Healey blurted out. "This isn't why we came here."

"This is the only way to find the pilot," Rodeo told him. "I can get the Chieftain's ear and he can tell me who in the tribe has the ability to multiply themselves."

"We could be wrong about the multiplying thing!" Healey yelled back. "You could be throwing your life away for nothing."

Rodeo barely glanced at him. "The pilot can help us prove that Admiral Joyce put out a hit on a Confederate Marshal and that he was after the Ziprothil. We have to find the pilot and the Chieftain's help is the best way to do that."

He turned away to face the open space in the center of the room.

"Don't intervene this time, Talon," Rodeo ordered over his shoulder. "Whatever happens, stay out of it."

"Aw, come on, man!" Talon growled.

Rodeo didn't look at him again. Rodeo faced Dane across the circle.

Dane didn't take his shirt off. His friends rubbed his back and shoulders on their side of the ring. They jostled him and yelled in his ears.

The noise in the house escalated to a din. Rodeo cocked his head, but he wouldn't be able to hear with all these voices yelling, cheering, and whistling.

Healey couldn't tell how much Rodeo could see on this planet, either, or if Rodeo could see at all.

In that moment, Rodeo didn't seem like a scrawny kid anymore. He stood straight, tall, and square-shouldered facing his old enemy. Dane was bigger, stronger, and obviously better connected, but Rodeo didn't back down.

Dane's friends pushed him forward and Rodeo took one step into the open ring. Dane danced around him in circles holding his fists in front of him. Rodeo didn't move except to angle his head back and forth the way he used to when he was blind.

He followed Dane's movements back and forth, but Rodeo didn't even raise his hands to defend himself.

Healey's stomach twisted in knots. He didn't care what Talon did. If this fight turned against Rodeo, Healey would step in.

He didn't know what he would do against a bunch of ferocious Chorions, but he would have to do something. He couldn't let Rodeo die.

The other boys pushed their way to the front and lined up right at the edge of the ring. They yelled at Rodeo and pumped their fists with the rest of the crowd, but the boys' voices got lost in a sea of noise.

Healey and Talon were the only people present who didn't seem happy about Dane and Rodeo facing off in a battle to the death. Everyone else in the house crowded around and more people packed inside until they filled the house to bursting.

Dane kept dodging here and there until, without warning, he rushed Rodeo and threw a punch straight at Rodeo's face. Rodeo reared out of the way just in time and Dane's fist whistled past Rodeo's nose.

Dane immediately followed up with a combination of punches that would have pulverized Rodeo into next week, but he dodged them all. He jolted his head back and forth from side to side and backward to avoid every punch.

In the middle of his combination, Dane vanished and instantly materialized behind Rodeo. Dane sprang forward to catch Rodeo from behind, but Rodeo reacted just as fast and threw an elbow over his shoulder.

He nailed Dane right in the face and Dane staggered backward. His hand flew to his face.

Rodeo still didn't turn around. He went back to standing in one place with his back to Dane and staring straight in front of him. Rodeo kept tilting his head from side to side and listening to every sound assaulting his sensitive ears.

Dane stumbled back into the ring and his expression hardened into a glare at the back of Rodeo's head. Dane clenched his teeth and vanished again.

He blinked into existence on Rodeo's left side and threw a punch at Rodeo's head, but Rodeo ducked it, and just as fast, threw a punch of his own into Dane's stomach.

Dane burst into a rapid sequence of movements, blinked out in one spot, and reappeared somewhere else just as fast. He attacked at each of these new places, but Rodeo either avoided Dane's assault or retaliated harder and faster than Dane. Every one of Rodeo's hits left Dane reeling.

Dane made ten of these moves in rapid succession until, at random, he appeared right in front of Rodeo. Rodeo reacted with impossible speed, kicked high and hard, and landed his heel into Dane's chin.

Dane's head whipped back, and for the first time, Rodeo attacked without mercy. He rushed Dane while Dane was still blinking the stars out of his eyes.

Rodeo seized Dane by the head, yanked him forward, and Rodeo dove for the floor taking Dane with him. Rodeo pivoted his weight on top of Dane's body and concentrated all his strength and weight on Dane's head to drive his face into the floor.

Rodeo reared on top of Dane and Rodeo bared his teeth in a deadly snarl. The house exploded in deafening cheers and yells when Rodeo vaulted onto his knees, seized the back of Dane's head, and started scraping Dane's face across the rough floorboards.

Just when it looked like Rodeo would scrape Dane's face clean off, a scuffle broke out on the other side of the ring. Four men who'd been supporting Dane broke out of the circle and charged Rodeo from behind. He didn't hear them over the noise.

Healey braced himself to intervene, but Talon got there first. He charged between Rodeo and Dane's friends. Talon extended his enormous arms to block these men from interfering with the fight.

Rodeo kept his back to the commotion, but the conflict escalated unbelievably fast. More people surrounded Talon and Dane's friends to get involved.

Random strangers showed up either to help to pull Dane's friends away or the onlookers tried to pull Talon away from Dane's friends to let them into the ring.

More people surrounded all the parties on both sides. Talon barely managed to use his huge bulk to block everyone from invading the ring.

People grabbed his arms and pulled him off balance. He roared as he toppled over, but he twisted his weight so that he fell backward into the crowd.

His fall created a domino effect and a mass of bodies fell around him. Everyone who'd been holding onto him went down in a sea of chaos. People punched and kicked each other, and in seconds, the crowd deteriorated into an all-out brawl.

People from the other side of the ring shoved to get involved, and in that moment, Rodeo launched himself off the floor. He left Dane lying face down on the floorboards. Healey couldn't see how much damage Rodeo did to Dane's already ruined face.

Rodeo leapt upright, brought his foot down in a crushing smash on the back of Dane's head, and drilled Dane's head all the way through the floorboards. The force of that kick shattered the boards and left Dane's head dangling from the neck through the hole toward the dirt below.

That one kick set off another chain reaction in the crowd. Everyone rushed inward from all sides. The empty space vanished as hundreds of people charged the center and Rodeo submerged beneath the tide.

Chapter 12

Healey stood outside the Kocha Chieftain's house and waited. Night had fallen while Healey and the Chorion Team had been inside.

Healey had been one of the very few who escaped the house before the whole shitshow went down in flames. He couldn't do anything to intervene, not even when Coon, Axel, Alla, Breeze, Laub, and Wolf all got pulled into the mayhem, too.

Healey had worked himself out of the house without getting hit by anyone, thank God. Everyone in there had been too busy fighting each other to pay any attention to him.

He stood outside and waited until the noise died down. Then people started coming out of the house one or two at a time. Nearly all of them had been injured and some supported each other to limp away to their own houses.

Then Laub and Axel came out with Coon and Wolf. Wolf had a bloody nose and Coon was limping. Laub and Axel were completely unharmed, and a few minutes later, Breeze came out looking as fresh as a daisy.

Alla took longer to show up, and when he did, his stomach had swollen to twice its normal size. He lowered himself painfully onto a nearby stump, rubbed his stomach, and groaned.

"Where's Rodeo?" Healey asked and then passed his hand across his eyes. "I don't want to know how bad it is."

"He's still in there talking to the Chieftain," Breeze replied. "This could take a while."

More people came out of the house and Healey caught a glimpse of the interior. Enough people had left that he could see into it and the lamps illuminated everything inside.

Rodeo sat on what looked like a box in the middle of the room. He had his back to the door and the Chieftain and his men stood around Rodeo talking.

Healey made a snap decision and went inside. Ten Chorions remained in there apart from the Chieftain's people. Thirty bodies covered the floor, but no one paid attention to them.

No one paid attention to Dane, either. His father and his father's entourage ignored the body entirely as if it wasn't there.

Rodeo sat hunched over with his arms wrapped around his stomach. Healey circled him and saw blood running down Rodeo's face. One of his eyes had been smashed in.

Talon stood next to Rodeo in a guarding posture and glared at everyone, including Healey.

"I'm telling you he landed in the northern mountains and he walked straight here," Rodeo was saying. "He wouldn't come here if he wasn't Kocha."

"I believe you, my son," the Chieftain replied, "but there is no one in our tribe with the ability to multiply themselves the way you say. I would know about that."

"Not if he's hiding his ability," one of the other men pointed out.

"If he's hiding his ability, then I wouldn't know he has it, would I?" The Chieftain turned back to Rodeo. "You have earned every bit of help I can give you, but I've never even heard of a man with the abilities you describe. I can send word to the other tribes and ask them, but if this man you seek is hiding his abilities from us, he would be doing the same with the other tribes as well. You must see that."

Rodeo gasped under his breath and turned his head away. "Damn it!"

"He must have been hiding his abilities even from his own parents," Talon pointed out. "His parents would have reported their child's abilities to the Chieftain."

"Not if the parents raised the boy somewhere else—apart from the village." The Chieftain cocked his head to study Rodeo. "You should go home and rest, my son. You cannot carry on this mission tonight. You've done enough. Go home and get the care you need. You can come and see me in the morning."

Rodeo rolled his eyes, groaned, and hauled his injured body off the box. "Yes, Your Excellency," he mumbled. "Thank you for your support."

"Of course, my son. You did very well to come and see me. It is good to have you back in the village. We've missed you."

The Chieftain laid his hand on Rodeo's shoulder and steered him away. Rodeo turned to the door and saw Healey standing there.

They locked eyes for an instant and then Rodeo turned back to the Chieftain. "Your Excellency, this is Confederate Marshall Lawrence Healey. He's under my protection. I expect everyone in the tribe to respect that."

The Chieftain shut his eyes and bowed his head. "Of course, my son. I will pass the word around the village." The Chieftain opened his eyes and turned to Healey. "Welcome, Marshall. Please consider yourself our guest."

"Thank you, Your Excellency," Healey replied and moved out of the way so Rodeo could hobble painfully out of the house. Healey and Talon had to wait for him to go first before they followed him. They met up with the other boys standing outside.

"Follow me," Talon told them. "You can come to my house."

He led the way through the village to a much smaller house. Talon opened the door and firelight flooded from inside.

He held the door open for Rodeo to drag his battered body inside. This house had been set up differently from anything Healey had seen before.

More of the long cushion couches surrounded a firepit in the center. One of the cushions had been unfolded on the floor across the room. Three children lay there asleep.

A woman stood by the fire with the flames glowing on her smooth cheeks, bright black eyes, and long, glossy black hair.

She rushed Rodeo the minute he walked. He winced when she hugged him. "You stay away for years and then you come into my house looking like this!" she exclaimed. "Do you have to get yourself killed the minute you step into the village?"

"Apparently," he muttered and collapsed on one of the cushions that still served as a couch. He groaned, winced, and pressed his arm against his stomach. "Where's Reese?"

The woman waved toward the door. "He's out there somewhere. He's probably busy with all the wounded. Talon can go get him for you if you really need him."

"I can wait." Rodeo leaned back on the cushion and groaned again. The woman started working around the house, brought a bucket of water over to the couch, sat down next to Rodeo, and started dabbing the blood off his face.

He didn't protest. Healey was just marveling at how close they seemed when Talon distracted everyone.

"Please sit down and make yourselves at home," he told everyone. "This is my sister, Dawn. Please...." He waved everyone toward the couches, and just to seal the deal, he shut the door with everyone inside.

Healey sat down on a couch across the room, but he couldn't help but see how much attention and care Dawn was giving Rodeo. She sat extra close to him. Were those his children asleep on the cushion? Healey wouldn't have been at all surprised.

Talon rummaged in a corner and came back with a bunch of stolen Confederate food like the packages of junk the crew had feasted on in Jairo's cave. Talon passed everything around to the guests and then sat down with them to eat it.

"What are we gonna do now?" Coon asked. "No one knows about our guy."

"I don't know about you, but as soon as Reese gets back, I'm going to pass out until tomorrow," Rodeo replied. "The Chieftain is right. We can't accomplish anything else tonight. If he doesn't know who the guy is, then this pilot must be very well hidden."

"Who's Reese?" Breeze asked.

"He's my husband," Dawn replied. "He has a healing ability. He'll tend to all the critical injuries and then take care of Rodeo when he gets back."

"Who is this man who can multiply himself?" Talon asked.

"He's a pilot," Bandit replied.

"He's working for our enemies," Axel added. "Someone put out a contract on us and this pilot is carrying it out."

"Or trying to," Coon finished.

Talon looked back and forth between them. "Did you all work for Ekol Thaine?"

"I didn't," Healey told him.

"He was the Sheriff of Pandora's Needle before all this started," Alla explained.

"And the rest of you?" Talon's gaze sliced from one face to another. "Where do you all come from?"

"I belong to the Etholla tribe," Wolf replied.

Talon burst out in loud, rolling laughter. "I guessed that."

Some of the others laughed, too. "They come from different parts of Chorion Osiris," Rodeo explained. "You know how it is. None of them comes from any other tribe."

"And did you all meet in Ekol's service?" Talon asked.

"We met on the transport going to Nyx Anonyma," Alla replied. "There's nothing more than that to tell."

Talon made a face. "There is always more than that to tell."

Just then, the door opened and another man burst in. "Where is he? Where's....." He broke off when he saw Rodeo lying there.

The stranger looked completely different from every other Chorion that Healey had seen so far. This new man had shaved his head and he looked a lot cleaner than every other Chorion on the planet.

The stranger rushed over to Rodeo, pushed Dawn out of the way, and laid his hand on Rodeo's chest. "I got here as soon as I could."

Rodeo collapsed back on the cushion, shut his eyes, and groaned again. "Thank you, man! Thank you!"

Everyone watched as the cuts, bruises, and scratches on Rodeo's face vanished. He sank into the cushion with a relieved sigh and his arms finally unwound from his midsection.

"It's good you finally killed Dane. Someone had to and you're the only one who could do it without incurring the Chieftain's wrath." The stranger stood up and cast a critical eye around the group before he saw Coon. "You—you got hurt in the fight, didn't you?"

Coon started to shrug, but the man crossed the room immediately, laid his hand on Coon's head, and held it there.

When he finished, he let his hand drop and looked around one more time. "I am Reese. You are all welcome to my home. Talon—are you hurt?"

"No, man. I'm fine."

Reese snorted, sat down next to Talon, and tore open a packet of Dominoes. "Unlike the men you killed, am I right? Lance is over there now vanishing the bodies."

"At least the Chieftain isn't upset about Dane," Rodeo remarked.

"He hates Dane," Talon interjected. "The Chieftain has been trying to find a way to get rid of Dane ever since you left. The Chieftain was more upset about you leaving than Dawn was."

Dawn threw her wet rag at her brother. "Stop it. Don't spend the whole time teasing me about Rodeo. You should all go to sleep now. It's getting late."

She went around the room unfolding all the cushions and giving everyone blankets to lie down and wrap up in. The guests had to share the big cushions among themselves.

Rodeo wound up sleeping with Breeze and Laub. Talon had to share his own huge mattress with Wolf and Healey.

Reese and Dawn finally retired to their own bed. The flames kept flickering on the rafters above Healey's head, but he heard Reese and Dawn whispering long after everyone else went to sleep.

Reese didn't act at all jealous about Dawn getting upset over Rodeo's departure. The dynamic between all these people left so many unanswered questions. Healey wasn't likely to get those answers, either.

One thing was certain. Healey was starting to understand now where Rodeo got his dominant personality.

Women gravitated to him. Men either loved him or hated him, but no one could ignore him.

The Chieftain honored Rodeo even more than his own son. That was one explosive combination. So why did Rodeo leave to become a hired gun for Ekol Thaine? He could have been ruling here instead.

Chapter 13

Healey stepped out of Reese's house and spotted the man standing off to one side. Reese held a basket woven out of twigs and rushes. One of his children squatted in front of him.

This one was a little girl, but she was dressed the same as the others. A hand-stitched dress of rough buckskin covered her down to her knees and she looked like no one had combed her hair since the day she was born.

"Are you ready?" Reese asked her. "You can do it. This one is easy."

The girl nodded. "I'm ready."

Reese pushed her away. "Take a few steps back. Give it some space. If anything happens, I'll be right here to help you."

The girl nodded again. "I can do it."

"Good." Reese took hold of the basket's lid. "Here it comes."

The girl backed away until she stood five feet away from her father. He leaned all the way back to keep his head away from the basket. Then he ripped off the lid and aimed the basket at the girl.

A long, snake-like body rocketed from inside, except that this was no snake. The creature's mouth stretched to three feet across with huge fangs lined in dozens of rows inside.

The monster flew straight for the girl and she raised her hand to block the creature from getting near her. She planted herself in one spot, gritted her teeth, and the monster flew straight into her hand.

The mouth closed to bite her in half....and then the creature disappeared inside her hand. Its long body slid into what would have been her arm except that her arm wasn't big enough to contain the whole creature.

"Fantastic!" Reese exclaimed as soon as the snake vanished. "You did it!"

She only shrugged. "It's easy."

"Are you ready to put him back out again?"

"Into the basket?" the girl asked.

Reese looked around. "Maybe Ray would like to take a turn."

"Who's Ray?" Healey interrupted.

"My brother." The girl turned to Reese. "We either have to do it now or put it back in the basket. If I keep it, I might use it later."

"We wouldn't want that," he told her. "It's better if he knows what's coming."

Healey didn't understand their conversation until Reese went into the house and came back out with his young son. The boy couldn't have been more than six.

Reese steered the boy over to his sister. "Sky has a merth in her hand, Ray," Reese told his son. "She's going to release it so you can fight it."

Ray rolled his eyes. "Not that again."

"Just take care of it and then you can go." Reese stepped away. "Are you ready? Put it out, Sky."

The boy and the girl glared at each other. Healey had to bite back a grin. He could just see the history between these two.

Ray compressed his lips. "Do it if you're going to do it. Get it over with."

The girl held out her hand, and without warning, the snake thing exploded from her palm. It widened its mouth and lunged for the boy to bite his head off.

The boy narrowed his eyes at the merth and the snake dropped dead right there in midair. Its long body flopped on the ground without even a twitch.

Healey stared at it, but it really was dead, just like that. The boy had a death glare—literally.

"That's excellent!" Reese gushed. "You both did excellently. You can both go play now."

The two children ran off in opposite directions. Reese picked up his basket.

"Do you do this kind of thing a lot?" Healey asked.

"We have to," Reese replied. "We have to train the children to be ready to defend themselves. They need to be ready to handle anything they might meet out there—or anyone they might meet in the village. We would be doing the children a disservice if we didn't prepare them."

Healey looked away, but he didn't argue. He was beginning to see that what he thought was horrific mistreatment of these children might just be the one thing that kept them alive until they grew to adulthood.

Reese read Healey's mind. "It isn't your way, but it is ours."

"It's just so different," Healey murmured. "It's hard to imagine anyone growing up like this, and yet....."

He trailed off when he saw Rodeo talking to another man across the village. The other man was young with shoulder-length sandy brown hair and piercing green eyes.

The two young men were about the same height and build and they obviously knew each other well. They smiled and laughed with each other and then Rodeo clapped his companion on the shoulder before they split apart.

Rodeo had grown up like this. He had grown up fighting these creatures and probably his fellow tribesmen. He'd had to fight for his life in battles to the death. What would it be like to grow up like that?

The rest of the Chorion Team had grown up the way Dodge, Shade, and Silver's boys grew up in the forest. These children must have seen it all—all the horrors and dangers this planet could throw at them.

Rodeo left his friend, crossed the village, and came over to Reese and Healey. "Any luck?" Healey asked.

"No one in the village knows of anyone with a multiplying ability," Rodeo replied. "Whoever he is, he isn't in this village."

"How are we going to find him?"

"I know someone who can help us, but he lives out in the jungle. We'll have to hike out there and visit him."

"How long will that take?"

Rodeo shrugged. "A day or two, but it will be worth it. If our pilot is anywhere on the planet, this guy will be able to find him."

Healey didn't necessarily believe that, but he didn't say so out loud. Some of the local children had discovered Breeze's secret superpower. Now he stood on the other side of the village entertaining them with his antics.

He was in the process of bending over and pulling down his pants when Talon returned from somewhere. "The Chieftain wants to see you, Rodeo."

"What for?" Rodeo asked.

"He didn't say. He only said he wants to see you this morning."

"It better be something about the pilot," Rodeo growled. "If it's anything else, I'm not interested."

"You tell him that," Talon replied. "You're the only person alive who can talk to him like that."

"You come with us, Marshall," Rodeo went on. "The Chieftain likes you."

"He does?" Healey asked. "Why? He doesn't know anything about me."

"He just does. He wouldn't have been so cordial to you last night if he didn't like you."

Healey couldn't argue with that, so he followed Talon and Rodeo back to the Chieftain's house.

Just as many people packed the place as before, but at least no fights broke out this time. New people had replaced those who died in last night's brawl and all the bodies had disappeared as though they were never there.

The crowd parted again to let Rodeo through, but no one stopped talking. They treated his arrival as an everyday occurrence.

He advanced to the Chieftain's cushion and all the men of the Chieftain's entourage stood up. The Chieftain waved Rodeo forward. "Come! Come and sit down, my son."

Rodeo sat down next to him. Healey didn't know what to do until Rodeo pointed his chin at the spot next to him. Healey sat down there.

"I want you to take Dane's place on the council," the Chieftain told Rodeo. "You've earned it. I need a man who knows how to get things done."

"I'm honored that you would bestow such a privilege on me, Your Excellency," Rodeo replied. "I would be honored to accept as soon as I find this man I'm seeking. I wouldn't be able to give the tribe the attention it deserves until I complete this mission."

The Chieftain gave a little gasp of annoyance. "Can't you search for him from my right hand? Why the delay? You can do both."

"My friends and I are going over the mountain to consult with Coots. If he helps me find the pilot, then I'll consider what I can give to the tribe."

"Then you accept?" the Chieftain asked. "I would be most delighted."

"I'll know better whether I can accept after I find the pilot. I wouldn't want to commit myself before then."

"Why is this pilot so important to you?" the Chieftain asked. "Is he more important than your own tribe—your own people?"

"I wouldn't be so valuable to you to take Dane's place if I didn't complete my mission," Rodeo replied. "I'm honored. I truly am. I must complete this mission by finding the man I seek. Then I'll know what I can commit to the tribe or if I can commit anything at all. With Your Excellency's permission, I'll go do that now."

"If you must," the Chieftain replied. "Come and report to me when you get back."

"Yes, Your Excellency," Rodeo replied, nodded to Healey and Talon, and left the house.

"Wow," Healey remarked after they got outside. "Are you sure you want to turn your back on this? This could be big for you."

"I didn't go to all the trouble of leaving home so I could crawl back to Chorion Osiris and watch these people tear each other apart," Rodeo snarled under his breath. "We're here to find that pilot and wring him for everything he can tell us about Joyce's plans. That's the only reason we're here. The only reason I went through that challenge last night was so the Chieftain could tell us who the pilot is. Now I find out the Chieftain doesn't know anything and the whole challenge was a waste of my time." He turned away. "We're going to see Coots. If he can't tell us anything, I say we leave this planet and go about our business. Chorion Osiris is no use to any of us."

Chapter 14

Talon and Rodeo rounded up the rest of the crew. Talon provided each person with a backpack full of supplies and they set off over the mountains.

Reese and Talon both came with the crew, but it became even more obvious as the day wore on that Rodeo was in charge—as if he'd ever been anything else.

He led the line back toward the west country where the crew had landed their gunship. He headed straight for it, but after midday, he turned south into a much deeper, more rugged stretch of mountains.

The crew hiked all day and camped in the open that night. Talon used two flint rocks to light a fire and everyone sat around it talking.

"Who's Coots?" Healey asked.

"He's a member of the Kocha tribe, but he doesn't live in the village," Talon replied. "He likes to keep to himself."

"How will he help us find the pilot if he's Kocha and no one in the tribe knows who the pilot is?" Healey asked.

"Let's just say Coots has some interesting abilities," Rodeo told him. "If he can't find the pilot, then the pilot isn't on the planet."

Healey didn't remind Rodeo that he'd made that claim before. He'd claimed that the Chieftain would be able to tell the crew where the pilot was, but the Chieftain couldn't tell them that.

Healey was beginning to question whether finding out the pilot's identity really mattered that much. Coon had enough evidence from the pilot's ship to prove that Joyce put out a hit on Healey and the Chorion Team. Why did they need the pilot, too?

Healey didn't say that out loud, either. Finding the pilot seemed to have become an obsession for Rodeo.

He seemed to take it as a personal insult, first that the pilot was a Chorion, that a Chorion would be working for Admiral Joyce, and that the pilot had taken refuge in Rodeo's own home territory.

Worst of all, Rodeo seemed to take it as a personal slap in the face that the pilot had so effectively evaded the crew until now. Rodeo seemed to want to find the guy just to prove that he could beat the pilot at whatever cat-and-mouse game they were playing.

Healey caught the other members of their team shooting Rodeo sidelong glances behind his back, too. None of them mentioned it, but they all questioned his mental state as much as Healey did.

The weirdest part was that Healey couldn't find anything wrong with Rodeo's mental state. If anything, he'd been acting more confident, more authoritative, more competent, and more determined than Healey had ever seen him before.

Rodeo had conducted this investigation with the skill of a military general. Healey just questioned if Rodeo should be conducting this investigation at all.

Healey could have pulled rank on Rodeo and gotten him to back down. That is, Healey could have pulled rank on Rodeo anywhere but here.

Healey took a back seat as long as they were on this planet. He couldn't really do anything else.

The crew woke up early the next morning, but as soon as they started walking, everything else started going wrong.

The crew had only been walking for fifteen minutes before Wolf spun around and snarled at the undergrowth behind them. Rodeo stopped, turned around, and cocked his ear at the surroundings. "What's wrong? Is something back there?"

Wolf only snarled again, faced front, and bashed his way forward, but fifteen minutes later, he did exactly the same thing. He jerked to the left, sniffed, and bared his teeth.

"Something's out there," he growled. "Someone is following us."

"I don't hear anything," Rodeo remarked.

Wolf sniffed a few more times and then tried again to shake it off. He kept walking, but in a little while, he took off his backpack, shoved it into Breeze's arms, and took off into the trees.

He ranged back and forth behind and on both sides of the party. He came back even more furiously agitated than before. "I'm telling you someone is out there following us," he roared when Rodeo tried to question him.

"I never said there wasn't," Rodeo replied in as calm a tone as possible. "If he isn't on the ground, where is he? If it's Viper, he could be in the trees.....or Jairo could be underground."

"It isn't Viper or Jairo!" Wolf snapped. "I would know if it was either of them."

"Then who is it? Do you recognize their scent?"

Wolf opened his mouth to answer and suddenly whipped around to glare off into the trees. "He's here," he muttered. "He's watching us and listening to us right now."

Rodeo angled his head from one side to the other. He didn't answer for a long moment of silence and then said, "I hear him. I hear him breathing."

"Where is he?" Wolf snarled. "I can't pinpoint him."

Rodeo shook his head. "I can't, either. Let's keep going."

The crew kept going, but a few minutes later, another deadly vine hissed out of nowhere and slashed Talon across the bicep.

He spun around with a roar, grabbed the vine before it could retract, and his fist dissolved it.

The vine gave a hideous shriek, broke off at the point where his skin burned it, and the vine whipped away into the undergrowth.

Wolf started growling again. Rodeo went over to him and laid a hand on his shoulder. Wolf jumped a foot in the air, spun around, and bellowed at Rodeo in fury.

Wolf slashed his fangs at Rodeo and made Rodeo back off. "Easy, boy," Rodeo murmured under his breath. "Easy. Take it easy. It's just a vine."

"It wasn't a vine—or not just a vine!" Wolf roared. "Whoever is following us is escalating. He's attacking us."

"You don't know that. It was a random vine strike. Reese, fix Talon's arm."

Reese placed his hand on Talon's shoulder and the cut closed up.

"Keep moving," Rodeo ordered. "We're moving too slowly."

The crew kept going, but Wolf didn't go with them. He took off into the bushes and spent half an hour sniffing around the undergrowth where the vine came from.

He was just on his way back to rejoin the group when a branch fell from a tree. It almost landed on top of Rodeo, but he heard it in time and jumped out of the way.

Wolf went nuts, charged over to the tree, and shimmied up it. Rodeo called everyone to keep going. Wolf stayed in the branches for a long time and the crew left him behind.

Healey had long since given up on Wolf rejoining the group. Healey had his work cut out for him deflecting one attack after another.

Healey wasn't sure if Wolf was right that someone was out there doing this, but the random attacks of predatory plants and ferocious deadly creatures definitely seemed to be escalating. The crew couldn't walk a dozen yards without something coming out to get them.

Wolf did come back, and when he did, he snarled and bared his teeth at everyone. He kept jerking right and left to glare into the undergrowth. "Did you find anything?" Rodeo asked.

"There's nothing there to find!" Wolf snapped. "Whoever is doing this keeps disappearing."

"Maybe that's because there's no one there and these are just random occurrences," Breeze suggested.

"There is someone there!" Wolf countered. "I smelled him, but he keeps vanishing. He can erase his scent trail whenever he wants."

"He isn't vanishing," Coon murmured. "He's using his copies to follow and harass us. He creates a copy to unleash one of these attacks and then eliminates the copy so no one can find it."

"If he eliminated the copy, wouldn't Wolf find the body?" Reese asked.

"Maybe there is nobody," Axel suggested. "Maybe he can just create the copy and erase it the same way. How should we know what he does?"

"We have to keep moving," Rodeo repeated. "We're almost to Coots's cabin. Stay with the group from now on, Wolf. Don't go looking for the guy. You'll only slow us down."

Wolf snarled at him again, but Rodeo ignored it, turned his back, and started walking.

The group climbed another mountain deep in the jungle wilderness and eventually found their way onto a narrow, beaten footpath winding through dense trees. Rodeo followed it to a rough, hand-constructed cabin perched on the very edge of the mountain.

An old man with greying hair sat on the step smoking something out of a carved stone pipe. He nodded when the party showed up.

"I saw you coming up." The old man waved at the step next to him. "Sit down."

Rodeo sat on the step next to him. Talon, Reese, and the other boys sat on the ground. Healey remained standing.

"It's good to see you again, Coots," Rodeo remarked.

Coots only nodded. "You, too. You've been gone a long time. I saw you come in the other day."

"Were you keeping track of our movements?" Rodeo asked.

Coots nodded. "I saw that ship come in up in Kocha. Then the pilot went down to the village."

"Did you see where the pilot went?" Rodeo asked.

Coots opened his mouth to answer, but just then, a much younger man climbed up the same path the crew used to get here. It was the young man Healey had seen Rodeo talking to in the village this morning.

He wore the same hand-sewn clothes made of skins, tattered fabric, and cobbled pieces of other unrecognizable garments.

He looked like he'd grown up in these mountains just like Silver's children, Mave's children, and all the other hidden Chorion children stashed away in these mountains.

"This is my son, Jace," Coots told everyone. "He's Rodeo's friend from the village."

Rodeo went around the group and introduced everyone except for Talon and Reese. Jace flipped his shoulder-length sandy brown hair out of his eyes when he shook hands with Healey. "Good to meet any friend of Rodeo's."

He went around the group shaking hands with the crew, but Wolf refused to shake hands. He glared at Jace until Jace moved on.

"Take a seat, son," Coots told him. "Rodeo and his friends are looking for the pilot of that ship that came in the other day."

"Have you seen him around?" Coon asked. "He can multiply himself into dozens of copies."

"I already told Jace that in the village," Rodeo interrupted.

"Maybe whoever it is doesn't belong to Kocha," Jace suggested. "Maybe he just wants to hide here because he knows no one will come looking for him here."

Rodeo shrugged. "Maybe. I don't know where to find him." He turned to Coots. "That's why we came to see you. Can you help us find him?"

Coots shrugged. "I can try."

Without a word of warning, his head shattered in a million tiny winking sparks of light. They exploded outward and vanished into thin air.

They left Coots's headless body sitting there on the step, but the body didn't fall. It kept sitting there and even tapped the stone pipe on the step to knock the ember out of its bowl. Coots's arm put the pipe in a pocket of his shirt.

"How long will he be gone?" Axel asked.

"As long as it takes," Jace replied. "He has to search the whole planet, so it could take a while. Did you hear about Fox's death?"

Rodeo scowled at the ground and nodded. "Viper told me."

"It was a tragedy. It affected Silver the worst. She was so happy when she knew she was having Fox's young....and then this happened. She's out there in the forest alone. She won't see or talk to anyone."

Rodeo didn't answer. He just kept glaring into the trees. The silence lasted a few minutes before all the tiny sparks of Coots's head reappeared, swooped together, and rejoined to form his head.

"He isn't here," Coots announced. "He isn't on the planet anywhere."

"LIAR!!" Wolf roared and lunged for Coots. Wolf bared his fangs and snarled in murderous fury. "YOU ROTTEN LIAR!!"

Healey was the only one standing up. He was the only one who could get to Wolf in time to catch him before he attacked Coots right there in front of everybody.

Healey collided with Wolf, but Wolf overcame Healey's strength. Healey fought him backward just long enough for the other boys to get there.

Even then, it took all their combined effort to stop Wolf from attacking Coots. The crew held Wolf at bay, but he kept throwing himself at Coots, roaring at him and calling him a filthy, stinking liar, and battling his friends to get to Coots.

In the end, Talon had to step in. He caught Wolf around the middle in one massive arm, hoisted Wolf bodily off the ground, and dragged him away kicking, spitting, and howling in fury.

Talon carried Wolf still thrashing toward the footpath. The others moved in front of him, shook hands with Coots, thanked him, and retreated.

Rodeo left the cabin last. He stayed behind talking to Coots and Jace for a few more minutes before he caught up with the crew.

Healey, Talon, Reese, and the boys were already halfway down the slope by the time Rodeo rejoined them. Wolf's enraged yowls echoed through the forest.

Rodeo pushed his way to the front of the pack and Talon lowered Wolf to the ground. Wolf exploded out of Talon's hold and turned his fury on Talon instead.

Wolf pounded Talon's huge chest with his fists. "Get the hell off me, you big bastard! Don't you ever lay your hands on me again!"

"Calm down, little brother," Talon rumbled. "I did you a favor by stopping you from killing that man."

"You bastard!" Wolf fired back. "You should have let me take him!"

"Keep quiet," Rodeo snapped. "He can hear you."

"Do you think I give a shit if he can hear me? I hope he does. He's a lying sack of shit, Rodeo, and you know it! He deliberately concealed the pilot from us!"

"I know that, boy," Rodeo returned. "I know it was well as you do, but getting in his face won't help anything."

"How do you know he's lying?" Healey asked.

"His sweat changed its smell," Wolf growled, "and his pupils fluctuated."

"I heard it, too," Rodeo added. "His heart skipped a beat when he said it. He knows where the pilot is and he lied about it."

"He had to be lying," Reese chimed in. "If he'd been telling the truth, he would have challenged Wolf for making that accusation."

"Then....you're saying Coots is working for Joyce?" Breeze asked. "That doesn't make any sense. You said you know both of those guys, Rodeo."

"I do. They've been living here all their lives. Coon's data shows that Joyce hired the pilot over a month ago and they met on another planet far away from Chorion Osiris. Someone would have noticed Coots or Jace leaving the area and then coming back."

"None of this makes sense," Healey muttered.

"What makes sense is that we aren't any further along than we were when we left the village yesterday," Laub pointed out. "This whole trip was a waste of time."

"There's nothing to do but go back to the village," Rodeo replied.

"You said yesterday we would leave Chorion Osiris if Coots couldn't help us," Healey pointed out. "You said that, if Coots couldn't find the pilot, then that meant the pilot wasn't on the planet and we would be better off leaving."

"But Coots did find him," Rodeo countered. "The pilot *is* on the planet or Coots wouldn't need to lie about not being able to find him. Coots probably heard me say that and decided to throw me off the trail by telling me the pilot wasn't here—which means the pilot is here. We can't leave yet. Come on."

Healey and the others exchanged glances, but Rodeo just walked off down the mountain. He didn't wait around for anyone to discuss it or agree with him.

The crew followed him one after the other. None of them was getting any closer to finding the pilot by standing around here.

Chapter 15

L aub groaned when the crew came in sight of the village on the crew's third day out. "Are we really coming back here?"

"We are," Talon replied and he and Reese strode ahead. They couldn't get back to their family fast enough.

"Any more ideas?" Healey asked Rodeo. "It looks like we're at a dead end."

"Something is bound to turn up," Rodeo replied.

"How long are we gonna stick around waiting for something to turn up?" Coon asked. "We should just pack it in and go. If you want to stick around waiting for something to turn up, you can do that alone."

A charge of tension went through the group. No one had dared to say that yet—not even Healey.

No one moved or gasped or exclaimed about how they wouldn't dream of leaving Rodeo behind. Every one of the boys must have been thinking the same thing.

"I won't argue with you," Rodeo finally murmured. "Just give it one more night. If we haven't found anything by tomorrow morning, we'll leave."

"Does that mean you'll come with us?" Alla asked. "It looks like you got a pretty good gig going here."

"A lot better than running from the law," Axel pointed out.

"None of you has to leave, either," Rodeo pointed out. "You could all stay."

They shuffled their feet. "Naw," Breeze murmured. "We'll go."

"I don't have anything to stay for," Bandit replied. "I've only ever been good at flying ships. I can't do that here."

"I'm going, too," Alla added. "Life was better on the outside before all this happened."

"Life is better on the outside even with all this other shit going on," Wolf chimed in. "We were right to leave. We all belong out there."

"Then we'll leave in the morning if we haven't found anything before that," Rodeo decided. "Come on. We can relax for tonight and let it go. We don't have to go off searching anywhere."

He strode into the village, returned to Talon's house for a while, and then went off somewhere else.

Healey and the boys took longer, but eventually, they returned to the village, too. There was nowhere else to go and nothing else to do.

Healey hung around Reese's house, shot the bull with him and Talon, and then wandered around the village.

No one messed with him. No one even spoke to him, which Healey supposed was a blessing in disguise. Word must have spread that Healey was under Rodeo's protection.

Healey headed back to Reese's house toward sunset and spotted Rodeo coming back from somewhere. "I just questioned ten other people and none of them has ever heard of someone who can multiply themselves."

"I'm starting to think maybe the pilot's ability is something else," Healey pointed out.

"How do you explain what we saw at Ultra Meridian?" Rodeo asked. "There were thirty people on one ship. Then there were hundreds. Then there were thirty again. There were thirty people on one ship that landed on this planet, but only one man walked away. Jairo would have told us if there was more than one—and Wolf only picked up one scent trail."

Healey shrugged. "I guess so."

"We're missing something." Rodeo narrowed his eyes at the village. "There's some piece of this puzzle we aren't seeing."

"So what do you want to do about it?" Healey asked.

"I don't know. The Chieftain invited all of us to a feast he's throwing tonight. It will be a big gathering with all the men from the whole tribe invited. We might see something there. Otherwise, I guess we'll just make tracks and see what happens. If we leave the planet, the pilot is bound to follow us. Then we might be able to catch him somewhere else."

"We should work on getting a better-armed ship," Healey pointed out. "That gunship won't stand up to the pilot's vessel."

"Finding another ship is gonna take money and resources we don't have. Let's concentrate on the step in front of us before we go making any bigger plans."

"If the step in front of us is going out into space against some unknown enemy in a better-armed ship than we have, then the step in front of us would seem to be getting something bigger and better-armed than he has. We'd get blown out of the sky otherwise. We can ask Jairo to hook us up. I'm sure he knows where we can get something bigger."

"All right. You ask Breeze about it." Rodeo squinted at the sky. "It will be dark soon. Bring the boys over to the Chieftain's house in an hour. He wants to see all of us there."

"Does that mean we're officially members of the Kocha tribe?" Healey asked.

Rodeo made a face. "You don't want to be a member of this tribe, Marshall. Even people like me who were born here don't want to be members of it. Why do you think we leave so young?"

Healey had to laugh. "All right. You got me. I don't really want to be a member of it, either."

"Of course you don't."

Rodeo went into the house. The other boys were all milling around the village at loose ends, too. They were all just counting down the hours until they could get the hell out of here.

Healey did the same thing. He wanted to get back to the business of meeting up with Lyons, Emmett, Beauty, and the Armageddon Core.

Healey wanted to make sure they really did have the Ziprothil—but that would only make the crew even bigger targets than they already were.

At sunset, they all went over to the Chieftain's house. It was already filling up with hundreds of people all jostling to get inside, but the Chieftain grabbed Rodeo and insisted that he sit with the Chieftain's entourage.

The rest of the crew got roped into sitting with the Chieftain, too, including Talon and Reese. Healey didn't see any women or children here, either.

The house had been set up with long tables two feet off the ground. The guests sat on cushions on the floor. Healey wound up sitting next to Rodeo with Reese on Healey's other side.

"Why aren't women invited to these events?" Healey asked Reese after everyone sat down.

"It's too dangerous," Reese replied. "They keep separate for their own protection. Fights are always breaking out between the men. Women are considered too valuable. It doesn't take much for an accident to turn deadly."

Healey couldn't argue with that after everything he'd seen and heard. These events seemed too dangerous even for the men taking part in them.

The servers who brought in the food for the guests were all younger men. They laid out platters of all kinds of strange food, placed everything on the tables where the guests could help themselves, and then the servers sat down at the ends of the tables and ate with everyone else.

Healey found himself looking around the room at all the men lining the tables. "Do you think the pilot could be in here right now?"

"I was just wondering the same thing," Rodeo replied. "Maybe everyone in this room is in on the ruse. Maybe they're laughing at us behind our backs because we're such chumps that we can't figure it out."

"Everyone?" Healey glanced over at the Chieftain. "Does that include our charming host?"

"Who would know better than he would who the pilot is? If he wanted to keep it from us, he would be in a perfect position to do that simply by not telling me who the pilot is."

Just then, the door opened and Coots and Jace entered. They both wore the same rough clothing they'd had on at their cabin.

They found places for themselves, sat down, loaded their dishes with food, and started socializing with those nearest them.

"Speak of the devil," Rodeo murmured.

"What are they doing here?" Healey asked.

"They had to come. They're part of the tribe. People will be coming in from all over the area for this."

"What's the occasion?" Healey asked. "Tell me he isn't throwing this feast because you're here."

"He doesn't need a reason. He throws them regularly for no reason. Maybe he wants to celebrate the fact that Dane is dead."

Just then, Coots exploded his head again. No one acted like a man's head exploding at the dinner table was anything out of the ordinary. Those nearest him kept eating, and in a minute, his head reappeared and he went on with his meal, too.

"I guess there's no chance that Coots could be the pilot," Healey remarked. "We all know what his ability is."

"It can't be Jace, either," Rodeo replied. "He's lived here all his life. He's never left."

"What's his ability?"

"I'm not sure," Rodeo replied. "He keeps it hidden."

"Couldn't he be the pilot, then? If he can reproduce himself an infinite number of times. He could have sent his copies to attack us at Ultra Meridian while a different copy was living here pretending that he never left."

"That would explain why Coots lied about the pilot not being on the planet," Reese pointed out. "Coots would have lied to protect his son."

"That would also explain why Wolf couldn't track down whoever was following us in the forest," Rodeo added. "Wolf said the guy kept disappearing. He probably sent his copies out and then retrieved them just as fast."

"What do you want to do about it?" Healey asked.

"Just keep an eye on things," Rodeo replied. "There's nothing we can do about it right now."

The crew continued eating, and in a little while, Coots and Jace left. The feast went on late into the night.

Rodeo talked to the Chieftain and his entourage about everything that was happening in Kocha territory and beyond.

Healey talked to Reese for a while, but after the second hour, Healey just relaxed and watched everyone in the room.

A few fights broke out with people using their abilities to attack each other. No one interfered with these fights except to push the combatants away from the tables.

Only once did the guests remove two men who were bothering the diners too much. Five hulking Chorions tossed the two men outside where they continued their skirmish while everyone else went back to eating.

Healey stopped eating long before the feast ended. After the fourth hour, Reese made an excuse about going home to check on his children. Healey used that moment to excuse himself, thank the Chieftain, and scamper, too.

They returned to Reese's house. The children were already asleep. Reese started whispering to Dawn again, so Healey went outside.

He stared up at the stars thinking everything over, and in a little while, Rodeo and the others came out of the Chieftain's house.

They stopped outside the door and stood whispering in hushed tones for a while before they walked away.

They returned to Reese's house, too, and then everyone went inside. They helped Dawn lay out all the cushions for the guests to sleep on and the boys flopped into their beds groaning and rubbing their stomachs.

"You didn't find out anything new tonight, did you?" Healey asked Rodeo. "That means we should leave tomorrow morning."

"No, I didn't find out anything," Rodeo replied. "Whatever happens, we'll definitely leave tomorrow. We won't need to stay here after tonight."

"Thank God!" Alla groaned and rolled over to face the wall.

Chapter 16

Healey fell asleep instantly the minute he hit his mattress. Exhaustion from the last three days of hiking over rough country caught up with him. The food he'd eaten at the feast weighed him down.

He couldn't think of what might have woken him up in the middle of the night. He didn't hear anything except the others around him breathing heavily and Alla snoring.

He shut his eyes and tried to go back to sleep, but he wound up opening them again and staring at the ceiling. His mind started working on the mystery of the pilot's identity, the Ziprothil, the Ithium, Davenport, Fiddler, Helios Sanctus, and everything else.

He was just telling himself to go back to sleep when an almighty blast struck the house from the side. The impact tore the roof off. One minute, Healey was looking up at the embers' orange glow on the rafters.

The next instant, he was looking up at the stars.....and then dozens of men swarmed over the walls, pounced down inside the house, and attacked everyone inside.

Healey threw his blanket off, but not fast enough. Ten men jumped on top of him, punched him all over, and then held him down while another man held a gun in Healey's face.

He barely yanked his head out of the way before the weapon went off. The shot blasted past his ear and tore a hole in the mattress. The stuffing flew in his face, but he couldn't pay attention to that.

Gunshots exploded in all directions and then Rodeo bellowed. "NOW, BOYS!!"

Healey didn't know what that meant. He was too busy fighting all these guys and then, out of nowhere, something struck the men attacking him.

Healey didn't see what it was until Breeze barreled past them and toppled seven of the attackers. They fell over each other and then someone's very powerful hand grabbed Healey by the collar and yanked him off the mattress.

Laub hauled Healey to his feet and shoved him into a group with Reese, Dawn, the children, Rodeo, and Bandit.

Rodeo pushed everyone toward a gap where the explosion had knocked down one of the house walls. Laub, Axel, Talon, and Wolf moved forward to fight the attackers off.

In the faint glimmer of light coming from the dying embers, Healey saw that every single one of those attackers was a carbon copy of Jace.

Coon had dropped onto one knee and plunged his arm up to the elbow in the dirt. Silver filaments threaded around his arm and twined downward to vanish into the planet.

Metal whips, chains, hooks, and random spinning weapons snaked out of the ground and cut down the attackers by the dozen. More and more copies came out of nowhere trying to fight their way through to assault the crew.

Breeze tumbled back and forth across the room knocking the copies over and making them easy prey for the other boys.

Alla stood on another side of the room devouring the copies as fast as his jaws could open and close. He swelled to an enormous size and didn't slow down for an instant.

Laub, Wolf, Talon, and Axel fought their way into the army of copies tearing them apart with their bare hands.

Talon dissolved the copies with his touch, but he couldn't keep up with their numbers. The copies' gunfire joined with Wolf's enraged yowls to create a deafening confused noise.

All at once, Rodeo stepped forward and bellowed, "JACE—STOP!!"

The copies paused for a split second. In that instant, Alla stretched his mouth to a huge gaping maw as big as the house, reared back, and dove for the copies.

He swallowed them all—or he would have. At the last possible second, Axel grabbed one copy and yanked it out of the way before the others vanished down Alla's throat.

The last copy instantly replicated it into dozens of its kind. They overran the house, but before they could attack again, Rodeo yelled out one more time, "Jace—stop!"

He did stop. All the copies froze for a second.

"We can keep this up all night, Jace," Rodeo went on. "Alla can keep eating your copies and we can keep killing them. You can't beat us. Just stop for a second and listen to me."

The copies stared at him and then one of them flipped his hair out of his eyes. "Say what you have to say, but I have a job to do. I have to end you boys. That's all there is to it."

"Admiral Killian Joyce hired you to follow us to the Ziprothil and then knock us off," Rodeo replied. "We found the evidence in your ship's logs."

That one copy shrugged. "I don't know who hired me. I just met the guy at Macron Calypso. He didn't say anything about him being a military man."

"Well, he is. He stole both an Ithium cartridge and the Ziprothil from Helios Sanctus so he could threaten the whole Confederacy." Rodeo took a deep breath. "I know you, Jace. I know you wouldn't have anything to do with that. You wouldn't go along with this if you knew what he was really all about."

That copy's eyes darted around the room and then all his other copies vanished into that one man. "Can you prove any of this?" he asked.

"Yes, I can and Marshall Healey here can back up everything I'm saying. Sheriff Mace Davenport confiscated the Ithium off a smuggler's freighter at Ultra Meridian. The only way the Ithium could have gotten out of Helios Sanctus is if some high-ranking military officer took it from there. Same with the Ziprothil. You know this, Jace. You're too smart not to put the puzzle pieces together."

"He said someone stole it from Helios Sanctus," Jace countered. "He said that's why he wanted me to get it back—to keep it quiet so it didn't cause a panic when people found out such a dangerous substance was missing."

"Son of a bitch!" Axel muttered.

"Did you follow the other crew away from Ultra Meridian?" Healey interrupted. "You left Ultra Meridian before us. Did you follow them to see where they went?"

"I didn't follow them," Jace replied. "There was no sign of the Ziprothil on their ship, so I figured you boys must have it. I figured you'd be better able to take it than a bunch of humans—no offense, Marshall."

Rodeo bumped Coon's shoulder and pointed at Jace. "Show him."

Coon pulled his hand out of the ground, stepped forward, and took the memory card out of his pocket. His filaments twisted into the card and he showed it to Jace. The screen blinked on.

"Is this the man who hired you?" Rodeo asked.

"Yeah, that's him, but he looked different," Jace replied. "He must have altered his appearance slightly."

"That's Admiral Killian Joyce," Coon told him. "He's been tracking us all over the Confederacy trying to retake the Ithium and the chip that sets it off. Now he has both. He only needs the Ziprothil so he can make all three into the biggest doomsday weapon ever created. If he succeeds in actually detonating it, he could wipe out most or all of the Confederacy."

Jace frowned. "I didn't know anything about that."

Healey turned to Rodeo. "Do you believe him?"

"Yeah, I believe him," Rodeo replied. "Jace is a good guy. He would never get involved in something like this."

"No way," Jace exclaimed. "I don't want to threaten the Confederacy."

"I could place you under arrest for trying to kill a Confederate Marshall," Healey interrupted. "Or you could come with us and testify against Joyce. If you really want us to believe you didn't know about this, now is your one and only chance to do the right thing. You can testify that Joyce hired you to assassinate me and these boys and to retrieve the Ziprothil for him."

Jace's expression cleared and he shook his hair out of his eyes again. "I can do that. I swear I didn't know anything about this."

"Then come with us," Rodeo urged. "We really need your help."

"Okay. Just let me send one of my copies back to Coots so he doesn't know I left the planet."

Jace copied himself once. The copy left the house and vanished into the night.

"You never told me you could do that," Rodeo exclaimed.

Jace shrugged. "I never told anyone—not here at least. It's better if people don't find out." He glanced at Reese and Talon. "I guess the cat's out of the bag now."

"You do the right thing and we'll keep your secret for you," Talon rumbled. "Don't make us regret giving you a chance."

Jace turned back to Rodeo. "So where do you want me to go?"

Rodeo waved toward the door. "We'll go now. Just.....help these people put their house back together. Then we can go."

"Sure," Jace replied. "Everybody step outside and I'll take care of it."

Healey and the crew stepped over the broken wall. Reese, Dawn, the children, and Talon followed and everyone assembled outside.

Jace produced dozens of his copies and they all got to work on the house. Healey couldn't see what the copies were doing. There were too many of them blocking the view.

"You don't really trust this guy, do you?" Healey asked Rodeo while the copies worked. "He tried to kill us. He shot us down at Ultra Meridian and he blew this house to kingdom come to wipe us all out."

"If you thought someone stole Ziprothil from Helios Sanctus to wipe out the Confederacy, wouldn't you try to stop them by any means necessary? Yes, I trust Jace. I've known him all my life. Joyce lied to him about what we were doing. Give him a chance. He'll prove himself."

"This is a terrible idea," Healey told him. "He could sell us out and we wouldn't get another chance. He could lead Joyce right to us."

"And if I'm right, Jace could be the one who saves us from Joyce. I think I know Jace a little better than you do."

Healey looked away. He didn't know Jace from a hole in the ground—except that Jace had been hunting the crew down for the last several days.

Nothing Rodeo said convinced Healey that Jace was a good person underneath it all. He looked like a huckster to Healey. Jace reminded Healey of the kind of innocent-looking con artist who would make up any old story to get himself off the hook. Then, when it suited him, he would strike later and finish the job.

He sure could work fast, though. His copies finished the house in no time and then he combined them back into one person who came over to join the rest of the crew.

He tossed his hair out of his eyes. "Do you want to go now?"

"Yeah, we'll go. The sooner we get off the planet, the better." Rodeo turned to Talon, Reese, and Dawn.

They all hugged each other. "Are you sure you don't want to stay until morning?" Dawn asked.

"I don't want to give the Chieftain the chance to try to talk me out of leaving," Rodeo replied. "It will be easier if he wakes up tomorrow and I'm already gone."

They all hugged again and then the three adults shook hands with Healey and the rest of the team.

Healey would have felt relieved to leave the village if Jace hadn't gone with them. His presence cast a pall over the crew—or maybe Healey was the only one who felt it. None of the other boys mentioned it or protested Rodeo's decision to bring Jace with them.

The crew filed out of the silent village. No one other than Dawn, Reese, and Talon saw the crew leave.

They headed back in the direction they came, back on the long trek to the ship where they could fly away and escape this planet for whatever dangers might be waiting for them out in space.

Chapter 17

Lyons ducked as a gunshot shattered the rock next to her head. Chips and shards peppered the side of her face. That pain spurred her to run faster.

She dodged corners and charged through steep canyons and ravines. She couldn't stop. The walls amplified the noise of hundreds of guns.

Emmett, Beauty, and the four clones of the Armageddon Core crowded behind Lyons. They all ran their fastest to get to the caves in time. The crew had to take advantage of the delay the Chorion Team was giving them.

Lyons kept running, but Flack grabbed Lyons's sleeve and pulled her into a side crevice. "This way!"

Lyons skidded sideways and the crew took off running in a different direction. The walls blocked the noise here, but not the danger.

Ricocheting shots pinged and whistled down the canyon. The crew wasn't out of the woods yet.

The four clones veered into another labyrinthian maze of chasms and then started climbing. The crew scrambled up a steep incline and ducked into a cave.

Friend led the way through multiple chambers, into a fourth chamber, and some invisible force yanked Lyons off her feet.

The momentum took her by surprise, and before she knew what was happening, she stumbled into the central cave of the Armageddon Core's secret hideout.

"Phew! We lost them!" Flack slumped onto a nearby crate. "Let's not do that again."

Friend hustled over to her computers. "Holy shit! Look at that!"

Emmett and Lyons went over to see what she was looking at. One of her machines showed a video feed of the canyon where the crew had just left the Chorion Team.

Healey and the boys blocked a tight crack and defended the route to the tunnel against what looked like hundreds of armed men. They wore masks over their faces to conceal their identities.

"Where the hell did they all come from?" Emmett demanded. "Rodeo said there were only thirty people on the ship that followed us."

"There were. Look." Friend pointed to another feed. It read back scanner data from the Valiant's battle and entry into the planet's atmosphere.

"Scanner data from the mystery assailant's ship still shows thirty crewmen on board," Friend reported. "Something fishy is going on."

"Then let's get the Ziprothil and get the hell out of here," Lyons told her. "Where is it?"

"It's hidden, but the minute I take it out of its hiding place, everyone and their mothers will be able to see where the Ziprothil is," Friend replied. "It will attract every corrupt Reserve Wing officer, bounty hunter, and criminal lowlife in the sector to come after us and steal it from us. If I take it out of its hiding place, everything Admiral Joyce has done to us will seem like a cakewalk in comparison."

"Which means we'll need a ship to leave the planet pronto," Flack added. "There's no sense in taking the Ziprothil out of its hiding place until we have some way to take it on the run."

"Where are we gonna get that?" Emmett asked. "There is only one operational ship on the planet and that's the mystery attacker's ship."

"What's wrong with that?" Frost asked. "We should go out there right now, steal his ship, and fly away in it. Then he'll be stranded here. Everyone else might come after us, but he won't be able to."

"His ship is too far away," Flack pointed out. "We need something closer."

"There is nothing closer," Emmett countered.

"There's Typhon Elexor and Mount Refractory," Friend suggested. "They both have ships and we can take the Skimmers there."

"Hell, no!" Lyons spat. "We are NOT going back to Typhon Elexor or Mount Refractory. I don't care if we have to hide on this planet for the rest of our lives. We aren't going back there."

"Then what's the option?" Frost asked. "We have no other way off the planet."

Lyons didn't know what to do, so she glanced around at the cave. She wouldn't have minded staying here for a long, long time—maybe forever.

The Armageddon Core had set it up with bedrooms for each of the residents. The clones also had plenty of food, supplies, and everything else they needed to live comfortably.

When she looked around, she saw movement on one of Friend's computers. "What's that?" Lyons inched a little closer to the screen. "Something's moving around the Ultra Meridian Jail."

The crew gathered around Friend's table while she adjusted the feed. Lyons couldn't figure out how Friend planted cameras all over the planet. She could even get a visual on places where she couldn't possibly have planted cameras.

She magnified the feed from the jail. It should have been abandoned since it had no sheriff anymore.

Friend slumped back in her chair. "It's only scavengers. They're harmless."

"They have a ship," Lyons pointed out. "And they're right over the hill."

"We should take a Skimmer anyway," Fizzle suggested.

"The scavengers would hear that coming," Emmett countered. "If we want to steal their ship, we should take it by stealth."

"Stealth—how?" Lyons asked. "It's in the middle of the Ultra Meridian planes—right where everyone can see anybody coming."

"That's easy," Emmett told her. "The six of us walk out there in plain view where the scavengers won't have any problem seeing us. They'll all turn to confront us and Beauty can sneak on board their ship and steal it for us."

Lyons glanced over her shoulder at Beauty. So did Emmett and the clones.

Beauty had located a large crate of food in the Armageddon Core's stash of goods. He'd pried the lid off and was just about to climb inside the crate to burrow into the food packages when he noticed everyone staring at him.

"Do you think you could do that, Beauty?" Frost asked. "Could you run around the other side of the Ultra Meridian Jail and steal those scavengers' ship while we distract them?"

Beauty stuck his foot into the crate. He really would have climbed all the way inside it and vanished under a mountain of food wrappers.

Lyons saw him about to make his escape, so she went over there and pulled him away by the back of the neck. "We're on a mission here. You eat afterward."

"I need to eat before the mission," he growled and wriggled out of her grasp. "One JuicyPie! Just one! I promise that's all I'll take."

"You take one JuicyPie and then you get us that ship," she snapped. "That's the deal. Otherwise, you won't get anything to eat for a month."

"Lyons!" Frost gasped. "You can't tell him that! He'll starve!"

Lyons snorted. "Hardly. Let's go get that ship."

The crew rifled the rest of the Armageddon Core's gear, found masks, goggles, and weapons, and armed up while Beauty ate.

Lyons pretended not to notice when he took more than one JuicyPie. In fact, he might have gotten one of the best meals of his life while she, Emmett, and the girls did all the work.

Beauty didn't need a mask or a weapon, though, so it didn't really make a difference in the end.

The crew reassembled in the main cavern. "So where's the Ziprothil?" Flack asked.

Friend laid aside her weapon, kicked some of the dirt on the floor, and revealed a metal plate buried under the dust. She pried it up and took another locked metal box from a hole chiseled out of the bedrock.

She held up the box and rotated it in her hand while she studied it from all sides. "I don't know how much protection this box will give us. I tried to surround the Ziprothil in as many layers of protection as I could. I guess the rock and the plate did the trick before now. I don't know how much time we have before someone detects it."

"We better get moving them," Lyons replied. "Let's move out."

The crew spent the next several hours trekking through more steep ravines and defiles to get back to the Ultra Meridian planes. The scavengers were still there by the time Lyons and her crewmates peered over the last ridge at the jail in the distance. It sure looked small from here.

"We need some way to hide the Ziprothil before we go out into the open," Flack suggested. "We don't want them to get the idea that we have it."

"Why not give the Ziprothil to Beauty?" Friend asked. "He'll be approaching the scavengers from another direction. The scavengers won't see him. He can hide the Ziprothil on the ship."

Lyons raised her eyebrows. "You want to give a potentially deadly toxic substance.....to Beauty?"

"That way," Friend went on, "if anyone captures one of us and questions us, we can truthfully say that we don't know where the Ziprothil is."

Lyons thought it over and Emmett frowned. "I suppose that could work."

"The alternative is taking the Ziprothil out there into a potential firefight where someone might shoot it, break the canister, and release the Ziprothil right here," Friend pointed out.

Lyons shrugged. "You're right."

Friend turned her back to the hillside and handed Beauty the locked box. Lyons would have liked to say something—like maybe giving Beauty a stern warning about how dangerous it was and about how the whole crew was putting their lives in his hands and how he needed to be extra careful with it.

None of those words seemed to fit the situation. If he didn't know by now, telling him wouldn't make him understand.

She only needed to look at him once to realize she didn't need to tell him anything. He bowed his head to look down at the box in his spindly fingers. He didn't turn it over to examine it.

Silence fell over the group of friends as the true gravity of what they were doing sank in. One wrong move on their part and the Confederacy would be over just as quickly as if Admiral Joyce released his doomsday weapon.

Flack brought everyone back to the job at hand. "Let's go," she murmured.

Beauty looked up. Friend and Lyons turned around to face the planes. "You stay here until we get out into the open, Beauty," Flack told him. "Then skirt around behind the scavengers and take the ship any way you can."

"Just make sure you take it in a way that it will still fly," Emmett added. "Don't damage it."

"I understand," Beauty growled. "I know what to do."

"All right. Let's go!"

Chapter 18

Flack got to her feet and the rest of the crew stood up, too. Lyons hefted her XQ and strode down the hill toward the planes, ready for anything.

The crew made it halfway across the planes before the scavengers noticed them. The scavengers didn't do anything at first. A few people went back and forth between the jail and their ship.

It was another Valiant, but this ship was nothing like the one Yuki Duetis gave the crew on Acrolith Diastema.

Parts of the hull had been patched with random mental plates welded in place. One of the engines had been replaced with something cobbled from a completely different model of ship.

Lyons didn't see anyone in the cockpit, but that didn't mean anything. How many other people did the scavengers have on board?

She really hoped Beauty would be able to take the ship by himself without damaging the Ziprothil cartridge, but the crew had already made that decision. She couldn't change her mind now.

Protective fury boiled over in her soul when she saw the scavengers dismantling the Ultra Meridian Jail. How dare they? This was Davenport's patch.

She wanted to preserve it for him so he'd have his outpost to come back to when this was all over. She couldn't for the life of her figure out why she thought that. He would never come back here. He would spend the rest of his life in Terminus Anathema.

No! She couldn't let that happen. She's already dedicated her best years to a life of crime. She had to turn things around by helping Davenport any way she could.

The scavengers stopped what they were doing when they saw the crew getting closer. The scavengers went on with their work for a while and then picked up their weapons.

Five armed men came out to confront the crew when Lyons, Emmett, and the four clones advanced. "What do you want?" one of the scavengers demanded.

"That's my friend's outpost you're raiding," Lyons countered. "You're stealing Sheriff's Service property."

"You ain't sheriffs," the guy fired back. "You can't stop us."

"Oh, I think we can," Lyons returned. "I'll give you a choice. You can put back everything you took or you can eat some of this." She dropped her XQ into her hands and aimed it at him.

"We ain't putting nothing back," another growled. "This is our site. You get your own."

"This is definitely not your site," Flack interjected. "Everything here belongs to Sheriff Mace Davenport. I don't think he'd be too pleased to hear that you were out here taking his stuff."

The guy's expression changed. His cheeks sagged and he cast a frightened glance around the plains. "Where is he?"

"He's on his way back here right now," Lyons told him. "If he comes back and finds his stuff gone, he'll go looking for the person who took it. We're his friends. If he asks us who ransacked the jail, we'll have to tell him the truth. Then he'll track you down and the results won't be pretty."

"No, don't tell him that," another guy cut in. "We didn't mean anything by it. We just gotta make a living, don't we? If we don't take this haul, we'll starve."

"I doubt that," Flack countered. "You didn't scavenger the Ultra Meridian Jail when Davenport was here and you won't do it now."

"So......" The first guy shuffled his feet. "You want us to put everything back? That could take hours."

"Do you have somewhere else to be?" Lyons asked. "We can wait all day."

The scavengers didn't answer. One of them looked over his shoulder toward their ship. Another two glanced toward the jail. Lyons couldn't tell from here how much of its contents the scavengers might have emptied out of it. It might be completely empty.

The desk was still in there. She couldn't see anything else.

"Oh, all right," the biggest scavenger muttered. "Have it your own way."

He started to turn away, but Lyons didn't relax. She kept her gun trained on him and for good reason.

He turned toward his ship, started to lower his weapon, and then whipped around and fired. Only his sudden move saved Lyons from getting plastered in the face with his gunfire.

She fired instinctively, and in a split second, a firefight erupted between the scavengers on one side and the crew on the other.

Lyons bombarded the scavengers with dozens of shots, but they kept firing back so fast that she couldn't tell if she landed any of her own hits.

Emmett grabbed her and pulled her behind the jail. The friends ducked out to shoot at the scavengers who backed away toward their ship.

They unloaded on the crew and hit the jail instead. Crashes, booms, and deafening bangs shook the building.

The scavengers inched a little farther toward their ship's hatch, but before they got there, the ship launched off the ground and pivoted its weapons toward the jail.

Lyons saw a man in a mask and goggles sitting at the controls. Beauty hadn't taken the ship the way the crew planned. Now they would never get off the planet.

The scavengers on the ground yelled, jumped up and down, and tried to grab the ship, but its engines were already howling to a screaming pitch and kicking up clouds of dust.

The ship wheeled above the scavengers' heads and a wicked blast of gunfire erupted from its cannons. The shot detonated the jail building right in front of Lyons, Emmett, and the four clones.

Lyons barely had time to dive on top of Emmett and tackle him to the ground. "Get down!" she bellowed and then the concussion pounded over her head.

The jail building dissolved in a spinning tornado of splinters, debris, and torn metal. The explosion left the six friends exposed, but the scavengers didn't pay any attention to Lyons and her crewmates.

The scavengers ran back and forth between trying to jump high enough to catch the ship and running toward the jail that wasn't there anymore. The scavengers clasped their heads and howled in horror that the jail was gone along with everything in it.

They ran back toward the ship, but when the dust cleared enough for Lyons to see what was happening, the ship rotated back in her direction and she saw through the cockpit window.

The scavenger pilot was gone. Beauty sat in his place and glared through the window at the scavengers. Beauty bared his teeth in a malicious grin, spun the ship around to aim its open hatch toward the wrecked jail, and turned the ship's guns on the scavengers instead.

They made one last rush to get back to their ship and he opened fire. He gunned down three of the scavengers and held the other four at gunpoint.

They still didn't get the message—not completely. They kept rushing forward to get to the safety of their ship, changing their minds and backing off, and then rushing forward again.

Beauty didn't fire again. He held the ship there with the open hatch pointed invitingly at Lyons and her friends. "Come on!" she yelled and jumped to her feet.

She pulled Emmett up and the four clones scrambled out of the wreckage. Lyons waited to make sure they all got to the ship in one piece.

She had to stop herself from making sure Friend had the Ziprothil. She didn't have the Ziprothil. Beauty had it.

Lyons herded everyone toward the hatch. The crew got close to the ship when gunfire erupted from somewhere out on the planes.

She didn't see where it was coming from. She ducked under her arms as gunshots smashed the ship's patched hull. Those shots zinged past her ears and she crouched low for protection. The ship's engine wash scoured her face and arms with dust. She couldn't see a thing.

The ship wheeled with another shriek of engines. All the scavengers flattened themselves to the ground as the ship's guns passed over their heads and Beauty turned in the direction of that gunfire.

The ship rocketed into the air hammering its guns into the distance. Lyons stayed where she was. Explosions vibrated through the ground underneath her. The ship was gone. If Beauty didn't come back for the crew, Lyons and her friends would be stranded here along with the scavengers.

She raised her head and squinted through her goggles to see the ship screaming back and forth across the plains. It bombarded some position out in the hills before the ship came howling back.

Beauty turned the ship backward one more time and lowered the open hatch to the ground in front of the friends.

Lyons didn't wait another instant. She grabbed her crewmates and they all charged on board.

"You might want to get your weapons primed and ready to fire!" Beauty called back from the cockpit controls. "The Ziprothil is definitely bringing the rats out of the woodwork."

Lyons didn't wait to hear any more. She sprang into her firing cradle just as the hatch slammed shut and Beauty fired the engines to rocket the ship into orbit.

The scavengers jumped up and down and waved their hands even more, but there was nothing they could do.

The Valiant started climbing, but the ship didn't even get out of the atmosphere before all hell broke loose. A Reserve Wing Dagger plunged across the ship's path. Then another three ships Lyons didn't recognize hounded the Dagger away and hammered it with gunfire.

"Who's shooting at us?!" Emmett bellowed.

"Everybody!" Beauty countered. "We got marauders and fortune hunters from every criminal organization in the galaxy fighting over us—and everyone is shooting at everyone else! Just get us off the planet! I don't care about anything else."

Lyons pulled her cradle around, but even then, she had to search to find the right target. There was no right target. That was the problem.

Reserve Wing Stalwarts hung in high orbit firing down at the ground. Daggers and Drifters hurtled back and forth shooting at the Valiant and at dozens of other craft all over Ultra Meridian.

They all traded fire with each other. Beauty dodged back and forth through the mayhem trying to avoid everyone. Most of what hit the Valiant was stray fire, but all the combatants landed plenty of hits trying to disable the ship and drive it back toward the ground.

"Where are we going, Beauty?!" Emmett hollered.

"Who cares?!" Beauty called back. "Nowhere will be safe with the Ziprothil on board."

"We need to find another place to conceal it," Lyons yelled.

"Any ideas?"

Lyons thought about it for a split second. That was all the time she had before she had to unload on another Dagger dogging the ship through the atmosphere.

"Take us back to Acrolith Diastema," she decided.

"Are you insane?!" Emmett roared. "You want to go back there after the way Yuki tried to shoot us down?"

"Acrolith Diastema is the closest outpost and we can trade this Valiant for another ship."

"We won't be able to do that without the whole Reserve Wing seeing us," Flack pointed out.

"There is no ship in existence that can hide the Ziprothil," Friend added.

"Then we'll just have to outrun them. Punch it, Beauty!" Lyons ordered.

He crouched a little lower over his controls and hit the throttle. Lyons didn't have to tell her friends to turn their guns to the front. Emmett and the Armageddon Core swiveled forward and all the gunners unloaded on any ship in the Valiant's path.

More ships converged from all over, but at least some of them thought twice about shooting at the vessel carrying the Ziprothil.

Nearly all the combatants pulled their punches and just tried to disable the Valiant instead of blowing it up right there in the atmosphere.

Plenty of the attackers did try to destroy the Valiant, but Beauty was picking up speed too fast. He rocketed out of the atmosphere and the gunners plowed a hole through the battle.

The Valiant broke out on the other side and kept on going, but not before a dozen ships split off to hunt the crew down.

Reserve Wing Daggers blasted their way out of the pack and would have fallen in right on the Valiant's tail. The marauders tried to do the same thing, but the Daggers outpaced them.

The marauders turned their guns on the Reserve Wing and distracted the Daggers and Stalwarts just long enough for the Valiant to punch through and sprint away to freedom.

Chapter 19

L yons unbuckled her harness, went forward to the Valiant's cockpit, and looked over Beauty's shoulder at the controls. "You aren't on course for Acrolith Diastema," she remarked. "Where are you going?"

He made a face and rolled his eyes. "If you want to go back to Acrolith Diastema, do it yourself. You promised me food if I stole the ship. I'm hungry."

He hopped off the pilot's seat and sloped off into the back. She sat down in the pilot's seat and changed the ship's course to Acrolith Diastema. It was the only outpost close enough where the crew could get a different ship.

Emmett came up to her and sat down in the seat next to her.

"Don't even say it," she snapped. "We can change ships without dealing with Yuki."

"I wasn't going to say anything." He pretended to mess with the controls. "You know Acrolith Diastema better than any of us."

She went back to what she was doing. "Besides, I kinda hope I do see Yuki."

Emmett only nodded. "I thought it might be that. Do you want me to come with you?"

"I think I better go alone."

Emmett waited a minute and then asked. "Can you scan anything farther distant—like maybe Helios Sanctus?"

"I already did," she told him. "But there are too many human life signs on the station. I wouldn't be able to tell if Fiddler is there."

He looked away and his voice cracked. "Thanks."

She squeezed his shoulder once. "We'll find her."

He only nodded down at the controls and didn't say anything. Lyons had already scanned Helios Sanctus searching for Adik life signs, but she didn't find anything.

That didn't mean Dice wasn't there. It didn't mean he was dead. She had to keep reminding herself of that. The Reserve Wing might have some way to conceal him to stop anyone from finding out that he was there.....or they might have moved him somewhere el se.

She had too many more important things to worry about right now. She turned her attention to Acrolith Diastema.

Emmett saw what she was looking at. "How do you want to do this?"

"I'm going to set down on that building right there and go out into town alone. You take the ship and keep on going."

"Go where?" he asked.

"I don't know. Go see about getting Davenport out of Terminus Anathema.....or maybe get closer to Helios Sanctus and see if you can find a way to rescue Dice and Fiddler. I don't care what you do. Just don't stay here."

"What about you?" Emmett asked. "We wouldn't just leave you behind."

"You won't be. I'll catch up in our new ship and then we'll all go on together."

He raised his eyebrows at her, but just then, Frost came forward from the back. "I think you better go get Beauty out of the food cupboard," she told Lyons. "We won't have anything left by the time he's done."

"It doesn't matter," Lyons replied. "We aren't staying on this ship."

"If something happens to you, we will," Emmett pointed out.

"Nothing will happen to me," Lyons replied. "Nothing bad, at least."

Emmett raised his eyebrows even higher. "What are you going to do?"

"Something I should have done a long time ago. Set us down on the building. I'm getting off."

She went into the back and reloaded her XQ. She heard rustling in one of the store cupboards, but she didn't interfere with Beauty's meal.

She made a deal with him that he could eat all he wanted if he stole the scavengers' ship. He held up his end of the bargain and got the crew off Ultra Meridian. Now it was his turn to enjoy himself.

Lyons opened the hatch when Emmett lowered the Valiant onto the rooftop she indicated. The ship looked so bedraggled that it fit right in with everything else in town.

"Be careful," Flack told her when Lyons stepped off the hatch.

"Don't worry about me," Lyons replied. "Just take care of yourselves and keep the Ziprothil safe until I get back."

"How will you catch up with us?" Frost asked.

"That will be for me to figure out. Don't worry. Everything will work out in the end."

Lyons turned away so she wouldn't see the grimaces of disbelief on their faces. She crossed the roof and turned back to watch the ship lift off. The sun was already dipping toward the horizon. It would be night soon. Good.

Now she was alone on the planet where she'd been born. Nearly everyone in town belonged to Yuki Duetis. If he turned against her, then everyone else would have turned against her, too.

Whether he turned against her wasn't a question. He did turn against her. He sent his ships and men after her to kill her and shoot her out of the sky. She didn't need to know anything else.

She could have gotten another ship and flown away in a matter of hours. She could have arranged it so that none of Yuki's people ever found out that she'd returned to this planet.

She wasn't about to do that, though. She grew up the daughter of a criminal overlord and those values ran too deep to just walk away.

Yuki grew up the son of a criminal overlord—the same criminal overlord who raised Lyons. Yuki should have known better than to screw with Lyons.

She waited for the ship to vanish into the atmosphere. Then she took the building's internal stairwell to the street, ducked into an alley, and darted from one concealed hiding place to another before she came to a different building.

She took another set of stairs to the basement where she pushed the door open. An old Zalvao sat hunched over a workbench peering at an ancient communications device. He looked up and blinked at Lyons.

"Lyons?!" he exclaimed. "Lyons! You're back! I never thought I'd see you again."

He hopped off his stool and hugged her. She had to laugh. "It's good to see you, Situr. You're one of the few people on this planet who's happy to see me."

"I shouldn't be considering how much money I owe you. Don't worry. I'm good for it."

He crossed the room, took a picture off the wall, and started dialing the lock on a safe built into the concrete wall.

"I didn't come to collect on the money you owe me," Lyons interrupted. "I mean, I don't want you to pay me in money. I need a ship."

"I can give you a ship, but I owe you more than a ship is worth. I would have to give you ten ships to make up the debt." He frowned and rubbed his chin. "Although it might depend on what ships you want."

"I need a ship that will conceal some very special cargo from any scanner from detecting it. We're carrying a Ziprothil cartridge and everyone can see it."

"Oh, that." He crossed back over to his workbench. "I heard something about that."

"Can you do it? Can you give me a ship that will conceal the Ziprothil?"

"Sure, sure. That will drive the price up, you know."

"I only need one ship that will conceal the Ziprothil—and the ship needs to conceal the fact that it's concealing it if you know what I mean."

Situr burst out laughing. "Of course. What would be the point if it didn't?"

She found herself grinning at him. "I missed you."

"I missed you, too." His smile drained away. "I don't suppose you could be convinced to come back here, could you—to stay, I mean? Nothing has been the same since....." His eyes darted away.

She didn't ask what he meant. "I wish I could, but I came back here to put things right. Things should improve after I leave."

He brightened up instantly. "Does that mean what I think it means?"

"I'm not going to ask what you think it means." She handed him her XQ. "I need a set of clothes and two handguns."

He walked away and talked to her over his shoulder. "It was so sad when your father died. He was such a strong, kind, intelligent man—such a powerful leader. Acrolith Diastema needs someone like that again."

Lyons didn't answer. She didn't have to. She heard what Situr wasn't saying. He would only say that if Yuki was *not* the powerful leader everyone needed him to be, but Lyons already knew that. No one knew Yuki Duetis better than she did.

Situr opened a closet full of all kinds of clothes. Then he opened another closet next to it that was full of all kinds of weapons, including some bigger than an XQ-85.

Lyons went into the clothes closet and came out wearing a knee-length poncho that covered all the rest of her body. She also selected an enormous hat that concealed her face.

She took two small handguns and stashed them under her poncho. "Now I'm ready to storm the castle."

Situr cocked his head to study her. "Are you sure you don't want some help?"

"No, it's better if I do this alone." She gave him a quick hug. "I hope things improve for you soon."

"They could only improve if you came back here."

"I'll do what I can. See you later.....and make sure you have our ships ready to go."

"They already are!" he yelled after her.

She hustled out of the basement and back to street level. She tucked her long hair inside her hat and bowed her head so no one would recognize her.

She made better progress through the streets even though they were all crowded with Yuki's people. She was the last person alive they would be looking for.

She paused at another intersection to look around and scan the terrain. She recognized quite a few people on the street.

She took a side street to the market and watched vendors, traders, and a few of Yuki's strongmen arguing, doing business, and drinking at some of the stalls. Nothing on this planet ever changed—until it did.

Once things changed, they changed quickly and they changed irrevocably. Things changed when Lyons's father died. Now they were about to change again.

She darted past a group of Zanides and hid behind another building. She peeked out and observed a mixed collection of armed aliens standing guard around the building where she and the Chorion Team had met up with Yuki.

The alien sentries guarded the entrance, circled the building, and she saw some of them standing on the roof. They patrolled the whole area to make sure no one came near the place without Yuki's permission.

Lyons watched their movements for a while and then doubled back through another series of alleys.

She took a different side street, slipped into an alley, and hid in a doorway until one of the sentries passed her hiding place. She had to take off her hat just to fit in the narrow doorway.

The sentry would have walked straight past her without even looking into that doorway. Yuki's people were getting way too complacent.

She raised her handgun, and the minute he stepped in front of the doorway, she shot him in the ear.

She snatched her hat, bolted across the alley, and concealed herself in a different doorway directly across from the one she just used.

She barely got in there before three more sentries came running to see what caused the gunshot.

They surrounded their fallen comrade and exclaimed over his dead body. They all turned their backs to Lyons and—Pop! Pop! Pop! She dropped them, too.

Chapter 20

L yons left all four bodies lying where they were, sprinted to the end of the alley, scrambled over a wall, charged down a different street, and circled the building from its other side.

The rest of the sentries rushed around the opposite corner to check out what caused the commotion. They left the building entrance completely unguarded. The fools.

Lyons slipped inside and eased the door shut behind her. A staircase led to the second floor where Yuki had entertained his guests.

Lyons tiptoed up the stairs and entered the large hall where she and Yuki had lunch. It was empty now.

She passed through it and climbed another set of stairs to an enormous apartment on the building's very top floor.

Lyons surveyed the large main room. It occupied a third of the building's top story. A wall on one side partitioned the apartment into different bedrooms with another internal stairway leading to some mezzanine rooms above this one.

The moment she stepped in, she heard moaning, screaming, smacking, and the rhythmic thump of bodies striking into each other. A female voice started sobbing in ecstasy and then spiked into screams.

Lyons rolled her eyes. Yuki never changed.

She climbed the internal stairs and came out in a small vestibule behind the mezzanine bedroom. From here, she could see more than she ever wanted to of Yuki's love life.

He lay stark naked on his back with one woman straddling his hips and another straddling his face. Their marble-white bodies undulated in blatant desire.

Lyons stayed where she was and watched for a minute. Thank the stars she'd never felt even marginally tempted to go any further with Yuki. This could be her right now.

She would rather live as a two-bit smuggler with no home in the world than to be one of Yuki's pampered pets. Lyons wouldn't have been surprised if he took over her father's empire just for the girls.

She waited for what seemed like a long time. The trio on the bed went through several different position changes until Yuki collapsed back on the bed with a satisfied sigh.

The two women fawned over him, smothered him in kisses and rubbed their bodies all over him, told him what an exquisite lover he was, and then, one by one, they left for the bathroom behind this bedroom.

Yuki stretched out on the mattress and shut his eyes. He sprawled on the bed without a stitch on him. Lyons couldn't have planned this better.

She threw off the poncho, pulled one of her guns, and strode out into the room. Yuki was so out of it that he didn't hear her stop at the foot of his bed.

She studied him at the end of her gun. Even shooting him like this seemed too good for him. She wanted to humiliate him before she put an end to him. The world would be a better place without him in it.

She waited for a minute and the two girls giggled in the other room, but he still didn't wake up. He might really have fallen asleep, but a second later, the toilet in the other room flushed.

He smiled to himself and opened his eyes. He froze when he saw Lyons standing there aiming a gun at him. "Enjoying yourself?" she asked.

The bathroom door opened and the girls froze in exactly the same way when they saw Lyons. She pivoted her gun in their direction. "I'll give you five seconds to get out of the room."

The two girls bolted for the stairs and Lyons moved her gun back over to Yuki. He stiffened slightly and then wilted back to prop himself on his elbow. "You should know better than to sneak into someone's bedroom waving a gun around."

"I'm not waving a gun around as you can see." She tightened her grip on the gun and raised it to aim at his face. "Did you really think you could get away with it, Yuki? Did you think you could hide from me forever?"

"What are you talking about? I'm not hiding from you." He stretched out on the bed and undulated his body in front of her. "Don't tell me you're jealous. You could have been in here with me instead."

She snorted. "Is there some reason Leron didn't come back from his mission to find the people who killed my father, Yuki? You were the only person who knew where Leron was.

Don't you think it's awfully convenient that he found the people responsible, reported their whereabouts to you, and then mysteriously vanished off the map? I don't know about you, but I find those three events highly coincidental."

"That's because they are coincidental," Yuki replied with a smirk. "That's what coincidental means. It means it's a coincidence."

"My father was shot in an alley less than a quarter of a mile from the center of town," she went on. "No one in Acrolith Diastema had more security than he did. No one could have gotten near him unless his security team already knew the person."

Yuki shook his head. "You have your facts wrong."

"Really? What about the fact that the security team wasn't even near my father when he got shot? What about the fact that someone fired gunshots less than a block away and the security team went to check it out? Then the three guards who were supposed to stay behind and protect my father got shot at point-blank range when they were standing less than two feet away from him. The three guards were all found with their weapons drawn and aiming away from my father—toward the sound of the commotion down the street. No one could have gotten that close to him unless the security team knew and trusted the killer. Someone created that diversion and then used their knowledge of the security team to get close enough to shoot them and my father."

"And you think the killer is me?" Yuki burst out laughing. "You're crazy."

"You think so? And then, after my father was dead, another hit team came after me. You and everyone else said it was because whoever killed my father wanted to stop me from taking his place. What do you know about that, Yuki? I was the only person who could have stopped you from taking over. You doubled down on the pressure for us to get together after my father died. You made a big deal about us ruling together and you also made a big deal about the danger of me trying to rule alone. Do you remember any of that? You were the one who stood to gain the most from someone knocking me off. You would have been the one to assassinate me to leave a clear path for you to step into my father's place."

He opened his mouth to answer back, but she'd heard enough. She lunged for him, seized him by the hair, and dragged him off the bed. As soon as she got him upright, she grabbed him by the back of the neck and shook him just to make sure he didn't try anything.

"Hey!" he shrieked. "What are you doing? Leave me alone!"

"I don't think so. You're coming with me. Now march." She shoved him toward the stairs.

"At least let me get dressed first!" he countered.

"Oh, no!" She laughed at him. "You're going like this."

She jabbed her gun into his spine and drove him downstairs, but she didn't stop at the large hall or the ground floor. She pushed him down some more stairs to the basement of the same building.

Half the aliens who'd been having lunch with Yuki earlier were down there. Seventy of his enforcers, guards, gunrunners, and officers stood and sat around talking, eating, and organizing their weapons.

The whole assembly stopped what they were doing when she drove him at gunpoint into the basement as naked as the day he was born.

He tried to cover himself up with his hands, but she gave him another cruel shove and he had to take his hands down to balance himself.

"Shoot this woman!" he bellowed as soon as he got inside.

She grabbed him by the neck, yanked him to a stop, and crammed her gun barrel into his temple.

"I am Rizarth Hudan's daughter and the rightful heir to his empire!" she yelled across the room. "Rizarth took this man into his home when Yuki was just a baby. Rizarth raised this man as a son and gave him everything. This man assassinated Rizarth in cold blood, pretended to grieve over his loss, took over Rizarth's empire in his absence, and then pretended to send out a scout to track down the people who killed Rizarth. Yuki then arranged for the scout to get killed so he couldn't come back to tell anyone what he found. If anyone disputes these accusations, let him speak now."

No one moved. Lyons knew most of the men in the room and they knew her. They also knew Yuki.

She clamped her hand on the back of his neck and murmured low in his ear. "Do you have anything to say in your own defense, Yuki? You know everyone in this room. Do you have any evidence to offer to clear yourself of suspicion in our eyes?"

He opened his mouth, but when he saw everyone glaring back at him, his voice failed. "I....." He broke off.

Lyons waited, but when he didn't say anything, she grabbed him and shoved him down on his knees. He didn't seem to notice. His petrified gaze remained riveted on the people in front of him—the people who made it possible for him to rule all this time.

They glared back at him. Not one person spoke up to defend him or even to suggest that he stay alive another day.

"I sentence you to death for the murder of Rizarth Hudan," Lyons announced, "and for the death of Leron Miwe, the scout you either killed yourself or arranged to have killed. I also sentence you to death for anyone else you may have killed on your rise to the top."

She stepped back, aimed her weapon at his skull, and paused. He huddled there on his knees, naked and defenseless. He didn't even turn around to look at her. He didn't call on their past relationship as brother and sister to save himself. Even he knew all of that was meaningless.

She fired, his body toppled sideways onto the floor, and a palpable wave of relief went through the room. No one stepped out to remove the body.

Lyons put her weapon down and faced the room full of guards, sentries, strongmen, enforcers, and officers. "I'm taking charge of this organization as of now," she told them. "There's a battle going on in the next solar system. The Reserve Wing is fighting to retake a ship with some of my friends on it. I want our entire fleet in the air on the double to defend this ship. Situr is providing additional vessels for us, so we'll need our own people manning them. I'll be with you. Let's go."

She waved toward the door and everyone took off for the stairs. No one stopped to pick up Yuki. No one looked sideways at him.

Chapter 21

Lyons strode on board a Cyclone-class battlecruiser manned by Yuki's people—except that these weren't Yuki's people anymore. They were her people.

A surge of power flooded through her when she sat down in the captain's chair on the bridge. She used to occupy this position on the *Echo Omicron,* but she only had a crew of three then.

Those days were gone. Now she was in charge of her father's criminal syndicate.

"Situr is sending word from the other Cyclones," one of her bridge staff reported. "The rest of his ships are ready to launch whenever you give the word."

Lyons turned around. The man who'd spoken was a giant Hidion who stood where the second-in-command bridge officer should stand. In fact, everyone on the bridge was a Hidion.

Lyons cracked a grin at the man who'd spoken. "It's good to see you again, Ignus."

He grinned back at her. "It's good to have you finally in charge, Ma'am. We've all been waiting for this day. We're ready to rock whenever you are."

"Take us out and send word to Situr to fall in formation with us."

Another Hidion named Vilo piloted Lyons's Cyclone. He lifted off the ground, and in a minute, thirty ships launched from all over Acrolith Diastema. They were the same ships that had come after the Valiant on Lyons's last visit, but now they flew on Lyons's orders instead of Yuki's.

Lyons checked the situation with the Reserve Wing. The patched Valiant carrying the Ziprothil stuck out a mile on the sensors. A flashing warning alarm went off every time the sensors swept the area with the ship flying in it. Everyone in the sector knew that that ship was carrying the Ziprothil.

The Reserve Wing had followed the ship away from Acrolith Diastema. The Reserve Wing kept trying to capture the ship with the Ziprothil on it. Every time they got close enough to put the ship in jeopardy, more marauders showed up and tried to snatch the ship for themselves.

"Order all our ships to surround that Valiant," Lyons ordered.

"Yes, Ma'am!" Ignus replied. "Moving in. The Reserve Wing is angling outward to defend the ship."

"Drive the bastards apart, force our way in, and take the Valiant on board this Cyclone."

The other Cyclones responded to her every word. They slammed into the Reserve Wing barricade and guns erupted on both sides. A crushing smash struck Lyons's ship.

"The marauders are taking advantage of our assault," Ignus reported. "They're trying to flank us to steal the Valiant."

"Wipe them out," Lyons ordered. "Destroy anyone who goes near that ship."

"Yes, Ma'am!" Ignus replied. "Our Cyclones are moving into position."

Lyons sat back and watched all these ships doing her bidding. She only had to give the word and they obeyed her instantly.

What was she thinking running away from Acrolith Diastema? She should have deposed Yuki long ago and taken control of her father's empire.

She wouldn't be in a position to help her friends right now if she hadn't been on the *Echo Omicron* when Davenport found the Ithium on board.

The Valiant did its best to defend itself, but the marauders outnumbered the ship and it was barely functional anyway. Its guns fired in every possible direction, but the marauders flew state-of-the-art vessels with countless weapons.

They surrounded the Valiant hammering the ship with all their firepower. The marauders were so intent on capturing the Ziprothil that they were completely unprepared for the Cyclones' onslaught.

Situr's battlecruisers punched through the marauder ranks, surrounded the Valiant, and swiveled outward to defend the ship. The Reserve Wing tried to break through, too, but so many other ships blocked their way that they couldn't get near the Valiant.

Lyons watched a mixed squadron of Cyclones and marauders hammer the Reserve Wing away. The two fleets worked together to drive the Reserve Wing off, but behind the lines, the Cyclones and the marauders battled each other for possession of the Valiant.

Stray fire crippled the Valiant's engines. The ship tried to limp away while the Cyclones and the marauders still duked it out for the prize.

"Get around the battle and take that ship on board!" Lyons ordered again. "Tell our Cyclones to stop fighting the Reserve Wing and move in to defend us while we take the ship on board."

"Yes, Ma'am! They're falling back now."

Lyons's flagship swooped around the battle. A dozen marauders tried to cut her off, but Vilo gunned the engines and circled behind them. They all moved in at once and he spun the ship around to stand its ground alone against all those attackers.

The Cyclone reversed and opened its cargo hold to take the Valiant on board, but the ship wheeled at that moment and opened fire on Lyons's ship.

"Hail the Valiant!" Lyons ordered. "Get them to....."

A punishing barrage struck the ship from the front as the marauders opened fire, but just as fast, Lyons's fleet whirled away from the Reserve Wing, sprinted across the battlefield, and laid into the marauders from behind.

Stray fire slammed into Lyons's ship and some of it hit the Valiant. One of its engines exploded.

"The Valiant is refusing our hails!'" Ignus announced. "The pilot is a human male and his return message tells you to spin on a lamppost."

Lyons had to laugh. "Emmett! Hack his communications system and put me through to him directly."

Ignus shook his head. "He isn't going to like it."

"He'll love it when he realizes who it is that's trying to take his ship on board. Do it."

Another bombardment from the Cyclones slammed a dozen marauders into Lyons's ship. They collided and banged Lyons's ship backward closer to the Valiant, but the ship only fired on Lyons's Cyclone again.

"They don't want to be rescued, Ma'am!" Ignus yelled over the noise.

"Get me Emmett on the double!" Lyons fired back. "We don't have time for this shit!"

"I got him! You're through now, Ma'am!"

She switched on the communications controls at her station. Emmett's voice came through the speaker and then the screen showed him fighting the Valiant's controls trying to steer the ship away from the battle.

"You can go straight to hell if you...."

"Emmett—it's me!" Lyons called. "It's Lyons. I'm on the Cyclone right in front of you. Hold your fire! We can take you on board. This ship will conceal the Ziprothil and then we can get you out of here."

"It's a little late for that, don't you think?" he sneered back. "Everyone knows we're carrying it."

"Just come on board!" she ordered. "Tell the girls to hold their fire. You won't make it another parsec in that ship."

He compressed his lips. "All right. You win. Just...."

Another brutal concussion of gunfire hit both ships. The strike didn't damage the Cyclone. "The Valiant just suffered a critical hull breach on its aft flank!" Ignus reported. "They have about five minutes of life support left."

"Take the ship on board! Hold your fire, Emmett! We're coming to get you."

Lyons cut the signal and the Cyclone backed away from the battle. The rest of Lyons's fleet surrounded the two ships and the Cyclone finally backed its cargo hold over the Valiant. The hold slammed shut with the ship inside.

"We got it, Ma'am!" Ignus reported. "The Valiant is on board and pressurized with breathable atmospheric gas."

"Get us out of here," Lyons reported. "Lay in a course for Terminus Anathema."

Everyone on the bridge looked up. "Ma'am?" Ignus asked.

"Terminus Anathema," she repeated. "I'm sure you've all heard of it and I'm sure you all know where it is. Order our fleet to stay behind and engage with these marauders so they don't follow us. I'm going downstairs. I'll be back in a few minutes."

She left the bridge, but when she got to the Cyclone's internal elevator, Ignus ran out to catch up with her. He stepped inside the elevator car with her. "Do you think it's wise to go to Terminus Anathema?" he asked. "The place will be crawling with Reserve Wing and Confederate Corps troops."

"I'm aware of that," she replied. "There's someone incarcerated there that I want to get out. Once we have him, we'll leave the area, but I doubt we'll be able to completely shake off the Reserve Wing. Did you check to see if this ship conceals the Ziprothil?"

He shrugged and looked away. "It conceals it from ordinary scans, but it's like your friend said. Everyone knows where the Ziprothil is. It's only a matter of time before someone starts using more sophisticated technology to track it. We won't be able to keep it concealed forever—or even very long."

"Then we better work fast. I want you to go back up to the bridge, search the Confederate Corps database, and locate a prisoner at Terminus Anathema. His name is Mace Davenport and he's human. He doesn't have a conviction. He was imprisoned without trial."

Ignus only nodded. "I'm not surprised."

"Find out which section he's in and then contact the prison superintendent to communicate our intention to free this prisoner. Tell the superintendent we're willing to do whatever it takes to get Davenport back—no matter what it takes. Is that understood?"

Ignus raised his eyebrows. "Who is this prisoner?"

"He's a friend of mine." The elevator doors opened and Lyons stepped out into the cargo hold. Ignus stayed inside the car and the doors shut with him in there.

Lyons strode over to the Valiant's rear hatch, but it didn't open. She tried the release, but nothing happened.

One of the ship's engines had been destroyed. Smoke came out of the other one and more smoke and steam billowed from hull breaches all over the ship.

Lyons finally gave up and fired one of her handguns into the hatch release. It popped and the hatch slammed down on the floor.

She peered in at the four clones staring back at her. Emmett was still up in the cockpit.

"Is everything okay, Lyons?" Flack asked.

"Everything's fine," Lyons replied. "Everything would have been a lot finer if you hadn't shot at me so much, but we can put that aside." She peered past them. Emmett still hadn't turned around. He sat with his back to them working on the Valiant's controls.

Lyons strode on board and stopped next to his chair. "You can stop working on this bucket of bolts. You're on board my Cyclone now. You're safe."

"You think so? Look at that." He pointed at the controls and her stomach dropped when she saw what he was pointing at.

The battle between Lyons's fleet, the marauders, and the Reserve Wing had spilled over with all three of them coming after Lyons's ship. Now the Reserve Wing and the marauders teamed up while Lyons's fleet tried to stop both armies from coming after Lyons's Cyclone.

Lyons's fleet kept dodging between her ship and all those attackers, but the two enemy fleets together overran her group in no time.

They kept surrounding the Cyclones, tying them up with brutal gunfire, and then charging around the Cyclones to make another run for Lyons's ship.

The three fleets played this game again and again with the Reserve Wing and the marauders leaving the Cyclones in the dust every time. The two squadrons worked in a coordinated effort to ditch the Cyclones where they couldn't protect the ship carrying the Ziprothil.

"Shit!" Lyons whispered. Then she spun away. "Come on! All of you get upstairs. I need you on the bridge."

"What about guns?" Frost asked. "Don't you need gunners?"

"I have that already. Come on!"

She raced back to the elevator with Emmett and the four girls. Lyons pretended not to notice that Beauty wasn't with them.

She should have taken the time to tell him to move the Ziprothil to another hiding place, but when she got back upstairs to the bridge, she realized that it wouldn't make any difference.

The Reserve Wing and the marauders obviously didn't have any plans to let the ship carrying the Ziprothil out of their sight long enough for the Cyclone to hide from them.

They kept hammering Lyons's fleet, overrunning them, and charging Lyons's vessel before the Cyclones could move in to defend it again.

"We got another massive problem, Ma'am," Ignus reported when Lyons returned.

"Not another one!" Lyons countered.

"Take a look." He showed her a scan of Terminus Anathema. Ships of every kind surrounded the planet and explosions popped off inside the prison structure itself.

A raging air battle blocked anyone from getting near the planet. Dozens of Reserve Wing vessels engaged in an all-out battle against a mixed collection of alien warships.

Their designations came from all over the galaxy, including Ekol Thaine's service, Calyx Elkanon's empire, half a dozen other criminal syndicates, and a bunch of others the Confederate database couldn't identify.

"Jesus Christ!" Emmett breathed.

"Word is going out on the wires that Calyx Elkanon is dead," Ignus murmured. "His organization is combining with Ekol Thaine's."

"That is gonna be one hell of a powerful organization," Friend remarked. "No one will be able to stand up to them."

"The Reserve Wing is giving it a pretty good effort," Emmett pointed out. "We better withdraw. They're bringing in another twenty Stalwarts."

"We can't raise the prison superintendents or anyone else at the prison," Ignus added. "The staff section has been destroyed and there are gun battles and explosions going off all over the island. It's impossible to tell which groups are prison staff and which are rioting prisoners. If your friend is down there, we won't be able to get near enough to the prison to get him off. We have to withdraw and find him another way."

Lyons's heart sank. She turned away feeling sick and nodded. Vilo steered the ship away only to run into the Reserve Wing and marauders trying to make another charge for her Cyclone.

Gunfire peppered the hull, and before she could say a word, the alien force that had been fighting over Terminus Anathema broke away and rushed the battle over Lyon's ship, too.

The Reserve Wing vessels that had been trying to defend the prison wheeled and gave chase, but they didn't get there in time before the alien force overran Lyons's position.

The fleet of the combined criminal syndicates flooded the battle. A chaotic soup of ships, gunshots, and explosions turned the whole area into a shooting gallery of everyone shooting at everyone else.

The Cyclones that had been following Lyons and trying to defend the Ziprothil got caught in the confusion. Gunfire rained all over Lyons's ship. "Get us out of this, Vilo!" she ordered. "Pull away from Terminus Anathema!"

"I'm trying to, Ma'am!" he yelled over his shoulder. "They don't make it easy....."

Another smash struck the Cyclone from starboard and the impact flung the ship across the battlefield. By sheer good luck, the impact hurled the ship closer to the edge of the battlefield and Vilo hit the throttle to burst into open space.

"Set course for Helios Sanctus," Lyons ordered. "How many spare people do we have on board?"

"About fifty," Ignus replied. "What do you want them for?"

"Send them all down to the hold and arm them up. We're going onto the station."

"You might want to check first and make sure our people are even on the station," Friend chimed in from the back of the bridge."

"I plan to," Lyons replied, "but we're still out of scanner range. Let's go."

Chapter 22

Lyons took advantage of the trip to Helios Sanctus to go back downstairs to the ruined Valiant. She searched the whole ship, but she didn't find any trace of Beauty or the Ziprothil.

She knew he was on board and that he still had the Ziprothil. She'd been able to detect both from the bridge. Now they were both gone. She would have to go all the way back up to the bridge to find exactly where on the Cyclone he was hiding.

She got a brainwave and went to the Valiant's cockpit instead. She switched on the scanners and they synched with the Cyclone's.

The Cyclone was still scanning Helios Sanctus. The ship had been too far out of range until now, but the ship had finally flown within scanner range to get a clear picture of the station.

The orders she'd given on the bridge translated to the Valiant's controls. The Cyclone scanned for Adik life signs.....and came up empty.

Lyons's heart sank when the scanners swept the station again and again. They always returned a negative result. There wasn't one single Adik life sign on the whole station.

She collapsed into the pilot's chair and slumped. He couldn't be dead. He couldn't be.

He'd been so weak and helpless when Admiral Joyce and Colonel Casey took Dice away from Ultra Meridian.

His life signs had been weak to the point of almost being undetectable when the crew attacked the *Trailblazer* to save him.

What if the Reserve Wing gave him too much truth serum and he died? He might already be dead. Then what would she do?

She couldn't think about that, but she found it impossible to think of anything else. Dice and Beauty had been her only family ever since she left Acrolith Diastema. They'd give her a way out. They'd given her a life when she didn't have any other.

The three of them had become bonded in a way Lyons had never been bonded to anyone except her father. Her father died and Dice and Beauty stepped into that place. She couldn't lose them—not now.

She stared at the scanner sweeping the Helios Sanctus again and again. It always came up negative. There were no Adiks on the station—none at all. Not even one.

She gulped down despair. What would she do if she couldn't get Dice *or* Davenport back? Where would she go? She'd spend the rest of her life on the run trying to hide a cartridge of Ziprothil that couldn't be hidden.

Now she'd put her father's whole empire in jeopardy on the hopeless chance that she could help Davenport and rescue Dice. She'd thrown away her father's legacy for nothing.

She should have just let Yuki run her father's empire. At least he had an empire under Yuki. Now no one had anything.

She didn't move before she heard footsteps crossing the hold outside. She didn't turn around when someone walked on board the Valiant and came forward to the cockpit.

Emmett sat down in the other chair and laid his hand on her shoulder. "You can't blame yourself for this," he told her. "You did everything to get here as soon as you could."

Lyons blinked down at her hands. "I couldn't save him."

"He isn't dead. We found records on the bridge. That's what I came down here to tell you."

Lyons's head shot up. "You what?"

"We found Reserve Wing records. The station suffered massive internal damage from an Adik rampage and the same records list Dice and Fiddler as escaped—along with one other prisoner who was locked up here with them. It looks like Fiddler found a way to trigger Dice to attack and then all three of them made it off the station. The Reserve Wing is undertaking a retrieval mission right now. Look."

Emmett went to work on the controls. Lyons struggled to contain her exhilaration while he patched the Valiant's controls into the Cyclone's bridge.

He pulled up a bunch of log records from Helios Sanctus. The footage showed Dice rampaging through the station destroying one deck after another and killing hundreds of soldiers.

He did so much damage that the footage cut out halfway through the attack. The station didn't record the fugitives making it on board a ship and getting away, but the records clearly listed both Dice and Fiddler as escaped.

Lyons frowned at the records. "It doesn't list the identity of the third prisoner. He's listed as classified."

"Who cares?" Emmett countered. "Dice and Fiddler are out there somewhere."

"Can you identify the ship they escaped in?"

"Sorry. We found the records of which ship it was, but there's no sign of it anywhere. Your friend Ignus ran it through the database of every Reserve Wing ship in the quadrant. The ship isn't in battle anywhere or any other place it could have gotten to in the time since the three of them escaped."

"That doesn't mean anything," Lyons countered. "They could have ditched the ship. They would be stupid not to."

"I don't care where she is as long as she's alive." Emmett went back to working on the controls.

Lyons studied the side of his face. "Thank you for coming down here to tell me. I would be lost if I thought Dice was dead."

"You and me both." Emmett shot her a look. "It's good to know they're out there somewhere, isn't it?"

"Yeah." Lyons threw caution to the wind and squeezed his arm. "I feel better."

He smiled at her. "We'll find them. I'm certain of it. The good news is that we're all looking for the same things. They'll be looking for Davenport and the Ziprothil. We have the Ziprothil and we're looking for Davenport, too. He's bound to turn up and then we'll all be together in the same place."

"Can you locate Healey and the boys?"

"I already tried that. I'm not reading any Chorions in the vicinity, either."

Lyons frowned. "That's odd."

Emmett shrugged. "What isn't odd about those boys? They could be anywhere."

"So what do you want to do now?" Lyons asked. "Everyone else in the sector knows we have the Ziprothil, too. What do we do with it? How do we put it somewhere no one else will be able to get it?"

"I know a few people, but I wouldn't trust them to hold onto it for us. The problem will always be keeping it out of the wrong hands."

Lyons made a face. "Maybe ours aren't the right hands for it, either."

"Then whose are? I can't think of anyone who would work as hard as we have to protect it."

"Neither can I—apart from Davenport."

"Yeah, it would be nice if we could find him, but wherever he is, he's in as much trouble as we are—if not more. He's a prisoner at Terminus Anathema right now because he tried to do the right thing."

"So who are these people you know?" Lyons asked.

"Just a few people I know from my early days. They might have a place where we could hide the Ziprothil—or us. I can tell you one thing, though. We wouldn't be able to roll up on these people with a fleet of Cyclones in tow. We might as well hang out a sign that announces to the world that we have the Ziprothil."

Lyons sighed and looked down at the controls. "Yeah. I know."

"We need to transfer to a smaller, less recognizable ship."

"That's what I was trying to do when I went to Acrolith Diastema," she told him. "But it somehow didn't turn out that way. It seemed like a good idea at the time."

"We might not be able to conceal the Ziprothil completely, but we can do better than this. Why don't you order your people to bring in a smaller, faster ship with better concealment? Then the Cyclones can create a diversion and we'll make our getaway. We might be able to put some distance between us and any pursuit. We can't keep traveling through space with three fleets of ships fighting over us."

That settled it. Lyons went back up to the bridge and gave her orders to Ignus. He took command of the Cyclone and the rest of Lyons's fleet.

It took eight hours for Ignus to bring in another ship for Lyons and her friends to take. Lyons still didn't know where Beauty and the Ziprothil were.

She spotted him on the ship's internal scanners, but she couldn't detect the Ziprothil. "How does he do it?" Friend asked over Lyons's shoulder.

"I learned a long time ago not to ask that question," Lyons replied.

"Maybe he ate it," Flack suggested.

Lyons groaned. "Don't even joke about that."

The other clones laughed. "It would make a good hiding place," Fizzle added.

"He's in the galley again," Lyons remarked. "I'll go tell him what we're planning to do."

She went down there, and as soon as she walked in, she realized how hungry she was.

She rifled the cabinets and found the Cyclone stocked with PureLife meals. That Yuki didn't spare any expense.

She started heating one up when she heard banging coming from a crate under one of the benches that lined the tables. They were solid rectangular benches fixed to the floor. The top cushion pulled away to provide storage inside the big box bench.

The compartment had been stocked with Peanut Surprise. These emergency rations came in a house-brick-sized block that weighed a ton.

Peanut Surprise contained all the essential nutrients to keep people alive and it tasted pretty good, too—or that's what Lyons had heard from people in the know. No one knew what the ingredients were. That was another question smart people didn't ask. Hence the name.

The blocks were as solid as a house brick, too. Anyone dying of starvation who needed Peanut Surprise to survive better hope and pray they had a hatchet to carve part of the block off to eat. A fully powered hydraulic jackhammer would have been better.

Lyons had never been in a survival situation dire enough to need to eat Peanut Surprise, but she'd held the blocks in her hand before. She could have dropped one from a thirty-story building and not damaged the block at all. The pavement underneath would have suffered at least a dent, but not the block.

Beauty must have hidden himself in this bench the instant the Cyclone took the Valiant on board. She could see that the entire bench had been loaded from top to bottom with blocks of Peanut Surprise and he'd worked his way through a third of the bench already.

Empty wrappers carpeted the floor of the compartment. Beauty crouched on top of the empty wrappers while he gnawed on another block. He screwed up his face and dug his eye tooth into the block, but she didn't see him doing any damage to it.

She snorted when she finally found him. "Are you making yourself sick again?"

"I'm eating," he growled. "I don't make myself sick when I eat."

"We're transferring to another ship, so you better finish eating before that happens. We also need you to take the Ziprothil on board the other ship when we transfer. We're hoping to find somewhere else to hide it."

He twisted the block back and forth trying to dig his tooth into it, but he couldn't even scratch the surface. She couldn't understand how he managed to eat so many blocks before now—not to mention how he continued to function with all that Peanut Surprise in his stomach.

Just then, the oven in the kitchen dinged and she went over there to get her PureLife meal. She put it on the table, sat down on the bench opposite Beauty, and started eating.

He eyed her over the top of the table. He kept shooting disgusted glances at the PureLife meal like he couldn't for the life of him figure out why she would eat that when she had all this wonderful Peanut Surprise on hand.

She glared right back at him, and in a minute, he hunkered down inside his bench where she couldn't see him. She heard growling, snuffling, and a few loud thumps followed by munching sounds.

She finished her meal and made an executive decision not to look when she passed him on her way back to the bridge.

A few hours later when the crew's new ride showed up, he presented himself in the cargo hold. He looked perfectly normal. His stomach was just as skinny as it had been before....and his hands were empty. He wasn't carrying the Ziprothil. Lyons decided not to ask about that, either.

The new ship was a Phoenix-class frigate. It was smaller than a Cyclone but just as well-armed. "The mechanics on Acrolith Diastema say it's shielded with Tekrite plating," Ignus told Lyons. "They say no one should be able to detect the Ziprothil through the hull."

"Famous last words," Lyons replied. "I guess we'll find out pretty soon. Are you ready to pull your diversion?"

"We won't have to. The marauders, the Reserve Wing, and everyone else are already following us. All we have to do is exist. They'll attack us or each other or maybe both. Then you can slip away in the confusion."

"I can't wait," Emmett mumbled.

"Let's get on board," Flack suggested. "We want to be ready when the time comes to make our move."

The four clones stepped through the side hatch. A line of cannons ran the length of the ship's lower deck.

The cockpit at the top sat at the front of the top deck with cabins and other compartments filling the rest of the top deck.

Lyons and Emmett went up to the cockpit while the four clones checked out the weapons. Lyons adjusted the scanners. "Can you tell if Beauty brought the Ziprothil on board?"

"The scanners are showing it in this hold at the same location as the ship, so I'd say yeah. It's a little late in the day to start questioning him, don't you think?"

Lyons shrugged. "I guess you're right."

"If we do get taken, there is no one alive who will be better able to hide it than he will be," Emmett pointed out. "Holy crap, here comes another contingent of the

Reserve Wing." He craned his head back and yelled down to the clones. "Strap in! We got company! Stand by to jump."

Lyons scrambled to fire up the controls. The rest of her people raced away to take command of the Cyclone. If this worked, she wouldn't see them again—which is what she wanted in the first place.

The Reserve Wing came in fast and hard with the marauders right on their asses. A bunch of syndicate vessels from Terminus Anathema came with them.

The Reserve Wing unloaded on the Cyclone and then the rest of Lyons's fleet showed up. The Phoenix jostled on its landing gear when gunfire struck the Cyclone.

Lyons held her breath counting down the seconds before the Cyclone released the Phoenix into open battle. She would have to get out of the chaos quickly.

Even that wouldn't help if this Tekrite shielding didn't work. If it didn't and everyone could still detect the Ziprothil, the Phoenix would be that much less able to defend itself than the Valiant had been.

The Cyclones plunged into the battle, and this time, Lyons's ship didn't hold back. Vilo dove right into the heart of the mayhem and the Cyclone's guns opened fire on everybody.

He piloted the ship through a swarm of attackers. Vessels on all sides fired on the Cyclone, but he flew too fast for anyone to hit him. Only Lyons and her crew could tell that he wasn't trying to get involved in the battle at all.

He plunged out the other side, took a barrage on his port side, and swung around to head back into the fight. The ship banked hard, and at the steepest part of its turn, the cargo hold slammed open and the Phoenix dropped out into open space.

Lyons punched the throttle to its maximum and blasted away into space. She kept the engines burning at their highest pitch and left the battle far behind. The gunfire and explosions vanished behind the Phoenix's vapor trail until nothing remained.

Chapter 23

"So where are we going this time?" Lyons asked Emmett.

"Head for the Pegasus Mines." He bent over the scanners. "No one is following us."

"That might be because they're all still tied up in the battle. Who do you know at the Pegasus Mines?"

He shrugged. "I know a lot of people there. I also know that the mine is stripping Tekrite at the moment. If your people are right about Tekrite shielding the Ziprothil, maybe we'll be able to hide it there among all the other Tekrite."

"I guess that's as good a lead as any." She entered the course. "So what are we going to do once we get there? Are we just going to hide out?"

"I worked there for almost a year while I was searching for Fiddler," he replied. "There are some very knowledgeable people there. They can help us find out where everybody is. Once we know that, the same people will be able to get us the resources we need to get our people back. Besides, we'll be able to work there to earn the money to buy those resources, which is just as important."

Lyons turned around in her chair to study him. "You really know this stuff, don't you?"

"I've been through it all before," he muttered. "I did it once. I can do it again."

"What kind of work will we be able to do there—apart from mining?"

He shrugged. "I'm sure you'll be able to find something. People with your skills can always find work."

"My skills! What do you mean?"

"Stealing, smuggling, bounty hunting, going on dangerous runs through space that no one else would be stupid enough to make—all the things you've been doing for the last however many years."

She didn't argue with him. She'd never discussed any of this with him or with anyone else on the crew. It would have been inevitable that someone would have figured it out.

She would need weapons for that, but when she went downstairs to check out what kind of supplies this Phoenix had, she discovered a weapons locker almost as packed as Situr's. Ignus had fitted out this ship with everything the crew could ask for and more.

She was in the middle of checking everything out when the four clones came upstairs. "Where are we going?" Frost asked.

"Emmett wants us to go to the Pegasus Mines," Lyons replies. "He says he worked there while he was searching for Fiddler. He says we can get information and supplies there."

"He would know." Flack helped herself to an XQ-62. Lyons watched Flack's hands going through the automatic routine of opening the magazine, checking it, and then closing it.

"Emmett thinks we can get work at the mines—I mean, not mining, but doing random jobs," Lyons went on. "Do you girls have any special skills—apart from Friend's computer skills?"

"Frost is really good at fixing ships and vehicles," Fizzle replied.

"I am not!" Frost countered. "Don't make it out like it's something special when it isn't."

"I bet you could get a job at the Pegasus mines," Fizzle returned. "I bet you could get a really good-paying job there—not like us."

"What does Emmett want us to do?" Friend asked.

"He didn't tell me what he wants *you* to do," Lyons replied. "He only said what he suggested I could do."

"Which is what?" Flack asked.

Lyons shrugged. "Stealing, smuggling, bounty hunting, going on dangerous runs through space that no one else would be stupid enough to make—all the things I've been doing for the last however many years."

Flack nodded. "That sounds good. I could do that."

"Is that what you've been doing all these last however many years?"

"Something like that."

Lyons turned to Fizzle. "What about you? What are you good at?"

"She's really good at tracking people—or anything else," Flack told her. "She can find anything or anyone."

"Only if they're on the ground," Fizzle countered. "If they're in space, forget it."

Just then, Emmett came back from the cockpit and joined them at the weapons locker. "What's the haps?" he asked.

"We were just discussing what kind of work we could get at the Pegasus Mines," Frost told him.

He nodded. "You girls will do fine at the mines. Useful skills are always in demand there."

"What did you do at the Pegasus Mines when you were here last time?" Flack asked.

"I had a legitimate job in the machine shop. It put me in a perfect position to talk to everyone, including all the people who *don't* have legitimate jobs with the mine."

"How does it work?" Lyons asked. "How are there so many people working on the fringes at an official Confederate outpost?"

"Even the people with legitimate jobs need ways to let their hair down and things to spend their money on," Emmett replied. "There are all the usual camp followers selling drugs, drink, women—anything anyone wants to buy. Naturally, that leads to a host of other professions these people need to support their business—which is where people like you come in."

Lyons jolted. "I'm not sure I'm entirely comfortable with how you keep talking about people like me."

"Why shouldn't you be comfortable with it?" he asked. "You are one. Why do you have a problem with it now when it might actually work in your favor to be that?"

Lyons didn't know how to answer that. He was right. She'd just used her underworld connections to harness a whole criminal empire for her own use. Why did she have a problem with it?

She didn't know what to say, so she looked down at her weapon.

"What's wrong, Lyons?" Frost asked. "Don't you want to go to the Pegasus Mines?"

"It isn't that. I guess.....I don't know.....I never told anyone this before—except for Fiddler....."

"Told her what?" Flack asked.

"I don't know. I guess I thought I was turning over a new leaf when I started helping Davenport. I thought I was leaving all that behind by doing the right thing....and now I'm going back to it. I don't know why it bothers me because I didn't have a problem killing Yuki and taking over my father's empire. Now I'm....."

Frost gasped. "You killed Yuki—Yuki Duetis?"

"Yeah, I killed him," Lyons muttered. "He.....he did a lot of things worse than just sending out his guys to shoot at us. He deserved it.....and then I took over my father's organization. Everyone wanted me to go back and rule it. I don't know where I am anymore."

Emmett laid his hand on her shoulder again. "You aren't that person anymore. You aren't doing this for your own gain. You're doing this to help Davenport, to hide the Ziprothil, and to find Dice. Remember that. Whatever change you made when you started helping Davenport, you're still doing it."

She nodded down at her hands. "I really wish I could believe that."

"If you can't believe it about yourself, you can believe me. I'm telling you it's true, so it is." Emmett turned to the four clones. "Are you all cool with going to the Pegasus Mines?"

"We're cool with whatever you decide, Emmett," Friend replied. "You've never steered us wrong yet."

He beamed at them all in what Lyons could only describe as fatherly affection. "You all are gonna be just fine there. You'll fit right in."

Just then, Beauty distracted Lyons by walking across the hall from one compartment to another. He vanished into one of the Phoenix's crew cabins.

"Where is he going?" Frost muttered.

"He isn't going to or from the galley," Fizzle pointed out.

"I'm not surprised," Lyons replied. "He ate at least thirty bricks of Peanut Surprise when we were on the Cyclone. He probably needs to lie down and sleep it off. That reminds me."

She sprinted up to the cockpit and ran a scan on the Phoenix in which the crew was flying right now. The internal scan showed the Ziprothil on board. So it was here.

Lyons couldn't figure out how Beauty kept it hidden, but she didn't care as long as he did keep it hidden.

When she left the cockpit, she heard Emmett and the four girls talking in the galley. Lyons followed the sound, but she stood outside watching them through the open door.

The five of them sat on two couches facing each other. They were talking about the Pegasus Mines and Emmett was telling them about his previous experience here when he'd been trying to find Fiddler.

The information he related didn't tell Lyons anything she didn't already know. The tone of their voices, though—not just Emmett's but the four clones', too—Lyons marveled at the closeness between them.

She'd known that he became a father figure to all of them—Fiddler and her four clones. Lyons had never seen it displayed like this before.

Emmett and these four young women could have been sitting in any living room in any home in the whole galaxy. They could have been any family—because they were one. They were family. He really was their father—the only father they'd ever had or would ever have.

The sight made Lyons's eyes sting with tears when she remembered what she lost when she lost her father.

She had to turn away and go sit in a different cabin by herself for a while until she pulled herself together.

Chapter 24

Lyons stood in the cockpit entrance and watched Emmett pilot the Phoenix through the atmosphere toward the Pegasus Mines. The mine sprawled across most of one continent on a planet far out of the way of central Confederate traffic.

Miles upon miles of huge mining machinery churned day and night. Heavy gas clouds in the atmosphere blocked the sunlight, so floodlights illuminated the structure around the clock.

Teeming cities of workers lived their whole lives right inside the mine complex. Even bigger teeming cities of other people surrounded the mine.

People had set up neighborhoods, villages, and smaller outposts inside the mine complex where the accessory communities could cater to the mine workers' needs.

The surrounding megalopolis sprawled across the countryside. This population wasn't connected to the mine at all. The whole system had grown and expanded to the point where the mine represented only a fraction of the overall economy of the place.

"We'll set down in the Nest Hangar," Emmett muttered to himself. "That's central enough to give us access to everything, but it's far enough out of the way that we should be hidden. It's also near the mine entrance. There's enough Tekrite around to shield the Ziprothil."

"Do we need any kind of permission to land here?" Lyons squinted through the cockpit window. "I didn't realize there would be so much air traffic around."

"None of them needs any permission. They come and go as they please. None of them belongs to the mine anyway."

"None of them!" Lyons took another look. "They're landing right on the structure."

"They can land anywhere they like as long as they don't interfere with the mine's operation. Do you see that one there with the death's head insignia?" Emmett pointed to a small velocopter landing on a high platform miles above the planet's surface. "That belongs to Xuiter Atholla. He practically runs this place."

"Do you mean the mine itself or the.....other stuff?"

"He imports almost all the drugs and drink. He also has a steady stream of girls from dozens of species that he rotates through the place. He handles assassination hits, kickbacks to mine officials, purchasing mining jobs, buying off the ruling council when it's called for—you name it. If it's happening here, he's in on it."

"Does he control it all?" Lyons asked. "Does he squash his competition?"

"He doesn't have to. If anyone else here is doing the same thing he's doing, they're doing it on such a smaller scale that he doesn't have to squash them. He's just doing so much more of it that no one can compete with him. He's too big to care about some small fry taking a piece of his action."

"Wow," Lyons breathed. "That sounds heavy-duty."

"Here we are. We're going in."

He tilted the Phoenix downward and flew between some towering silos, pipes, and scaffolds in the mine's superstructure. He soared between them and passed through a line of enormous pistons thumping downward through gargantuan cylinders.

They landed at the bottom of their cylinders with a deep, ground-shaking thud, but the cylinders muffled the sound. Only the steady thump, thump, thump of vibration translated through the air and shuddered the Phoenix as it passed.

Emmett flew past the cylinders, around another collection of towers, and into a hangar at least two hundred feet off the ground. More aircraft came and went from every part of the mine. Lyons couldn't tell which of those craft actually belonged to the mine and which didn't.

Emmett landed on the floor in a broad hangar with dozens of other craft in it. They came from all classes, including some Reserve Wing vessels and others Lyons didn't recognize.

"Do we have to pay for this?" she asked Emmett.

"We will pay for it. I'll talk to Tror about getting my old job back. If that fails, I can get something else by the end of the day. I'll pay for the hangar using that." He shut down the engines and turned away from the controls. "You and the girls should go out into town and sniff around. See what you can find."

He walked out. Lyons heard him talking to the clones and then he opened the hatch. He crossed the hangar and immediately started talking to a bunch of guys who were hanging around in there.

They came from dozens of different species, but he walked right in on their conversation like he belonged here. He didn't hesitate even for a second to move right back into his old place like he'd never left.

Lyons went back to the galley where she found Frost and Flack eating breakfast. "We're at the mine," Lyons told them. "Emmett is out there talking to some people about getting his old job back. He says for us to go out into town and see what we can find."

"We talked about this last night," Frost replied. "I'm going to the machine shop with him."

"I'll go with you, Lyons," Flack replied. "You and I will probably be looking for the same kind of work."

"I sure wish Emmett would tell us where to look," Lyons replied.

"I'm sure we'll figure it out." Flack grinned at her. "Come on. This should be fun."

"Fun?" Lyons repeated. "You think this will be fun?"

"It will be fun to explore a new place. What could be wrong with that?"

Lyons tagged after her. Lyons could think of a lot of things more fun than exploring a den of criminal iniquity on the farthest reaches of space. Emmett made this place sound like a boil on the ass end of the respectable universe.

Flack bounced around having the time of her life. Lyons went straight to the weapons locker. She didn't plan to set foot off this ship without plenty of weaponry.

Emmett came back on board and told Frost and Friend that he had jobs for both of them. He stopped by to let Lyons know they were leaving.

Then Fizzle came over to the weapons locker and decided to go with Flack and Lyons to see the sights and attractions this thriving hub of civilization had to offer.

"Has anyone seen Beauty recently?" Lyons asked.

"I haven't seen him since yesterday," Frost replied.

"He isn't in his cabin," Emmett replied.

"And he isn't in the galley," Friend reported.

"He's probably hiding from us," Lyons remarked. "He doesn't want us to put him to work."

"Then he's smarter than he looks." Emmett turned away. "I'll see all you fine ladies later. Have fun out there and don't get into trouble."

Lyons snorted. Getting into trouble would be the only thing they did around here.

She, Flack, and Fizzle left the ship. One of the kind mechanics working in the hangar directed the three women to a hallway that led to an elevator that took them to the ground.

Then it was just a question of walking across town before they found....something.

"So what are we looking for?" Fizzle asked.

"You're the tracker here," Flack pointed out. "Find us someone who can tell us where we should go."

"Very funny," Fizzle chided.

"You said it would be fun to just stumble around with no clue where we were going or what we were supposed to be doing," Lyons interjected.

"I changed my mind," Flack replied and Lyons had to laugh.

"What was it like for you at Helios Sanctus?" Lyons asked. "What did you do there?"

"Not a lot," Fizzle replied. "We mostly just hung out with Fiddler."

"But we were a lot younger then," Flack chimed in. "We were only three or four when we met her."

"She was the greatest," Fizzle went on. "She always came up with games and stories to keep us entertained. She basically got us through it all by herself."

"She still is the greatest," Flack corrected. "Her and Emmett both. None of us would have made it without them."

"You seem really close to them," Lyons remarked.

"That's because we are," Fizzle replied. "They're all we have."

"What about you?" Flack asked. "What was it like for you to grow up at Acrolith Diastema?"

"It was pretty wonderful—mainly because I didn't understand my father's business," Lyons replied. "He included Yuki in his business and taught Yuki everything he needed to know to take over the empire after my father couldn't do it anymore, but my father kept it hidden from me. I don't know. Maybe he thought he needed to protect me from it—which he did."

"What do you mean?" Fizzle asked.

"I found out later that he had other crime lords coming to him wanting to marry me to seal alliances with him. They were coming around making proposals for me even when I was a little kid. They didn't care about me. They just wanted to get in his good books so he wouldn't treat them as his enemies. Then I got older and I found out what his business was really like. That's when I decided to leave."

"Whoa!" Flack breathed. "That's heavy."

"Yuki thought I was being naïve because I had a problem with it. Everyone wanted me to take over the business after my father's death, but I couldn't stand that, so I left."

"But.....didn't you basically get back on a criminal crew when you joined up with Dice and Beauty?" Fizzle asked. "Isn't that kinda the same thing?"

"Yeah," Lyons muttered. "It is. I guess that's the point."

"What is?" Flack asked. "I don't see any point."

"I didn't change. That life was all I knew. I understood Dice and Beauty so it made sense for me to join up with them and keep doing what I knew. I didn't change until this whole Ithium thing started. Now I'm out here looking to do the same thing. Maybe I haven't changed at all."

"Yes, you have," Fizzle insisted. "Emmett is right. You're different because you're doing it for different reasons. You're doing it for the right reasons and you're doing it because you want to do the right thing. Right? You didn't even want to do the right thing before."

"You're right. I didn't." Lyons studied them. "What about you? Did Emmett teach you to do the right thing?"

"No, Fiddler did," Flack murmured. "She taught us so many things in the lab."

"I sure wish I knew where she was," Fizzle choked. "We gotta find her."

"Emmett says she and Dice escaped from Helios Sanctus," Lyons reminded them. "That means she's out there somewhere. They both are."

"He told us that," Flack replied.

Lyons threw back her head. "Okay. We need to find work so we can go get Dice and Fiddler. That's why we're here, so let's get it going. Where do we go first?"

"There's a tavern on that street corner over there," Flack pointed out. "We could try going in there."

"Yes! Good idea." Lyons turned off and the three women went into the tavern.

Chapter 25

Aliens crowded the bar even at this time of day. Maybe a tenth of the patrons were human. No one here belonged to the Reserve Wing or any other branch of the Confederate Corps.

The miners stuck out a mile in uniform jumpsuits darkened with dull grey rock dust. The dust clung to their hair and skin and made their eyes stand out much brighter than they should have.

The aliens also divided themselves by their clothes instead of by species. One group wore all black with black hoods over their faces. Another group wore a silver uniform one sleeve of which came in a different color to indicate the person's rank.

Each group used different insignia to announce their affiliation with whatever group they belonged to. "It sure would be nice if we understood all their insignia," Flack remarked. "We should have brought Emmett with us."

"We'll just have to find out for ourselves," Lyons replied. "Let's go up to the bar and talk to a few people."

"We don't have any money to pay for drinks," Fizzle pointed out.

Just then, one of the human guys in a mine uniform came up to them. "Hello there!" he began. "Can I buy you ladies a drink?"

"Uh....okay," Lyons replied. "Thank you."

He held out his hand to her. "My name's McCoy. Where are you from?"

"I'm Lyons." She shook his hand. "This is Flack and Fizzle and we're from....um....you know.....here and there."

He cracked a grin. "Oh, I know! That's what they all say."

He went up to the bar and ordered without asking Lyons and the two clones what they wanted. He came back with four different drinks. Smoke billowed from one of them and another fizzed so badly that it bubbled all over the floor.

"Come over here to my table," he insisted.

Lyons followed him to a standing table near the back of the bar. He set the drinks down and the three women gathered around where they could observe everyone in the establishment.

"What is this?" Fizzle put out her hand to the smoking drink.

"Don't touch it!" The guy shot out a hand to stop her. "You have to wait until it stops smoking. If you disturb it before then, it might overreact and explode."

Her head shot up and her eyes widened. "You want us to drink something that might explode?"

"That's nothing." He pointed to the fizzing drink. "The Silent Killer has been implicated in several unexplained and mysterious disappearances."

"Actually, we were hoping you might be able to tell us where we could find work," Lyons interrupted. "And maybe you could explain to us who all these people are and which groups they belong to."

"What kind of work are you looking for?" McCoy asked.

Lyons exchanged glances with the two clones. "You know......Stealing, smuggling, bounty hunting, going on dangerous runs through space that no one else would be stupid enough to make—all that kind of thing. We've been doing it for years."

He only nodded. "Then you want the Ambition over there." He indicated the aliens in black. "They handle all that kind of thing."

"We heard Xuiter Atholla controls everything on the planet," Lyons told him. "How do they relate to him?"

"They're a branch of his organization. They handle transportation in and out of the mine. Everyone around here works for him except for the people who work for the mine. Some people work for him *and* the mine if you get what I mean."

"What about you?" Lyons asked. "Do you work for him *and* the mine?"

McCoy shrugged. "A man has to make a living somehow."

"So what do you do for the mine?" Flack asked.

He cracked a grin. "I might be involved in a little transportation, too."

"Could you set us up with the right people?" Fizzle asked.

"I might be able to." He picked up one of the other drinks that didn't seem as dangerous as the others. He sipped it and put it back. He didn't push the three women to drink the other drinks.

"So how did you end up working at the mine?" Flack asked.

"I was on a transport crew from Acrolith Diastema delivering Usium charges to the mine. We didn't know the captain was wanted by Xuiter Atholla for a deal that went wrong years before. We landed here to deliver our cargo and a hit team knocked off the captain, so we were stranded. The rest of the crew went over to Ambition and I eventually found out about an opening at the mine, so I took it."

Lyons stared at the guy in astonishment. "You came from Acrolith Diastema? Who did you work for there?"

"I was in Rizarth Hudan's organization starting when I was fifteen. We were halfway here when we found out he'd been murdered and Yuki Duetis took over. None of our crew wanted to go back if he was in charge, so we just found it easier to stay here and work for Xuiter Atholla. He's a good boss. He takes care of loyal people."

"That is one hell of a coincidence," Flack began. "Lyons here is from...."

Lyons laid a hand on her arm to stop her. "If you have connections with Ambition, could you set us up? We don't have any money. All we have is our skills, but we're really good at what we do. We won't let you down—or whoever it is we work for."

"Yeah, I could do that. Wait here." McCoy downed his drink and shouldered his way back into the crowd at the bar.

"Why didn't you tell him who you are?" Flack asked after he left. "He could help us."

"He already is helping us and I don't want to use my past as the reason I get a job," Lyons replied. "He wouldn't get us a job if he knew who I was anyway. Xuiter Atholla might find it threatening if Rizarth Hudan's daughter showed up in town."

"Do you know about him?" Fizzle asked. "Did you know McCoy on Acrolith Diastema?"

"I don't remember him, but there was an older McCoy on my father's payroll. I wasn't involved in my father's business, so maybe the younger McCoy was already working off the planet by the time it all went down. Then he just stayed gone. I don't know."

Just then, a scuffle broke out among the aliens at the bar. Lyons didn't see what caused it. She was busy examining the other three drinks trying to decide if one of them was safe to drink.

She heard shouting voices and then the smash of breaking glass made her turn around. A bunch of aliens from different groups shoved each other back and forth.

McCoy got caught in the commotion, tried to break out, and then one of the aliens shot out an appendage from his midsection that hammered his adversary right in the chest.

The appendage appeared out of nowhere and smashed the other combatant backward with incredible force. The impact made the victim stagger and he fell against four other patrons including McCoy.

They all toppled against the bar with the other four on top of McCoy. He got trapped under the pile of bodies.

The attacker launched another flurry of appendages that erupted from all over his body. He pummeled his victim down on top of the other patrons so no one could get up.

Other patrons jumped in to pull the attacker away only to get hit by more of his flying appendages. The bar disintegrated in a whirlwind of flying arms and legs and people hurtling away from the guy as he knocked everyone away.

McCoy tried again and again to free himself from the stack of bodies on top of him. As soon as someone got free, they fell to the ongoing assault not only from the first attacker but from everyone else getting pulled into the fight.

Lyons sprang forward to grab him. The four patrons who'd fallen on top of him managed to get clear and join the crowd of other combatants trying to restrain the first attacker.

Another of the same alien species came out of the crowd and the tornado of flying limbs put everyone in danger. No one could get near either of them without getting hit.

Lyons, Flack, and Fizzle sprang between McCoy and the two aliens. Lyons turned her back to the fight and ducked her head to avoid lashing punches and blows coming from behind her.

Flack and Fizzle jumped forward to block her and she shoved McCoy back toward their table. He stumbled clear and then all four retreated out of range.

"Thanks," McCoy panted. "I owe you one."

Lyons surveyed the fight getting more chaotic. It blocked the whole bar so no one could get near the doorway. "Is there another way out of this place?"

"Yeah, follow me." McCoy tossed back the other of the three remaining drinks—not the Silent Killer or the other one that had stopped smoking now.

Lyons, Flack, and Fizzle walked past them and followed him to the back of the bar where they exited onto a small platform dotted with miniature aircraft.

"Get in," McCoy told them. "I'll take you to see a friend of mine."

He pulled a remote controller from his pocket and pointed it at one of the aircraft. It had four seats surrounded by a glass dome and the engine and its housing underneath the dome.

The engine powered up when he pushed a button on his remote and the dome popped to let the four passengers climb inside.

"Cool!" Fizzle remarked when they strapped into their seats. "I've never seen one of these before."

"That's because I invented it," McCoy told her. "This is the only one of its kind in existence."

"Wow!" Flack exclaimed. "You could patent it and make a mint."

"I already did patent it," he told her. "Xuiter Atholla is going to mass produce them for me. We're going to be business partners." He shot her a grin over his shoulder. "That's who I'm taking you to see."

Lyons didn't have time to ask all the questions that came to mind. He fired up the engines, the dome snapped back into place, and he took the little craft's controls to lift off the platform.

The craft levitated over the street where Lyons and the two clones had just been walking. The craft buzzed upward into the maze of scaffolds, conduits, and pipes running all over the mine.

"Are you really taking us to see Xuiter Atholla?" Fizzle asked from the back.

"He'll be able to assign you where he wants you," McCoy replied. "He's always looking for good people to do jobs for him."

"What can you tell us about him?" Lyons asked. "Is he ruthless and bloodthirsty or benevolent like Rizarth was?"

McCoy spun around. "You think Rizarth was benevolent?"

Lyons looked away. "I wouldn't know about that."

"Xuiter is a crime lord like any other, so yeah, I would say he's a lot like Rizarth was. If you know anything about Rizarth, you'll know what Xuiter is like."

"I guess I don't really know anything about Rizarth Hudan," Lyons murmured. "Just what I heard."

"That's Xuiter's place over there." McCoy pointed to an enormous building amongst the towers and silos of the mine superstructure."

"Why is his place part of the mine?" Fizzle asked.

"He's part owner in the mine—but no one knows that," McCoy replied. "He's what you might call a shadow investor, but he really runs the mine, too. There isn't much on this planet that he doesn't own."

No one said anything else until McCoy landed his little craft on a platform high on the building's steep sides. The platform stuck out of a terraced patio attached to a giant penthouse apartment that covered most of the building's top story.

McCoy popped the dome and got out. "Come on inside. Xuiter will know what to do with you."

"How do you know him so well?" Lyons asked. "How do you know such a big shot well enough to land at his private apartment?"

"This isn't his private apartment. This is just where he does business—and I told you I'm going into business with him. Xuiter and I go way back."

Lyons exchanged glances with the two clones. Something about McCoy's story didn't add up, but Lyons didn't say that out loud. How could he have gotten so deep in Xuiter Atholla's pocket if McCoy had been working as a mine transporter all this time?

Going into partnership with Xuiter Atholla didn't explain McCoy just walking in on Xuiter Atholla unannounced like this.

Huge sliding doors opened from the patio into the apartment and McCoy strolled right in like he came here all the time. He crossed an enormous living room to a corner in the back.

McCoy turned the corner and stopped in front of ten aliens and two more human men standing around talking. They all wore business suits instead of the uniforms Lyons had seen on the ground.

The apartment had been partitioned into rooms in the back. The aliens gathered in front of a door leading to one of the rooms. McCoy sauntered up to the aliens, but right then, another human man came out of the room and shut the door behind him.

He consulted a computer device in his hands and tapped on it. "You're next, Shainyx. You can go right in. Xuiter is ready for you."

"What about Thewi?" one of the aliens asked. "He didn't come out."

The human raised his eyebrows and pierced his counterpart with a hard stare. "Are you going in or not? You don't want to keep Xuiter waiting. If you don't want to go in, I can send in Ineron instead."

Shainyx shut his mouth, pulled open the door, and vanished inside. The human guy tapped on his device a few more times and then spotted McCoy. "What can I do for you, Mr. McCoy? Do you want to go on the list?"

"I came to introduce these friends of mine. This is Lyons, Flack, and Fizzle. They're looking for work in the smuggling, transporting, and high-risk line. They have experience and they just helped me out of a jam. I'd like to give them my recommendation." McCoy turned to Lyons. "This is Vor. He handles Xuiter's schedule."

"You don't need to see Xuiter to get on the high-risk payroll." Vor tapped his device again. "I can give you an assignment for today. If you accomplish that, I can bump you up the roster for more complicated assignments. How does that sound?"

"Great," Lyons exclaimed. "Thank you. What's the job?"

"McCoy will show you to a hangar on the tenth floor of this building. It's full of all kinds of spacecraft, but there's only one Dynopter in it." Vor pulled a card out of the back of his device. "Plug this into the controls and it will show you where to go. You'll need to infiltrate the Ward Ruins' stronghold in Thobriz Sector, neutralize anyone you find inside, retrieve the Grora Orb, and bring it back here." He handed over the card. "You'll find all the information on this."

Lyons looked back and forth between him and the card. "Um....okay."

"You'll find all the weapons and supplies you need on the Dynopter." He turned to one of the other aliens in the group. "Did you bring your proposal for the new gymnasium project?"

McCoy pulled Lyons away. "Come on. I'll show you where the hangar is."

Chapter 26

McCoy led Lyons back out to the patio to his little craft. She kept casting backward glances into the apartment, but she couldn't see anything from here. "What the hell just happened? We didn't even get to see Xuiter."

"That happens sometimes," McCoy replied. "If Vor can handle it, he does. Anyway, you got your job. Get in and I'll take you downstairs to the hangar."

Lyons climbed back into her seat, but she couldn't stop staring at the card in her hand. "What was all that about the Grora Orb?"

"I have no idea," McCoy replied. "I guess you'll find out when you get to the Dynopter and read the card."

"How are we supposed to assault someone's stronghold and neutralize them when we don't have any weapons or anything?" Flack asked from the back seat.

"If Vor said the Dynopter was fully armed, he meant it," McCoy replied. "He wouldn't send you out without everything you need. Here's the hangar."

McCoy lifted off the patio, sailed down dozens of stories, and landed his little bubble craft in a different hangar much closer to the ground.

Everything Vor said turned out to be true. Drifters, Nitrols, two Daggers, and a bunch of unidentified alien craft crowded the hangar, but there was only one Dynopter.

"This is where I leave you," McCoy told Lyons before they got out. "You can take it from here. If you need to find me, just go back to that bar. Let me know if you need anything or if you have any problems."

Lyons found herself beaming at him. "Thank you. We owe you big time for this."

He grinned back at her. "Naw. Let's call it even for you pulling me out of that fight."

Lyons held out her hand. "I hope I see you again."

"Me, too." He shook her hand and then popped the dome on his craft.

Lyons, Flack, and Fizzle got out. He shut the dome and flew away somewhere. "I guess we just go on board and see what the card says," Flack remarked.

The Dynopter wasn't much bigger than McCoy's little craft. The Dynopter also had four seats, but each seat had a cannon attached to it.

They swiveled outward from the Dynopter's armored sides and the engines hanging from the two wings had been built for speed, maneuverability, and combat.

"This is more like it!" Flack exclaimed when she pivoted her cannon from side to side.

Lyons sat down in front of the pilot's controls in the front seat and slotted the card into the dashboard.

It brought up a screen that displayed tons of information, including maps and schematics of the entire Pegasus Mine complex, the surrounding neighborhoods, who lived where and which groups controlled which territories, and a detailed exploded view of the Ward Ruins' stronghold in Thobriz Sector.

Then the card showed her a whole ton of information on the Grora Orb. From what Lyons could tell, the Orb didn't have any special value other than the fact that it was the only one of its kind.

Criminal elements had been stealing, killing, and battling across the galaxy to get the Orb from each other and any law enforcement agency that happened to get their hands on it.

The Ward Ruins were another small syndicate who'd annihilated the Ivory Screech and stolen the Orb from them. Now Xuiter wanted it just so he could say he owned it.

Lyons switched back to the layout of the Ward Ruins' stronghold. "Can you tell where they're keeping the Orb?" Fizzle asked.

"Of course not," Lyons muttered. "That would make it way too easy."

"Then we'll need to capture one of them and make them tell us where it is," Flack added. "That's going to add a whole new level of complexity to this job."

Lyons rifled the rest of the information on the card. The very last document showed the proposed payout for returning the Orb to Xuiter.

"Holy mother-lovin' shit!" Flack breathed. "We are so doing this job!"

"The question is how to do it." Lyons went back to the stronghold layout. "These levels here are all residential. The Ward Ruins wouldn't store the Orb there."

"Unless one of them is keeping it under his pillow," Fizzle pointed out.

"Hey, look at that." Flack pointed at a schematic of the bottom four stories of the stronghold's structure. "The very lowest level is fortified with reinforced concrete and weapons placements. I bet you that level is their strongroom. The orb must be there."

"The job orders us to neutralize anyone we find inside the stronghold," Lyons reminded her. "That includes everyone in the residential areas."

"There must be a thousand people in there," Fizzle countered. "No way could the three of us go up against all of them."

"Then there's only one solution," Lyons replied. "We have to take them all out at once."

"How do we do that?" Flack asked.

"Simple. We vaporize the building with explosives. If we're right about the Orb being in their strongroom, blowing up the building won't damage it. Then we can take out anyone who's left in the strongroom, find the Orb, and go."

Fizzle frowned at the display. "Vor did say we would have access to any supplies we needed to get the job done."

Lyons and the two clones went into the very back of the Dynopter and checked out the weapons lockers. "There are plenty of weapons, but no explosives," Lyons observed. "Let's go tell him what we want. Then we can fly out to Thobriz Sector and case the stronghold."

Vor was as busy as ever when Lyons flew the Dynopter up to Xuiter's apartment. Vor treated Lyons's request for explosives as the most normal piece of business imaginable. Maybe he was in the habit of passing out massive amounts of explosives to his operatives every day of the week.

He directed Lyons to another level of the same building. Xuiter's storehouse covered three stories of the building with every kind of weapon, explosive, ship, part, supply, and piece of gear Lyons had ever seen.

Xuiter's quartermaster gave Lyons and her friends a pass to help themselves to literally anything they wanted. Lyons could have gone on the shopping spree of her life except that the Dynopter wouldn't hold it all.

She, Flack, and Fizzle loaded the Dynopter with four enormous crates of explosives. "Don't crash, Lyons," Fizzle told her. "Whatever you do, don't crash that ship."

"Let's get out to Thobriz Sector and get this stuff unloaded," Lyons suggested. "I don't want to fly around with it any longer than I absolutely have to."

She flew the load out to Thobriz Sector. It was one of the seedier neighborhoods on the mine's outskirts.

She landed on a building roof a block away from the Ward Ruins' stronghold. It occupied another building among dozens of identical buildings. No outward sign gave any indication that the building was anything special.

Lyons switched on the scanners. "Shit!" she muttered. "It looks like we aren't alone."

Flack and Fizzle gathered around and the three women stared as four Reserve Wing Daggers landed on the street near the stronghold. The four pilots got out, but they didn't go near the Ward Ruins' building.

The four officers split up, fanned out across the neighborhood, and questioned a few different people. Then the pilots loaded up and flew away.

"Do you think someone told them we were here?" Fizzle asked.

"How could they?" Flack countered. "No one knows we're here."

"Everyone at the bar saw us," Lyons pointed out. "And now we're working for Xuiter Atholla. We're wanted by the Reserve Wing. Someone might have reported us."

"What do you want to do?" Fizzle squinted at the building in the distance. "Do you want to abort the mission?"

"We can't," Lyons replied. "We have nowhere else to hide the Ziprothil, and as long as we're on this planet, we need work. We probably aren't ever going to find anything as good as working for Xuiter Atholla. I say we go through with it, give him his Orb, and get paid. If the Reserve Wing starts giving us a hard time, we can think about pulling out and going somewhere else."

"I'm with you, Lyons," Flack told her. "We're already here with a Dynopter and a crap ton of explosives. We might as well go through with the job and get it over with."

"We'll divide up the explosives and lay them around and inside the building," Lyons went on. "We'll detonate them remotely and then storm the strongroom before the dust settles. Got it?"

The two clones nodded. The three women went into the back, divided the explosives between them, and stashed as many charges as possible in their clothes.

Lyons went out onto the street and cast a glance right and left. She was just about to cross the street to the Ward Ruins' building when she spotted the same four Reserve Wing Daggers hovering over a different part of the neighborhood. They were still here.

They didn't come close enough to interfere with her job, though. She couldn't back out now, so she darted across the street.

Flack and Fizzle split off to the right and left. Lyons went straight to the building entrance and walked right in. The Ward Ruins were so concerned about staying inconspicuous that they didn't guard the place.

Lyons realized why once she got inside. The building's interior looked like any other normal apartment building. Families lived in all the apartments. Children ran and rode their miniature bicycles up and down the hallways, played, wrestled, and drew on the walls.

Lyons passed through one hallway after another. She should have dropped her explosive charges all over the building, but the farther she went, the more she realized she couldn't do that.

She was supposed to be changing her ways. She couldn't blow up this building. She didn't care what happened. She couldn't be the one who killed all these people. She wouldn't be able to live with the guilt.

She couldn't let Flack and Fizzle do it, either. Lyons didn't believe for a second that Flack or Fizzle could actually trigger the detonation that wiped out all these people.

She passed through four more floors, but she kept seeing the same thing everywhere. She hesitated to go back to the ship and tell the other two that she was changing her mind, but the evidence of her own eyes left her no choice.

She left the building and met up with Flack and Fizzle on the sidewalk outside. None of them said anything until they returned to the Dynopter. "We can't go through with this!" Lyons murmured under her breath. "That building is full of families, children, old people, and pregnant women. No way are we blowing up the whole building! We have to come up with another plan."

"We saw the same thing through the windows," Fizzle replied. "I wasn't sure how to break it to you, but we can't go through with this, either."

Lyons let out a shaky sigh of relief. "Thank goodness you didn't lay the charges."

"What do you want to do?" Flack asked. "We still need to take the Orb back to Xuiter."

"I say we just assault the strongroom in the basement," Lyons replied. "We know everyone in it will belong to the Ward Ruins. We can neutralize them, take the Orb back to Xuiter, and explain that we aren't in the business of killing civilians. If he has a problem with that, we'll take the consequences."

Fizzle dipped one nod. "I'm with you."

"That means we have to go into the strongroom with guns blazing," Lyons reminded her.

"I still say we should capture one of them and make him tell us where the Orb is," Flack added.

"We'll do it if it works out that way," Lyons replied. "We might not get a chance, in which case we'll just have to lay down everyone in there."

Both clones nodded. "Got it," Fizzle agreed.

The three women returned all their unused charges to their crates and took out the biggest XQs they could carry. Lyons loaded her pockets with ammunition cylinders instead. Then she went to the cockpit and checked the schematics again.

"There are three stairwells leading down to the basement," she told the other two. "I'll take the main one and start shooting. Everyone down there will turn and come after me. That will leave the other two stairwells unguarded. You two can storm in, shoot all those people in the backs, and then the three of us will work our way through anyone left behind. Understand?"

The clones nodded again and the three women split up. Lyons paused on the street outside to check right and left.

Now would be the perfect time for the Reserve Wing to make its appearance, but they didn't. She didn't even see the Daggers in the air. They'd vacated the area.

Chapter 27

Lyons strode across the street and into the Ward Ruins' building. Flack and Fizzle broke away and circled the building on its outside to head for the other two stairwells.

This plan would put Lyons in the heaviest line of fire, but she didn't care about that anymore.

She entered the stairwell and started climbing down. Adrenaline pumped into her veins and she tightened her grip on her XQ.

She descended four floors before she heard voices coming up from below. Five men rounded the next landing.

Lyons reacted automatically, lowered her XQ, and opened fire. They were completely unprepared. They all carried their weapons slung over their shoulders. None of them even got a chance to aim their weapons at her.

She gunned them down, but the noise echoing through the stairwell reverberated through the whole building.

She took off running down the stairs as fast as she could, came to the very lowest level, and burst through a door into a hail of gunfire coming from all directions.

Twenty armed men knelt and stood in front of the stairwell. They all unloaded on her and she dove back inside the stairwell for protection.

She pulled the heavy fortified door closed in front of her, but their gunfire still tore the door and the surrounding walls apart.

She ducked behind the wall as gunshots punched through the door. They would have slaughtered her if she hadn't reacted so fast.

She huddled there behind the Ward Ruins' own fortifications. Their shots exploded the wall to smithereens, but its reinforcements protected her.

She waited until the men inside stopped shooting before she darted to the other side of the door. They all opened fire again, and this time, she propped the door open and fired back through it.

The deafening crash of her shots ricocheting around the room smashed more walls in there and then she heard screams. The noise inside the strongroom spiked off the charts and she heard gunfire coming from another direction.

She dared to look around the corner and saw bodies falling all over the place. Flack and Fizzle stormed in from two directions and caught the Ward Ruins in the middle.

Lyons sprang out of her hiding place and added her fire to theirs. The three women cut down all the men standing guard, but Lyons saw right away that this was only the beginning.

Another wall sectioned off the lower basement. A space of fifteen feet separated that wall from the stairwell door she just used to enter this place.

A single heavy reinforced door occupied a central position in the middle of that wall. It had to be guarding something valuable.

The three women devastated all the men standing guard. Anytime the guards turned one way to defend themselves, the other two women hit them from the other direction. The whole battle ended in a few seconds.

Lyons advanced into the room. Bodies carpeted the floor, but when she checked the door, she found it locked with multiple different locking mechanisms, each one more complex than the last.

"Over here!" Flack called from across the room.

Lyons turned around to find Flack and Fizzle holding one of the defenders at gunpoint. The man lay sprawled on the floor with his head and shoulders propped against the wall by the side stairwell that Flack used to get down here.

The guy had been shot through the upper shoulder. Blood poured down his shirt front and he shivered all over in a cold sweat. "Please.....don't......don't kill me....." he panted. "I.......I have......a family....upstairs."

"We just want the Grora Orb," Lyons told him. "Tell us where it is and we'll let you live."

"I can't.......I don't know...... where it is......" His eyes darted to the fortified door and then he did it again. He glanced in that direction in a significant hinting way that told Lyons all she needed to know.

This guy couldn't just outright tell her where the orb was. The Ward Ruins would kill him for betraying them if Lyons and her friends didn't do it first.

"How do we get inside?" Fizzle asked.

"I don't......have the...combination...." His eyes slid down this time—to his belt.

A clip held his keys to his belt with the keychain tucked into his pocket. Lyons unclipped it. "Go upstairs to your family," she told him. "If anyone asks, tell them you don't know anything about what happened here. Tell them you never worked for the Ward Ruins."

He nodded and panted once, "Thank.....you......."

He pushed himself off the floor and staggered away to the stairs. Lyons took his keys to the fortified door. Only one of the locks used a key. The others used combinations and different code dials.

She tried four of the seven keys on the ring before she found the right one. She fitted it into the hole and turned.

Clunks and clicks echoed from inside. Flack and Fizzle leveled their guns at the door and then Lyons pushed it open with her own weapon raised.

The door swung inward to reveal one large room that had been set up as an apartment. A giant blob of an alien sat on the couch. He was all alone.

One large mouth opened in the top of the creature's shapeless body. The creature didn't have any eyes or any other feature.

The Grora Orb sat on a small round pedestal on the coffee table in front of the alien. Mist swirled inside its black depths. Lyons couldn't see any other feature about the thing.

She, Flack, and Fizzle spread out through the room and aimed their guns at the alien, but it didn't have any eyes even to see the three women. Its gelatinous body jiggled slightly. It wasn't capable of any other movement.

Flack lowered her weapon, went over to the coffee table, and picked up the orb. "Is this what all this trouble is about? It's nothing."

"People wanting it is what makes it valuable," Lyons told her. "Let's get out of here before we......"

At that moment, another mob of guards poured into the room. The three women had left the fortified door open. Gunmen flooded through it—or they would have.

Flack and Fizzle both had their backs to the entrance and Flack didn't even have her weapon up. Lyons was the only one who could react in time.

Her arms jerked her weapon up before she realized what she was doing. She opened fire and all the invaders ran into the path of her gun.

They toppled onto each other and blocked the entrance, but Lyons still heard people in the outer room. They hid behind the walls waiting for the three women to come out.

Lyons rushed the doorway, plastered herself against the wall, and fired her gun around the corner without looking.

She sprayed a dozen bursts out there, but she still heard people. She glanced around the room at Flack and Fizzle. Flack pocketed the orb and the two clones inched over to the door so all three could get out of here at the same time.

The three women barely got into position before the blob let out a roar through its mouth and then sprouted appendages just like the alien in the bar.

They burst from every part of the creature's body and shot across the room toward where the three women crouched.

The appendages hit Flack and then one of those boneless arms smashed Lyons across the side of the head. She staggered into the wall and the appendages snaked all over the place to go after the two clones.

Flack and Fizzle spun around to defend themselves. Lyons raised her weapon, and without thinking, she fired into the only target available.

Her shots punched into the alien's squishy body. Unimaginable goo ejected from the punctures. The creature roared again and quivered all over before it went limp, slumped, and then the whole enormous bag of jelly squished off the couch and onto the floor.

Lyons, Flack, and Fizzle stared at it in horrified fascination as the thing oozed between the coffee table and the couch. Its body—or whatever held all that goop into one single shape—started to dissolve and the jelly inside it spread into a puddle that saturated the carpet.

"Ick!" Fizzle murmured.

Lyons cleared her throat with difficulty. "Okay! That's all taken care of. Now we just gotta get out of here."

She turned back to the door and heard the people out there whispering to each other.

She took a chance and inhaled a deep breath. "Your alien friend in here is dead!" she yelled into the silence. "We're getting out of here, so unless you want to throw your lives away for nothing, you might want to get the hell out of here before we walk through this door! We'll shoot anyone we see on our way out of the building! Do you hear me? You alien is dead, so you'll be throwing your lives away for nothing."

She waited, and a few whispered conversations later, she heard footsteps running for the stairwell. The doors slammed and silence fell once again.

"Are you okay?" Lyons panted to the other two. "Did either of you get hit?"

"We're okay." Fizzle raised her hand, but she stopped short of touching Lyons's face. "You don't look so good."

"I'm fine. Let's get the hell out of here."

Chapter 28

Lyons sat down in the pilot's seat of the Dynopter and fired up the engines. Her head was starting to hurt, but she shook that off. She and the two clones had completed the mission. They were going home in triumph.

She glanced over at Flack. "Do you still have it?"

Flack patted her bulging pocket. "Not too bad for our first day's work, huh?"

Lyons had to laugh. "Emmett will be impressed."

She lifted off the Dynopter and flew back to Xuiter's hangar. The sun was going down by the time the three women returned all the explosives to the quartermaster and then took the building's internal elevator back to Xuiter's apartment.

Vor stood outside Xuiter's private room. Vor was alone. No one else was around waiting to talk to Xuiter at this time of day.

Flack put the orb in Vor's hand. "There it is, exactly the way you ordered."

"We neutralized everyone in the strongroom," Lyons explained. "We aren't in the business of annihilating innocent children and civilians, so we didn't take down the whole building. If you have a problem with that, we shouldn't be working for Xuiter in the first place."

Vor looked back and forth between them and the orb. "I don't have a problem with that. You can come back tomorrow and I'll give you another job."

"What about payment?" Lyons asked.

He took another card from inside his device. "Here you go. You earned it."

"We left the Dynopter in the hangar where we found it," Fizzle told him.

He nodded. "You can leave it there. You can take it out on jobs, but leave it here between times."

That left the three women no choice but to walk back to the tower where they'd left the Phoenix. They made it to the building by full dark and took another elevator up to the hangar.

Lyons stepped out into the hallway and instantly sensed something wrong. She didn't know why. She heard men's voices coming from the hangar, but that was nothing unusual. She'd heard men's voices before when Emmett landed here.

These voices sounded different. She pulled Flack and Fizzle against the wall and the three women inched toward the hangar. They flattened themselves into a corner and peered out.

Lyons's worst nightmare came true when she saw five Reserve Wing officers circling the Phoenix. They went inside through the hatch, came out, and walked around the ship again and again aiming their scanners at it.

"The scanners are reading the Ziprothil on board," one of them remarked. "We've searched the whole ship, but we can't find it."

"We'll keep an eye on things," another replied. "When the fugitives come back, we'll collar them and get them to tell us where the Ziprothil is. That worked last time. It will work again."

The first officer nodded. "Sounds good. We'll report to the admiral. He might have another idea about how he wants to handle these people. Let's go."

They turned away from the Phoenix and Lyons saw for the first time that they'd landed a Dagger in the same hangar. The officers' ship was the only Dagger in the place. It was one of the Daggers Lyons had seen on the street earlier.

She didn't give herself an instant to hesitate. She couldn't let these men leave to report the crew's whereabouts to Admiral Joyce.

She sprang out of her hiding place and opened fire with her XQ. She caught three of the officers by surprise. Her gunshots made them jerk and convulse before they fell across the floor.

The other two officers spun around to defend themselves, but Flack and Fizzle advanced behind Lyons and all three women opened fire on the last two officers. They went down, too.

"We gotta warn Emmett and the others!" Lyons exclaimed and hustled back to the Phoenix. "Flack—get on board that Dagger and program it on autopilot to fly out over the city. I don't care where it goes. Just get it away from here—and put those bodies on board before you send it out."

"I'm on it!" Flack put her XQ down and she and Fizzle went to work.

Lyons sprang on board the Phoenix, ran one quick internal scan to make sure the Ziprothil was still here, and then strode through the ship yelling at the top of her lungs.

"Beauty! It's me! It's Lyons! I know you're here and I know you can hear me! I need you to come out of wherever you're hiding and leave the ship—and bring the Ziprothil with you! It's an emergency! Come out now, Beauty! I wouldn't bother you if this wasn't important!"

Nothing happened for a second and then one of the ceiling panels slid back. Beauty's head emerged pointing straight down toward the floor. "What's so important?" he asked.

"The Reserve Wing found us. Bring the Ziprothil. We need to get out of here."

"Give me a minute to go get it." He pulled his head back in, replaced the ceiling panel, and vanished.

Nothing happened for a second. Lyons waited, but when he didn't come, she turned around to go back to the cockpit. She planned to scan the Pegasus Mine for any other Reserve wing activity, but when she turned around, she jumped in surprise when she almost stepped on Beauty standing right behind her.

She gasped in shock for a second and her hand flew to heart. "Beauty! Don't do that!"

"You said you wanted me to come out."

She eyed him while she tried to catch her breath. "Do you have the Ziprothil on you?"

"I wouldn't have come if I didn't. You said you needed to take it off the ship."

She studied him. He didn't have anything in his hands and she didn't see anywhere else on his person that he might have stashed it.

She didn't want to think about where he'd been hiding it, so she let the matter drop. "Come on. We gotta go."

She went back outside. Fizzle was still hauling the dead officers on board the Dagger. Lyons spotted Flack through the cockpit window. Flack bent over the controls programming the ship to fly away on autopilot.

She came out and met up with Lyons, Beauty, and Fizzle. The ship launched itself out into the sky and vanished.

"We need to find Emmett and the others and warn them," Lyons began.

"We need to find some other better hiding place for the Ziprothil," Flack countered. "It obviously isn't hidden well enough."

"What do you suggest?" Lyons asked. "Maybe Tekrite isn't as good at shielding it as we thought."

"Maybe nothing will ever be able to shield it," Beauty muttered.

"So we just keep running around with it until the Reserve Wing catches up with us?" Lyons countered. "We have to do something with it. The Reserve Wing knows now that we're on this planet. They'll only send out another crew to steal it from us."

"Let's find Emmett and the others and see what they say," Flack suggested. "We have to find somewhere to stay tonight."

"Where are they?" Fizzle asked.

At that moment, Emmett, Frost, and Friend came out of the elevator. Lyons and her group hurried down the hall to rendezvous with them. Lyons filled in Emmett on what just happened.

"We need to find a place to spend the night," he remarked, "but we have no way to pay for it."

"We got some money," she told him. "We did a job for Xuiter Atholla and we just got paid."

Emmett raised his eyebrows. "That was fast."

She grinned at him and handed over the card. "We're going back tomorrow morning to do another job for him."

"Good for you. This is great." He put the card in his pocket and led the group all the way back down to the ground.

The party passed through the streets, and in a little while, Emmett flagged another Dynopter to take everyone to a hotel in one of the outlying neighborhoods.

The Dynopter landed on a high platform and the party entered another large open space like Xuiter's apartment. This one obviously served as the hotel lobby.

Emmett approached the desk and booked the whole crew into another large apartment with multiple bedrooms. He also ordered a huge meal to be brought up for everyone. He paid for everything out of Lyons's funds.

The crew retired to their apartment. Beauty vanished into the many rooms while Lyons, Emmett, and the four clones relaxed in the lounge.

"We were just speculating on how we can get hide the Ziprothil," Lyons told Emmett. "The Tekrite isn't concealing it the way we hoped it would."

"I agree with you," he replied. "I've been racking my brain to find another way."

"What about putting the Ziprothil down the mine?" Frost asked.

"Anywhere we hide it is going to run the risk of someone else finding it," Friend pointed out. "Then we would have no control over where they took it or what they did with it. I say we keep it with us."

"Then we need a better way to hide ourselves," Flack pointed out.

"Why don't we ask Beauty where he keeps hiding it?" Lyons suggested. "He's been able to hide it from detection more than once. He should be able to tell us."

Emmett looked around. "Where is he?"

Lyons went to look for Beauty, but no amount of calling, ordering, or pleading would make him come out. She searched the whole apartment, but she couldn't find him.

"We should have asked him a long time ago," Fizzle grumbled.

Just then, their food came. Emmett spread it all over the coffee table in the lounge and the crew started eating.

"Beauty is missing out," Friend remarked. "I thought this food would bring him out of the woodwork if nothing else did."

"He won't need to eat for a month after all the Peanut Surprise he ate on the Cyclone."

The others laughed and got down to their own food. Emmett had spared no expense and ordered some of the Confederacy's finest delicacies.

Lyons helped herself to a huge stack of fried Goliv ribs with Zilowi sauce dripping off them. She took a bite and the juice gushed down her chin. "Oh.....my......God!" she groaned. "I haven't had these in ages."

Flack grabbed a roasted salty and sour Dalarus pigeon. She bit into it without even taking the feathers off it first. "We should eat like this all the time."

"If you keep working for Xuiter, you probably will," Emmett replied. "I'm sure he does eat like this all the time."

Fizzle bit into a Thao beak and crunched it up between her teeth. "What does he look like? We didn't get to see him."

"No one sees him," Emmett replied. "Some people think he doesn't exist and Vor runs the operation by himself."

"Wouldn't the people who go in to see him tell everybody that?" Lyons asked.

Emmett shrugged. "Maybe that's part of the deal. Maybe you have to keep the secret if you want to do business with him."

"We met someone who will be doing business with Xuiter," Flack told everyone. "His name is McCoy. He designed this...."

"McCoy!" Emmett snapped. "Are you sure that's his name?"

"That's what he told us," Lyons explained. "He works for the mine."

Emmett snorted. "He doesn't work for the mine."

"He was wearing a mine uniform and he was covered with dust," Flack told him.

"He did say he worked for Xuiter, too," Fizzle pointed out. "McCoy said he was kind off.....well, he didn't exactly say he was on the fence, but he implied it."

"You want to stay away from that guy," Emmett growled.

"He seemed nice," Lyons interjected. "He bought us drinks, and when we told him we were looking for work, he was the one who introduced us to Xuiter—I mean, he introduced us to Vor. That's how we got the job—on McCoy's recommendation."

Emmett shook his head. "McCoy doesn't work for the mine. He's a mover and a shaker. He's a player in the big leagues. He might be as big as Xuiter. If he works for Xuiter, that only explains why Xuiter is so big."

"Then what was McCoy doing pretending to be a miner in a local watering hole?" Flack asked. "He got stampeded in that fight and he didn't even fight back."

"Then that explains it," Emmett replied. "He was probably going streetside to check out the local scene. All these bigshot gangsters send their people onto the street to pick up whatever the small fry are talking about. McCoy would be stupid not to do the same thing."

Lyons didn't say anything about that. All this talk about organized crime and its syndicate lords brought back memories of Acrolith Diastema—and not nice memories, either.

She went on with her meal. She couldn't reconcile what Emmett was saying with her impressions of McCoy. He'd seemed so normal with his little bubble craft.....

Then again, the bubble craft alone seemed to suggest there was more to his association with Xuiter than just some invention.

The others kept talking. Emmett, Frost, and Friend had found jobs for themselves, too, but their conversation made Lyons wonder. How long would the crew stay on this planet, now that the Reserve Wing knew they were here?

Emmett, Frost, and Friend might have to walk away from their jobs even before the three of them started working.

The others stuffed themselves with food and still didn't make a dent in everything Emmett bought for them.

The clones went off to their rooms, but Lyons stayed where she was. She couldn't have slept now if she wanted to.

"What's on your mind?" Emmett asked.

Lyons looked up and realized they were alone together in the living room. She looked away. "Nothing."

"Of course there is. Are you worried about the Ziprothil? We all are."

"It isn't that—I mean, it isn't only that."

"What is it, then?" he demanded. "You better get it off your chest before your head explodes."

She spun around and laughed at him. She'd gotten so much closer to him than she ever would have imagined.

"It's really touching how you've become a father to all these girls," she began. "You're the salt of the Earth, Emmett."

"What was I supposed to do—leave them at Helios Sanctus? And then, once we left it, I couldn't exactly jettison them into space by themselves. They were just kids then."

"I mean now. You still act like their father even now that they're all grown up. You treat them all the same way you treat Fiddler—like they're your own daughters."

He shrugged and now it was his turn to look away. "They are my own daughters—as much as anyone can be. I spent all that time looking for Fiddler. Now I know I was looking for all of them. Helping them has been the greatest privilege of my life. It's been wonderful watching them grow up and now...." His voice cracked and he broke off.

Lyons stared down at her empty plate. "They're lucky to have you."

"I'm just as lucky to have them," he countered. "I wouldn't be able to function without them."

Lyons didn't answer.

"What's bothering you?" he insisted. "You've been in another world since....."

She looked up. "You mean since Acrolith Diastema? I've been thinking about my own father. I know he felt that way about me. I guess.....I guess I never really knew him. He kept his dark side hidden from me."

"He did it to protect you."

Lyons nodded. "I know."

"Do you think things would have been different if you'd known? You might have grown up hating him for what he was."

"So instead I came to hate him for what he was after his death. What difference does it make?"

Emmett inclined his head the other way. "Do you really hate him? It seems like you love him. If I had to guess, I'd say you love him a lot."

Lyons couldn't look at him. Tears stung her eyes. "I guess I do," she croaked.

"You killed Yuki in revenge for your father's death," Emmett went on. "That tells me all I need to know about how you feel about your father."

Lyons gulped down a lump in her throat. Why did she kill Yuki if not in revenge for her father's death?

She could have killed Yuki to free Acrolith Diastema from his tyrannical rule. She could have killed him to restore the balance in the underworld. She could have killed him for trying to kill her to stop her from taking over her father's empire.

She didn't kill Yuki for any of those reasons. She did it to give him a taste of what he did to her father. Yuki earned her father's trust and then stabbed Rizarth in the back. Someone had to take revenge and Lyons was the only one who could do it.

She loved her father. That was the painful truth. She loved him more than anything. She loved him more after she found out about his business than she'd loved him to begin with.

Finding out who he was and what he'd been doing for a living all these years—it only made her love him more. It made her wish she'd known sooner.

Emmett's low murmur broke in on her thoughts. "I don't know anything about your father, but I do know you and I know about fathers and daughters. I'd bet anything I own that your father would be very proud of the person you've become."

Lyons snorted to cover up her gnawing pain. "You mean because I became a criminal like him? That's rich."

"I meant after that. I meant the person you are now. I would be incredibly proud if I had a daughter like you."

He stood up and left the lounge heading for his own room. He shut the door behind him. Only then, now that she was completely alone, could she bury her face in her hands and let out all the anguish in her heart.

Chapter 29

Lyons sat up and looked around the apartment. She'd fallen asleep on the couch and no one else was awake yet. A dozen dishes still sat on the coffee table with all the leftovers from last night, but she didn't feel like eating them.

The lights from the mine streamed through massive windows on one side of the lounge. She went over to them, slid open the balcony doors, and stepped out onto the terrace.

She, Flack, and Fizzle would go back to Xuiter's apartment today and hopefully get another fat payday. How long would this go on before disaster struck again?

The crew had been on this planet less than a day before the Reserve Wing caught up with them. She didn't trust their luck to last because they didn't have any.

She let the wind blow through her hair while she thought over where they could hide the Ziprothil. Maybe she would ask Vor to make that the payment for the crew's next job—a hiding place for the Ziprothil.

That would defeat the purpose like Friend said. Lyons telling Vor she had the Ziprothil would announce to the whole criminal underworld that she had the Ziprothil. Any hiding place he provided for her would also get broadcast to the four winds. She didn't even have to question that.

Emmett and the clones woke up pretty soon. They all gathered around the table to eat. "Why isn't Beauty here?" Friend asked. "He must be getting hungry by now."

Lyons stuck her head into one of the other bedrooms. "Beauty!" she hollered. "We're going to eat all the food!"

Emmett pulled Vor's payment card out of his pocket and tapped on it. "The scans show that he's still in the apartment."

Lyons gasped. "That thing has scans?"

"Check it out." He passed her the card. It turned out to have a bunch of different features including communications, access to the Confederate database, and a few other useful applications.

She read the scans of the apartment. The readings indicated that both Beauty and the Ziprothil were in the room Lyons just checked, but no matter how much she looked and searched, she couldn't find him.

"He's a slippery little eel," Lyons muttered and handed the card back to Emmett.

"Do you think he's avoiding us because we want to question him about how he hides the Ziprothil?" Friend asked.

"He isn't hiding it," Lyons pointed out. "It's right there on the scans. Anyone can see exactly where he is."

"Except that they can't," Frost argued. "Seeing him on the scans doesn't mean anything if we can't find him in real life—or if the person who wants to steal the Ziprothil can't see him in real life."

"None of this helps us hide the Ziprothil long-term," Emmett pointed out.

"So we're right back where we started," Flack finished. "We're nowhere."

"At least we have the resources to hide it if we need to. We aren't running around the galaxy with nowhere to go and no place to do it. We have someplace to stay. We have food and money and a ship and....."

He broke off when a ship flew past the terrace outside. Its engines howled and it sent a blast of wind through the open doors.

Lyons glanced up and then went back to eating. It took her a second to realize that the ship wasn't flying past the terrace outside. It swiveled onto the terrace, and before anyone realized what was happening, the vessel turned its guns toward the apartment and opened fire.

The first catastrophic implosion took out the apartment's outer wall and opened a yawning cavity so the ship could unload on the apartment at will.

Lyons dove for those nearest her. She tackled Frost and Fizzle onto the floor between the couches. "Get down!" she roared.

Everybody ducked for cover as a Reserve Wing Dagger bombarded the apartment with dozens of shots. They exploded the back wall punched through into bedrooms and then blasted one of the couches off the floor.

It cartwheeled into the air and slammed down in the middle of the room. Only a miracle prevented it from falling on top of one of the friends huddling for cover behind a different couch.

Stuffing exploded into the air. Broken glass, shattered plaster, concrete, broken tiles, and splintered woodchips revolved through the apartment as one devastating explosion after another destroyed the apartment and everything in it.

Lyons huddled under her arms and covered Frost and Fizzle with her body. One of those shots would take her out and there would be nothing she could do to save herself or any of her friends.

In that moment, her mind switched somewhere else. Where was Beauty?

The Reserve Wing must have been able to see that he had the Ziprothil in this apartment. Shooting at it could trigger the Ziprothil right now, but maybe the Reserve Wing didn't care about that.

The Dagger kept unloading into the apartment for at least five minutes before the gunners cut their fire.

The ship hovered there for a second and then its engine noise changed. Lyons dared to peek over the couch behind which she'd been hiding. Her stomach dropped when she saw the ship setting down on the terrace outside.

She glanced around. She'd left her XQ by the door. None of the crew's other weapons were anywhere within reach.

She shot to her feet and sprinted across the room trying to get to her weapon in time, but the ship unleashed one more bone-crushing blast into the back wall.

The concussion hurled her across the room and she landed hard on the floor. "LYONS!!" Flack yelled and then a dozen male voices bellowed out through the destruction.

"Don't move!!" A dozen Reserve Wing soldiers stormed the apartment aiming their own weapons everywhere. "Get your hands in the air! Get down on the ground! Don't move!"

Lyons rolled over onto her stomach and tried to push herself onto her hands and knees. Her head spun and her ears rang.

She jolted when one of the soldiers strode over to her and crammed his foot into the back of her neck to push her back down on the floor. "I said don't move!" he barked.

She struggled, but then she felt the cold barrel of his weapon pressed against the back of her neck. She twisted her head around and saw soldiers standing over all her friends—except Beauty. He still wasn't here.

Another howl of engine noise punctured the silence and a Nitrol touched down next to the first Dagger. Lyons's blood boiled when Admiral Joyce stepped down from the ship along with half a dozen other officers.

He strolled into the apartment and looked around with a satisfied grin. He barely glanced at the clones. Then he noticed Lyons lying there. "You! You were so helpful with the Ithium. You can tell me where the Ziprothil is."

"I don't know where it is, you son of a bitch!" she roared. "I've been trying to find it the same way you have!"

"Tsk, tsk, tsk," he clucked. "You brought it to this apartment......"

"My crewman has it! Now he's lost! We saw him on the scans and now he's gone! You can check for yourself!"

One of the officers standing behind Joyce came over and handed him a similar card to the one Vor had given Lyons. Admiral Joyce frowned at it. "He's in the next room. Go get him."

The soldiers swarmed into the bedroom that Lyons just searched. "I told you he isn't in there!" she bellowed. "I don't know where the hell he is! Get off me, you cocksucker!"

The soldier jammed his foot tighter into her neck and made her roar with pain and indignation.

Joyce waved to his soldiers. "Search the whole apartment."

The soldiers spread out, and when they still didn't find either Beauty or the Ziprothil, they used their ships' scanners. "It has to be in this apartment somewhere," Joyce growled.

"It's moving around, Sir," one of the officers told him. "The scans show it right in this room—but that's impossible."

Joyce smacked his lips in annoyance and waved at Emmett and the clones. "Get them up."

The soldiers yanked Emmett, Lyons, and the four clones to their feet. The soldiers shoved everyone together in a group and Lyons and her friends held onto each other.

She started to ask Flack, "Are you all right?" but Joyce told her to shut up.

He lunged for them, grabbed Friend by the elbow, and dragged her away from the rest of the group. Before anyone could say a word, he pulled a gun and aimed it at her head. "Tell me where the Ziprothil or she dies."

"No!" Emmett struggled against the soldiers who held him back. "Leave her alone!"

"I already told you everything!" Lyons shrieked. "You can see where the Ziprothil is as well as we can!"

"That isn't good enough. Your crewman is following you around and......"

Right at that moment, Emmett broke the soldiers' hold and rushed Joyce and Friend. Emmett made it halfway there before another soldier stepped in, raised his rifle, and smashed Emmett across the face.

His knees buckled. "EMMETT!!" Flack and Frost both screamed, but they couldn't get near him with all the soldiers guarding them.

Emmett collapsed on the floor. Joyce rolled his eyes, raised his gun one more time, and fired into the side of Friend's head. "NO!!" LYONS screamed, but it was too late.

Friend went down, too. The other clones screamed Lyons couldn't hold back her tears. "NO!!" she shrieked one more time, but no one could change what had already been done.

"Who's next?" Joyce turned back to Lyons and the remaining clones. "Only four more to go. This won't take long."

The sight of Friend lying there dead blurred in Lyons's tears. If Joyce didn't listen to her now, he never would. He didn't kill Friend to get the Ziprothil. He did it because he wanted to.

He surveyed the four women trying to make up his mind when one of the officers called out, "Sir! The Ziprothil is reading on board our own Nitrol! Whatever is carrying it is on board the ship right now!"

Joyce turned around and raised his eyebrows. The officer came over and showed him the scans on the card, "That's impossible!" Joyce exclaimed. "It was here a second ago. Go check it out."

The officers went back on board the Nitrol. They didn't come back.

Joyce tapped his foot and then waved at the soldiers. "Finish off these five. We've wasted enough time with this already."

One of the soldiers stepped up behind Flack, raised his rifle, and fired. He fired three times in rapid succession and dropped all three clones right there.

Lyons buckled under the weight of heartbreaking despair. She fell on her knees next to them, but she couldn't even bring herself to touch them. They and Emmett were all she had left.

The soldier pivoted behind her and raised his gun to shoot her in the head, too. She didn't care anymore. What was the point of all this struggle if she couldn't even save those closest to her?

Tears poured down her cheeks. They were all gone—all four of them. At least she would be dead soon, too.

Just then, one of the officers came back. "The Ziprothil is definitely on board the ship, Sir, and so is the alien carrying it. If we take off now, we'll take it with us and we can find it and the alien later."

Joyce waved to the soldiers. "Load up, all of you. We got what we wanted."

He returned to the Nitrol. Some of the soldiers went with him. The rest got on board the Dagger.

Howling wind pelted through the open doors, but Lyons didn't even care when both Reserve Wing vessels flew away and vanished into the sky taking Beauty and the Ziprothil with them.

Chapter 30

Lyons hunched on the floor shaking with sobs. It was all gone. Everything she ever cared about—all gone.

Only Emmett remained. She finally crawled over to him, but she was crying so hard that she couldn't even see how bad his injuries were—like she would be able to do something even if she could see.

She rolled him over. Blood covered his face. "Emmett....." she choked.

She couldn't even decide why she wanted to wake him up. She didn't want him to wake up and see the four bodies lying on the floor.

She broke down in sobs just thinking about it, but in a second, he stirred on his own. He groaned, rolled onto his side, and sat up. His hand flew to his head and he growled in pain when he touched his own face.

Lyons dreaded the moment when he finally saw. He turned around and frowned when he saw her sobbing her eyes out. "You okay? What's wrong?"

"I'm sorry.....Emmett!" she howled. "I'm so sorry!"

"What are you sorry about? What happened to the.....?" He glanced around the destroyed apartment. That's when he saw them.

He blinked at them in disbelief for a second. Lyons couldn't even speak. The devastation in her heart hurt too much.

"No, no, no," Emmett muttered and crawled over to Flack. He touched the back of her shoulder.

His voice strained and then spiked a register as the misery broke loose. "No! No! No! No!"

He groped from one body to the next touching them and then he broke down completely. "NO!!" he whimpered and burst into racking sobs.

He picked up Frost and her body flopped in his arms. He held her and rocked her, but he had to put her down and pick up Fizzle next.

He kept going from one body to another bawling in agony trying to hold them all at the same time. He finally came to Friend, picked her up, and his shoulders shook with sobs while he held her.

He stroked the side of her head and then ran his hand down her arms. Lyons wept in silence watching him. Not even the knowledge that Fiddler was still out there somewhere could make up for this loss.

Emmett pulled Friend's body against him, buried his face in her blood-stained neck, and crushed her in his arms while he cried. He was still crying when he laid her back on the floor, caressed his hand down her cheek one more time, and then patted down her pockets.

He came to the inside pocket of her vest, pulled out a computer chip stashed there, and he stuffed it into his own pocket before he sat back on his heels.

He buckled over with another outburst of wretched sobs, now that he could see all four of them lying dead in front of him.

He'd risked everything including his own life to save them and give them some kind of life worth living. He'd given them the only family and the only years of freedom they'd ever known. Now they were all dead in the space of minutes.

Lyons stopped crying first. The pain in her heart cut too deep even for tears. She watched Emmett sob over his lost children. She didn't try to comfort him or bring him back. There was no coming back from this.

Lyons passed her sleeve across her eyes and looked around. The apartment was completely demolished along with all the furniture, the food—everything.

Then she spotted her XQ still standing in the corner by the door. The blast that knocked her away from it had made the gun slide to the floor, but it was still there.

What an insult that the soldiers didn't even try to remove it. They didn't care if Lyons armed herself. She would never be able to stop them. She would never be able to stop Joyce.

Now he had all three elements—all the elements that Davenport and his crew had worked so hard and sacrificed so much to keep out of Joyce's hands. All their efforts had come to nothing and now the Armageddon Core was all dead, too.

Lyons spotted the payment card lying across the room. She got to her feet, too numb with pain and misery to feel a thing.

She picked up the card. It still displayed the scans of the apartment that she and Emmett had been looking at when the Reserve Wing showed up.

The scans didn't turn up Beauty or the Ziprothil anymore. They really were gone. Did Beauty hand over the Ziprothil to Admiral Joyce?

Beauty wouldn't do that. The soldiers searched that Nitrol, but they couldn't find Beauty or the Ziprothil. Was this Beauty's way of keeping it hidden—again?

Lyons heard a strange noise and turned around. It took her a second to realize that what she was hearing wasn't a noise. It was silence. Emmett wasn't crying anymore.

He turned his bloodshot eyes to the terrace and glared out at the Pegasus Mine. He didn't even try to wipe the tears off his face. He got to his feet, strode over to where the sliding glass doors had been, and narrowed his eyes at the horizon.

Lyons recognized that look. It was the look of pure, burning, hate-fueled rage. It was the look of a man driven by the thirst for revenge.

Lyons crossed the room again, picked up her XQ, and then went into what was left of the bedrooms. She collected all the clones' weapons and returned to the lounge to find Emmett coming toward her.

She handed him two XQs and he stopped there to check them. Neither of them spoke as they left the apartment, returned to street level, and walked back to the hangar where they left the Phoenix.

Lyons didn't look right or left on the way there. No one was looking for her anymore. She wasn't carrying anything that Joyce or his henchmen wanted.

They'd left her and Emmett alive. Now it was up to the two of them to make Joyce regret that as his last, most fatal mistake.

Nothing prevented Emmett and Lyons from going out there, finding Davenport, Dice, Fiddler, Healey, and the Chorion Team, rejoining, and doing whatever was necessary to stop Joyce before he carried out this plan of his. This crew was the only one left that could stop him.

Emmett and Lyons took the elevator to the hangar, went on board the Phoenix, and they both went straight to the cockpit. They sat down side by side and went to work firing up the engines, prepping the ship, and taking off.

The Pegasus Mines held nothing for either Emmett or Lyons anymore. Everything important was out there waiting for them to go find it. Once they did, it would be time to track down Joyce and finish this job once and for all.

<u>End of Book 6.</u>

Keep Reading

U ltra Meridian Series: Book 6: Atlas Arcane

Sheriff Mace Davenport was just trying to do his duty by keeping a doomsday weapon out of a criminal mastermind's hands. Now Davenport is under arrest and on trial for his life. He's charged with waging armed insurrection against the Confederate Reserve Wing—the same Reserve Wing that has been trying to set off the doomsday weapon all this time.

Davenport's struggles across known space haven't been in vain, though. His friends and allies are everywhere he least expects to find them. They've been waiting for the chance to come out of the woodwork and make sure both he and his enemies get the justice they so richly deserve.

In the final showdown for the fate of the free world, one man's relentless dedication to the law will be tested to its limit in the ultimate fight to bring down the ruthless forces set to destroy him.

You can find it at your favorite book retailer.

Sign Up Once--Get all Theo Mann's free books including brand new releases

S ign Up Once--Get all Theo Mann's free books including brand new releases

Humanity on the brink of annihilation.

A mysterious package, a corrupt officer, and a conspiracy that goes all the way to the top? What could possibly go wrong?

When a routine mission goes horribly wrong, Warrant Officer Ewing Archer and a handful of faithful friends get trapped in a battle to save the last survivors of Earth.

The human race has abandoned the ecological disaster of Earth. Now all that remains is a network of interconnected ships, stations, and satellites surrounding the planet.

But when war breaks out, Archer becomes a firebrand that could destroy it all....or save it.

Sign up at www.theomann.com to read it for free

About Theo Mann

I write 70 books per year—and yes, before you ask, all these books are my original creative work. Nothing written under my name is AI-generated or ghostwritten because I write better than AI and any ghostwriter out there.

People don't read fiction for entertainment or to escape from reality. People read fiction to see their humanity reflected in another person's character and story.

This is my promise to you. When you read my books, you'll see your own humanity reflected in the characters and stories. I take this commitment to my readers very seriously. My books are an intimate form of communication between us. I would never disrespect my readers by turning that over to a machine or another writer. This is my bond between me and you as my reader.

I write 20,000 words per day as my daily work output. If anyone with a public platform would like to challenge me to prove this in a controlled environment, feel free to contact me on this website's contact page.

I worked as a professional ghostwriter for fifteen years. Now I'm on a mission to set a Guinness World Record by writing 700 books over the next ten years and 1400 books over the next twenty years, all originally written by me. See my website for the full book list.

I'm also the author of *Proof for the Existence of God* and the *Crimes Against Fiction* blog. You can find all my nonfiction work at www.crimes-against-fiction.com.

If you have a story idea, or if you would like me to explore a series in more depth, or if you'd like me to explore a character by writing a spinoff series about that character or world, leave me a message on my website's contact page. I answer all reader emails, so ask me anything, tell me what you liked and didn't like, and let me know where you'd like your favorite series to go. I would love to hear your ideas and find out what you'd like to read next.

Find out more at www.theomann.com.

Also by Theo Mann (so far)

Standalone Novels

Kingdom of Heaven

The Verge

Series

Onyx Series (Books 1-6)

Prideland Series (Books 1-4)

Ultra Meridian Series (Books 1-7)

Hellhounds Series (Books 1-7)

Battlefleet Series (Books 1-4)

Highland Heroes Series (Books 1-6)

Battalion 1 Series (Books 1-5)

The Network Series (Books 1-6)

Corrupted Coil (Books 1-5)

Rise of the Giants Series (Books 1-10)

The Edge of Chaos Series (Books 1-5)

The White Series (Books 1-7)